Set in the world of contemporary art, Guy Kennaway's new novel delivers his trademark absurdities and laugh out loud moments.

As the globe's most successful super-dealer, Herman Gertsch spent his charmed life jettiing between his galleries in Zurich, London and New York, fawned over by artists, curators, politicians and the uber-rich.

As Herman's empire grew, nothing seemed to get in his way, until he made the calamitous decision to open a gallery in a rural English backwater. Here, Herman encountered John 'Brother' Burn, a penniless hippy known as the slipperiest man in south Somerset, and therefore the western hemisphere.

In the riotous comedy of errors that follows, Kennaway pours mistaken identity, Amazonian tribesmen, Swiss food, DMT, Arab Royalty, million dollar paintings and worthless tat onto a spin painting of a story that dazzles with surprises and leaves you feeling reassuringly warm about art and life.

THE
ACCIDENTAL
COLLECTOR

GUY KENNAWAY

MENSCH PUBLISHING

Mensch Publishing
51 Northchurch Road, London N1 4EE, United Kingdom

First published in Great Britain 2021

Copyright © Guy Kennaway, 2021

Guy Kennaway has asserted his right under the Copyright, Designs and
Patents Act, 1988, to be identified as Author of this work

A catalogue record for this book is available from the British Library

ISBN: PB: 978-1-912914-36-4; HB: 978-1-912914-22-7; EBOOK: 978-1-912914-23-4

2 4 6 8 10 9 7 5 3 1

Typeset by Newgen KnowledgeWorks Pvt. Ltd., Chennai, India
Printed and bound in Great Britain by CPI Group (UK) Ltd, Croydon CR0 4YY

Disclaimer

A phrase that I always find annoying is *you couldn't make it up*. Any decent novelist could make anything up, and this book is proof of that. All events, characters and places in *The Accidental Collector* were made up by me, and do not exist in what some call real life. Friends who know me will attest that my imagination is a great deal more effective than my memory, and it is from my imagination that this story derived, not my memory.

The book is dedicated to Paul, my friend

I

It is a truth universally acknowledged, or at least by all those who know the gig, that a single man in possession of no fortune, marrying a wealthy woman, is in want of a decent cover story.

Herman Gertsch was just such a man. Newly wed and in his late twenties, Herman had curly brown hair, long eyelashes, a wide mouth and an easy smile. Normally of sunny disposition, Herman felt distinctly moody as he sat surrounded by empty armchairs in the less exclusive extension of the bar at the Mont Cervin Hotel in Zermatt. It was the midpoint of the skiing season in 1989, when snow was plentiful and cheer abounded, but Herman simply stared at the press of men in the other half of the bar whose backs were turned to him. He had earlier tried to ease himself into the group, standing on its edge, tipping his head to one side, nodding and smiling, trying to catch the thread of their conversation. He had retreated when a tall, patrician Englishman called Ludo stepped back onto his toe and said, 'I'm so sorry, I do apologise, I didn't see you there,' and then turned his back, blocking

Herman's entry into the group with a roar of laughter which Herman was currently trying to convince himself had not been aimed at him.

In the bevelled mirrors of the salon, Herman's lustrous corduroys had the shine and length of a brand new garment. He didn't look or feel sleek like the suntanned playboys, aristocrats and billionaires of the inner bar who casually leant against the bright red leather stools as they swapped big stories. An Italian count called Gianni was being teased for dropping his pants in a restaurant jape. Herman turned to look through the plate glass window: the sharp tips of the Alps were gilded in late sun, and a glowing shadow that had descended the white hills was calmly crossing town. Happily exhausted skiers walked towards their showers, massages and steams. Herman swirled the dribble of whisky in the tumbler that must have weighed about half a kilo, and which made him, like his clothes, feel smaller than he really was.

Herman came from a poor and respectable Swiss family in a town called Interlaken at the bottom of the Alps. When he had skied as a child, he hadn't been anywhere like the Mont Cervin Hotel or even Zermatt. He and his brother slept behind a curtain in a cramped apartment well below the snow line, and had taken the cog train to ski on a handful of short runs. His mother made him a packed lunch and gave him 50 centimes for a hot chocolate. His father had been the station master at Interlaken; Herman had done well enough at school to attend university in Berne, where he met Marie.

His face brightened and he stood up.

Marie was at the entrance to the salon. Herman waved and a warm smile lit her soft, classic features. Long chestnut hair framed a face of calm and composure, an impeccable complexion and a kind mouth. As Herman pulled out the sturdy Swiss chair for her, she murmured thank you.

'I'm so glad you're here,' he said as he kissed her on the cheek. 'I've been sitting on my own. You look wonderful.'

The bar manager, a good-looking chap called Roman, never seemed to bother with Herman, but a waiter with an alarming Adam's apple appeared from nowhere. He took Marie's order for a coupe of champagne, bowed, clicked his heels and departed.

'What a great last run that was,' Marie said, her face flushed with Alpine air and fast skiing. 'Are you all right? You look thoughtful.'

'I've been worrying,' Herman said.

'What about?'

He took a breath. 'I think I need to get a job.'

'A job?' said Marie, her drink stopped in mid-air. 'Why?'

'What would you think of me working in a little restaurant, like a stubbe? Just a traditional Swiss one, serving Walliser teller, raclette and fondue? Wouldn't that be fun?'

'A restaurant?'

'Not a big one. About twenty covers. A little stubbe with steamed up windows.'

'But what about the hours? You'll never be at home. I'll miss you.'

Herman thought for a bit. Then his face lit up. 'You could work there too! We could have uniforms.'

'I don't think so,' said Marie. 'Herman, really! It's a bit of a bonkers idea. Do you have any idea of how hard work it is to run a restaurant?'

Herman looked deflated.

'*Meine Liebe*,' Marie put her hand on his arm. 'I didn't mean to hurt you.'

'A stubbe might be impractical, I do see,' Herman said. 'But I still think I need something to say when strangers ask what I do. They see me in all these places and assume I must be some big, high-powered businessman or something. I want to say I do something.'

'Why?' said Marie, 'You don't want to be like them. Successful businessmen are almost always complete idiots.'

'I suppose it's about not getting any respect,' Herman said. 'It happened with Georgio, today at lunch,' Herman said. Georgio was the perky, blue-eyed Romanche ski instructor whose tight little buttocks Herman was getting fed up with following all day long. 'When we stopped for lunch he asked me what I did. I found myself stammering for a reply.'

'What did you say?'

'I actually said something stupid,' admitted Herman.

'What?'

'I said I was a writer.'

Marie raised her eyebrows. Then she took a good glug of champagne.

'Well I had a think about what I had done recently and the only thing I could think of was writing that piece about badgers for the conservation group.'

'That was so interesting, I adored that,' said Marie.

'Well the European badger is a lovely little fellow, and as you know much maligned and misunderstood. Anyway I told Georgio I did a little bit of writing, hoping I wouldn't have to explain any more, and he asked me what the titles of my books were and I swallowed and thought about pretending to fall over in the snow to stop the conversation and then went bright red as I said I wrote mainly for magazines. Typically, Georgio is mates with a successful writer. Bernard Cornwell, no less. Georgio taught Bernard's children to ski and has done loads of glaciers with the man himself, all by helicopter. Turns out Bernard is coming to Zermatt next week and Georgio wants to introduce us, unless I already knew him. It was a nightmare.'

Marie put her hand on Herman's arm.

'And I thought about meeting Bernard Cornwell and telling him about my 500 words on the European badger …' Herman muttered.

'I'm sure he would be fascinated,' Marie said. 'I was.'

'And after that conversation, Georgio stopped carrying my skis and started talking to you all the time. If I had a proper job, none of it would have happened. The man practically ignores me.'

'The thing is,' said Marie, 'if you had a job we wouldn't be able to come away skiing for weeks at a time, or go on the boat whenever we want. You would have to be at an office. And offices are such boring places.'

'Yes, well I understand all that. It's just that I'm feeling a bit unhappy because I never have anything to say when someone asks me what I do.'

'Can't you say nothing?'

'Not really,' Herman scratched the side of his head. 'A man needs a decent answer. For my own peace of mind. I think it's getting me down.'

'Oh darling,' Marie stroked the arm of Herman's brand new après ski cashmere sweater. 'I think you do loads. You walk the dogs, you row me on the lake, you tell Otto to clean the car, and you keep a jolly good eye on Fritz in the garden.'

'I know but they're not real jobs.'

'I understand,' said Marie.

'I had to get it off my chest.'

'But a job could be a bit of a problem,' said Marie.

'Yes, I realise it's an inconvenience,' he sighed. 'It's a bit unfair it doesn't happen the other way round.'

'Oh it does, Herman. You must have noticed lots of wives of rich men think they have to have jobs. Think of Julianna, and Rosa. I never can work out why they bother,' Marie said. 'Talk about making life more complicated than it needs to be. I mean, what is the problem of doing nothing but having fun? And think of Donatella with her spa, and Ulla with her healing centre. I doubt a single yoga studio would exist if it wasn't for some rich woman needing to look like she was clever enough to run a business. And of course it's the same with men who've inherited money. They often have camouflage careers. Some write books, or in extreme cases poetry. Half the novels published only exist because someone felt guilty about having a lot of money.'

'Maybe I could do that,' Herman said.

'But you would have to actually write a book or a poem, if you went that route,' Marie said.

Herman's brow furrowed. 'Yes. It took me three weeks to do 500 words on the badger.'

'I've got an idea,' said Marie. 'How about you just say you have a job? Without actually having to do or produce anything.'

'How do you mean?' Herman said.

'Have just a job title without an actual job. Might that work?'

Herman thought for a bit.

'You are clever darling,' he said. 'That's a brilliant idea. I could just say I was a doctor, for instance.'

'I'm not sure that's the best pick,' said Marie.

'Oh yes, I see why,' said Herman. 'That could go badly wrong. I know, a helicopter pilot! I love choppers. Oh no, that's no good either.'

She smiled at him. There wasn't a bad bone in his body. 'We'll think of something.'

Marie's grandfather was the founder of a Swiss precision engineering firm that you or I have never heard of but which was sold by Marie's mother for well over two billion euros, not that long ago, though this money did have to be divided between Marie and her mother, who then died and left her half to Marie.

After inheriting this fortune at twenty-one, while she was at university and going out with Herman, Marie had had a few meetings with lawyers in anonymous foggy lowland towns outside Zürich and tied up her fortune discreetly and cleverly. She grasped soon that with the amount of money she had and the advisers she chose, mainly old, kind and patient men, she could happily be secure with only two meetings a year.

No one, including Herman, knew how much she possessed, and after repelling the first hedge-fund managers, financial advisers and private banks who all came hunting for it, the men in new suits finally gave up and declared that she probably didn't have much anyway. Which was just as she liked it.

'Now come on, drink up and let's go to dinner. We can have one of their yummy Corton-Charlemagnes.'

'With some veal, and hollandaise,' said Herman, holding out his arm for her.

'Or Chateaubriand', said Marie thoughtfully, 'then we could have a Nuits-Saint-Georges! A really good one.'

'And half a bottle of Yquem with that chocolate soufflé,' said Herman.

On the way out of the bar, Herman signalled to Roman to put the drinks on his bill but the bar manager blanked him. Wait till I have an important job title, Herman thought.

After a wonderful rich, luxurious dinner in the style of Escoffier, the two of them sat rather red-cheeked and jolly sipping their Sauternes as the waiter laid a new linen tablecloth over the old one, lifting the glasses, condiments and cutlery over the roll as he unfurled it. Herman took Marie's hand and did the thing he most enjoyed in life, looked into her deep brown eyes.

When they left the restaurant, the night was stippled with slow and fluffy snowflakes. The path to the street was dusted with powder, so Marie gripped onto Herman whose new boots wouldn't let them down. The two of them were warmed in their coats and in their souls by the feeling of being well skied and well fed, their blood full of oxygen and fine Burgundy. Ladies in thick furs walking their lap dogs were lit by the glow from the ski equipment shops. High above the village, the headlights of the piste machines criss-crossed in the darkness, readying the slopes for the next day.

Herman and Marie entered the hotel to a friendly greeting from the concierge. As they passed the bar Herman spotted Gianni, the Italian count, wearing a necktie as a bandana, standing on a bar stool trying to stop a ceiling fan with his head.

The next day was bright and cold, perfect for a day's skiing. Purists loved a fall of fresh powder on a precipitous run to ski deeply through all day without a break, but Herman and Marie were happy to ski on a well prepared piste on a gentle slope down to a cosy hut in which to enjoy a vertiginously high-calorie lunch.

Everyone on the station platform was gloved and goggled except the train driver in his soft boots and buttoned coat. When the train doors opened, Georgio nipped ahead to bag a seat for Marie, while Herman followed in the crush with the skis. On the ascent out of the village they passed close to the furry white balconies of the apartment blocks, and snow-laden branches of the spruce and larch. Occasional breaths of wind knocked dollops of snow onto the pocked ground. At the top station they tramped through a concrete tunnel to the sound of ski boots clanging on metal grilles, and emerged into the thin and biting air under a dark blue sky. A fit Alsatian lolled in the sun on a bank of snow. People threw their skis down with a whumf before stepping into them, adjusted the grip on their poles, gave a final check to sunglasses, hat and pockets, and pushed off down the slope.

At the bottom of the first lift, Herman and Marie spotted some old friends from Berne, Adrian and Heidi. While Heidi and Marie were chatting in the clattering queue, Georgio managed to fix it so that he could sit with them on the three-person chair. Herman didn't mind being left with Adrian, a slow, thoughtful man who owned an art gallery in Zürich, and who adored Marie and knew her family. He and Adrian were whisked off on the chair with an empty seat between them and their wives in front.

Herman carefully pulled off and stowed his gloves between his thighs while he reached for his tubes of creams, applying suntan lotion to his face and salve to his lips.

'How's married life?' Adrian asked.

'I love it,' said Herman. 'Marie is so wonderful.'

'You are a lucky man.'

'Extremely. I keep thinking I am going to wake up and find I am a trainee hotel manager at a hospitality college in Lausanne.'

'Was that what you were going to do once?'

'It was certainly an idea,' said Herman.

'You don't need to do that now,' laughed Adrian. 'Do you?'

'Well actually, I was just saying to Marie last night that I wouldn't mind a job, even if it was just to have something to talk to people about if they asked. She suggested I just got a job title, and I thought that a jolly good idea.'

Adrian chuckled.

Herman blinked. He was having one of his ideas. And this felt like a good one.

'Hey,' said Herman, 'You've got an art gallery, haven't you?'

'I have.' It was a quiet and cultivated spot of contemplation for Adrian, visited every now and then by wealthy Swiss to purchase items of real beauty.

'I don't suppose there's any chance I could work for you?'

'I don't have a job vacancy I am afraid.'

'I don't mean actually have a job. The thought! Imagine me selling art!'

That is exactly what Adrian had been doing, and it wasn't pleasant.

'I don't know a Picasso from a … from a … I can't even think of another painter!'

'It does take a real love of the subject to do it,' said Adrian.

'But that's the thing, I wouldn't actually do anything. If people asked I would just say I worked with you and then move onto other subjects, like the European badger.'

'What if someone asked about an artist who was showing at the gallery?' Adrian asked.

'I would say that that wasn't my department and they should talk to you, and generally give you a good puff before switching the subject.'

'Time to get off,' said Adrian raising the bar, inching forward and gliding diplomatically down the slope away from the conversation.

Adrian and Heidi were not staying in the Mont Cervin. They were in the Monte Rosa where there were fewer old Russian men with pneumatic blondes, and many more children larking around in the lobby. Adrian, a tall, almost bald man, elegant and refined, was stretched out on the bed with his hands behind his head, dozing as he watched the news. He was woken when Heidi came in wearing a towel turban and a voluminous white gown.

'Wasn't it wonderful to bump into Marie and Herman,' she said, 'lucky things staying at the Mont Cervin.'

'Yes. They looked well. Though something rather embarrassing came up when we were on the chair lift. Herman asked me for a job.'

'What do you mean? He doesn't know the first thing about art, and he certainly doesn't need the money.'

'I know.'

Heidi disappeared into the bathroom. Adrian crossed his thin ankles and let his eyes close.

He was woken by his wife. 'It would be wonderful to help him, as a favour to Marie. She's always so kind and generous to us.'

'I know that too. I am in something of a dilemma,' said Adrian.

'Herman's incredibly sweet. You must be able to find something for him to do. I can't believe he'd be able to get a job anywhere else. He's too kind for this world, that's his trouble. He's perfect for Marie because she doesn't have to worry about money. You must have something … wake up.'

'I'm not asleep. I'm listening. A thought crossed my mind. I may not have to find him something to do. He said he only wanted a job title, not an actual job.'

'What do you mean?'

'He just wants to be able to say, "I'm a director of an art gallery in Zürich" to people who ask. He doesn't want any money or any duties.'

'Why on earth?'

'To have something to say when people ask him what he does.'

'Yes. I understand now,' said Heidi. 'Well you have to help him.'

Adrian uncrossed his long legs and sat on the edge of the bed rubbing his face. 'I suppose as long as he doesn't ever talk about art or business it might not be a problem.'

'Please do it. For me,' Heidi said.

'All right. I'll talk to him tomorrow. As long as he doesn't try to stick his oar in.'

'Hello! Herman Gertsch, I work for Krietman Stoop, art dealers, Zürich. Herman Gertsch, Krietman Stoop, wonderful to meet you. May I freshen that drink? Do you mind if we don't talk shop as I'm on holiday? Yes, such an important time. Work-life balance, you know. Wonderful snow.' Herman was chatting gaily to himself as he hurried up Zermatt's high street with the sound of sleigh bells tinkling in the air. He weaved through the fur-clad old biddies and round the carousels of postcards on his way back from the pharmacy with some cosmetics for Marie. He liked being sent on errands and liked getting it exactly right.

'Sorry,' a voice said, 'were you talking to me?'

It was Ludo, the tall Englishman from the hotel.

'Hello!' said Herman. 'Actually, I was just congratulating myself on getting a rather good job.'

'I'm very pleased to hear that. What line is it in?'

'Oh – art dealing. With Krietman Stoop in Zürich. I've been made a director.'

'Good for you. Must dash. See you in the bar tonight, yes?'

After delivering Marie the creams and unguents she had requested, Herman dressed and hurried down to the hotel bar, bursting with anticipation and confidence.

When he entered the inner bar with the polished red stools and deeply buttoned banquettes, Roman, the tanned head barman, was leaning across the brass bar and speaking in conspiratorial tones to some of the tall, loud guests. Herman stood behind them and tried to join in, but Roman didn't even flick him a glance of those charismatic eyes.

Some more men arrived: Gianni, and Ludo, who pushed in front of Herman and shoved him further out of the group. Herman found himself standing beside a black-clad, short and frankly fat man with a face made kind by eyes that slanted down as though in sadness. The man was doing what people always did when they felt a bit self-conscious: he was pretending to be interested in a painting.

Herman heard one of the tall, loud crowd whisper, 'Where did that come from? I think they let someone's driver in by mistake.'

Out of sheer sympathy for the underdog, Herman gave the man a smile.

'My name's Herman,' he said.

'Khaled,' said the man. 'Do you mind if I talk to you? Then people will think I've got a friend here.'

Herman laughed. 'I know what you mean. It's a bit stuffy, this place. I'm sure they're actually all very nice when you get to know them.' Trying to think of something else to say, Herman said 'Interesting picture.'

'Fascinating,' said, Khaled. 'Old Zermatt. Do you know anything about art?'

'Absolutely nothing I'm afraid,' Herman laughed.

'What is it that you do, if you don't mind me asking?' Khaled said. At that moment, Ludo broke away from the knot of men at the bar and came towards Herman with his glass raised. 'Here's to the new venture', he said, maintaining a deadly course.

Herman gulped. 'What do I do?' he said. 'Well that's the funny thing. I actually work for an art gallery,' he laughed.

'Where is that?' Khaled asked.

'Zürich. Krietman Stoop,' Herman said.

'Telling him about your gallery?' shouted Ludo. 'Well it's blue chip. Hello, any friend of Herman's a friend of mine. I'm Ludo.' They shook hands.

Khaled introduced himself.

'You're a dark horse Herman, I'll give you that,' said Ludo. 'I like your style. Here's to you.'

When Ludo had pushed off again, Herman said, 'You're probably wondering why I said I knew nothing about art. The thing is, I don't like to do business when I am on holiday. It's not fair on my wife. So that's what I always say to put people off the scent.'

'Of course. Very sensible. Family must come first.'

'Talking of which,' he said, 'there is my wife. Please excuse me. Good to meet you. Have a good evening.'

Marie and Herman went to sit down in the sensible Swiss chairs near the windows. Herman told her how successful his first foray into the world of having a job title had been.

'It was a bit tricky for a moment, as I got used to it, but it was nothing I couldn't handle,' he told her.

Half an hour later, Khaled approached in the company of a pretty young woman wearing a head scarf.

'May I introduce my wife, Emira,' he said.

They made introductions, and then Khaled said, 'Emira is a great admirer of your gallery.'

'It is Krietman Stoop, yes?' she asked.

'Oh yes,' said Herman, 'in Zürich.'

'I was thinking of going there. Where exactly is it?'

Marie, seeing Herman's blank face, said, 'Koeniger Strasse, near to the Museum Strauhof.'

'If you want to visit, the best thing is to give Adrian Krietman a ring. He knows more than me about the place,' said Herman.

'He is your assistant?' Khaled asked.

'No no no, golly no. He really knows more about everything than me. He's the man to talk to.'

The conversation took a turn to the day's skiing, the weather and restaurants in the village of Zermatt, ground that Herman was less likely to fall flat on his face on than the art world. After excusing themselves to move on to their dinner reservation in another restaurant, Khaled and his wife walked happily through the crisp night air of the village.

'He is a good man to buy art from,' Emira said to her husband. 'I have a feel for these things. Did you see that diamond his wife was wearing? He is very successful. And yet modest. And so young. Extremely impressive.'

'Yes,' said Khaled. 'I liked him. You know he told me he knew nothing about art, because he doesn't like to do business on vacation. Isn't that admirable?'

A few days later, Herman and Marie were on a chairlift, ascending through the tops of pine trees under wisps of cloud in brightening and dimming sunshine. Herman glanced at the chair behind them to see Georgio on his own, and smiled. He had even made the man carry his skis to the station. As the chair rattled over a pylon and swung forward and back, he patted Marie on the beautiful curve of her full thigh and gave her a little kiss.

Herman's phone sounded. It hardly ever rang. With his teeth he pulled his glove off, and patted pockets.

'Uh-oh,' he said. 'It's Adrian. I hope he's not in a bate with me. Hello,' he said as the chair swooped up and rattled over another pylon's little wheels before settling back into an even swing.

'Hello!' said Adrian. 'How are you, my associate director?'

'Am I in trouble?'

'Not at all. Do you know someone called Prince Khaled Salime Al Deshani?'

'No.'

'Well he knows you. He said he met you at the Mont Cervin last week with Marie. He's short and plumpish.'

'Khaled! Is he a prince? Well I never. Everyone thought he was a chauffeur.'

'There aren't any cars in Zermatt.'

'They're not very bright, that lot.'

'Well, I'm pleased to tell you that you have just made your first sale. He and his wife have just bought four paintings. Total value 450,000 swiss francs.'

'Golly.'

'Yes. Your commission is 35,000 dollars.'

'Wow. Look, I've got to get off a ski lift now, but thanks for telling me.'

He slid the phone into his breast pocket.

'What was that?' Marie asked as they lifted the galvanized safety bar and edged forward in the seat. The rope net passed underneath them, and suddenly their skis were back on the snow and they were sliding down the ramp.

'I've made my first sale,' Herman shouted.

Marie pulled up beside him. 'Oh, you are clever. Congratulations.'

'I feel very pleased with myself,' Herman said. 'Come on, let's ski. Dinner's definitely on me tonight.'

Adrian commissioned some exquisitely understated business cards embossed with Herman's name and phone number. Within days of having them sent up to Zermatt he regretted it. Krietman Stoop gallery, tucked in a silent cul-de-sac off an expensive shopping street, was discreet to the point of being invisible, deliberately to deter the passer-by. Adrian's ideal day would be spent alone in the gallery communing with his art library, uninterrupted by human interference. Occasionally he liked to walk around the show, unspoiled by anyone showing interest.

Since supplying Herman with the business cards, Adrian had twice been disturbed by the doorbell ringing (he never left the door unlocked), which was bad enough in itself but, even worse, it presaged the noisy arrival of people who wanted to know all about the exhibition. Adrian didn't mind a rarefied discussion with an art historian or established connoisseur over some recondite detail, but he didn't do sales pitches to ill-educated rich people.

The first couple came in and dumped some glossy shopping bags with soft rope handles right in the middle of the gallery, where they jarred so acutely Adrian felt a migraine come on, and had to dab his brow with a handkerchief, hoping the people would get the message and leave. They didn't. Something inside Adrian whimpered when he heard the woman say, 'that one would look great in the den with the new drapes.' The second couple were depressingly young, and also totally ignorant, and asked tedious questions, mostly about the artist's life rather than the work. Adrian found it distasteful talking about biographical detail, which to him was irrelevant. To make matters worse, both couples bought work. Neither had any kind of collection to talk of, and they seemed to see buying art as a retail rather than an artistic, philanthropic or even spiritual activity, as Adrian considered it to be.

The sad truth was that Adrian's favourite clients, the lovely old collectors with deep knowledge and inexhaustible wealth, were getting thin on the ground. Some had died without passing onto their offspring the family habit of buying from Adrian to extend the collection, and others, more alarmingly, had appeared to have run out of money to spend on paintings and sculptures.

Herman and Marie remained in the mountains for a full month, and only left the Mont Cervin when the pistes near the town broke out in green blisters, and all you could hear at the bottom of the runs was the shriek of skis on sheet ice and rock. The streets in Zermatt turned grey and gritty, with grimy sponge cakes of the last unmelted snow clogging the gutters. The tourists thinned out. The hotel staff, in their baggy uniforms stained with the grime of a hard season, grouped up by the shrunken ice sculpture to collect tips and say goodbye to the departing guests.

Marie and Herman, feeling strange not to be in ski kit during the day, took the train down to the plain. From the soft seat in the quiet carriage they watched waterfalls hurl thaw water into the churning grey rivers.

They lived on the lake near Zürich in a house called Delincourt, which looked like a cross between a doll's house and a wedding cake, though was rather bigger than both. After walking through the rooms and checking the improvements they had set in hand before going skiing, they trod the pea gravel path to the jetty and looked back at the lights in the windows, agreeing how pretty it looked. Herman held the rope tight as Marie climbed into the boat, and then followed her in with a bit of a wobble, took the oars and guided them away from the shore. The lake was calm, and the ripples made bendy repetitions of the house on the water. Marie enjoyed the knock of the oars in the rollocks and the dripping water from the blades between gulps.

Back inside, they looked at their mail. Marie sat at her desk, as she had rather more than Herman, who opened his on the sofa.

'Look! Adrian has invited us to an opening!' Herman said.

'He always does,' said Marie, not looking up.

'Really?' said Herman.

'Mmm,' said Marie, tipping a sheaf of envelopes, letters and card invitations into the waste paper bin.

'I think we should go,' said Herman. 'I mean, it could be fun. I should see the place. I talk about it enough.'

'Isn't the job over?' Marie said.

'Oh no. I can see it is going to be very useful for some time. It's next week. Let's go.'

The vernissage at the gallery was thinly attended. Adrian liked it that way, as he was keen to get the thing over and done with as quickly as possible. Before it had started,

23

he had watched his secretary arranging a matrix of wine glasses on the tablecloth and said, 'that's quite enough. Hide the rest.'

'What if we run out?'

'Say the wine is finished.'

Marie and Herman looked around the show. Herman barely registered the pictures but had strong views about the catering arrangements, which he decided were inadequate.

When he got Adrian on his own, he said, 'Have you ever heard of an artist called Martino Zachman?'

'Alive or dead?'

'Alive.'

A flicker of pain crossed Adrian's face. 'What does he do?'

'I have no idea,' Herman said.

Adrian picked a magazine off the desk, and went to its index. Then he flattened the publication on the desk.

'Well he can't draw,' he said.

'A couple of people asked if we could get them some of his work,' Herman said.

'What did you say?' said Adrian, alarmed.

'What did I say? I asked them how their day's skiing went.'

Adrian smiled.

The next day, Herman was in a meeting with the interior designer about a remodelling of the boathouse when the most extraordinary thing happened. Martino Zachman called.

'Guten Tag!' The artist sounded upbeat and spoke in German. 'Ludo Daventry, my great friend – you know him don't you? – mentioned you were the best gallerist in

Switzerland. I am looking for a show and of course I need the best gallery.'

'Ludo!' exclaimed Herman. 'I love Ludo. Wonderful skier. Do you ski?'

'No. I hate that shit,' said Martino. 'I only like to work and fuck.'

'Ah! Well, there's a thing,' Herman blushed.

'So – I have a show with you or you blow the chance?' said Martino.

'To be honest it's my associate, Adrian, who decides all that kind of thing.'

'Talk to him. Ring me back.' And he put down the phone.

Adrian sounded tired when Herman spoke to him. 'The thing is I don't think Martino Zachman is any good. He's flashy and he's fashionable. But it's just not my scene.'

'But people want to buy his pictures,' said Herman. 'People I know.'

'Yes,' said Adrian absent-mindedly, 'people who don't know anything about art. Not collectors, not real collectors who understand the history and the threads of painting and sculpture. People who have studied, people who love art for what it is, and not because, well, because they have some empty walls that need covering.'

Adrian's mind returned to the auction catalogue open on the desk he had been leafing through when Herman had disturbed him. It was not contemporary. It was a quiet sale of minor Renaissance works on paper. He had been studying a particularly delightful ink sketch of a Madonna and Child, no more than 25cm square, but which could have come from the hand of Fra Angelico. Something deep inside Adrian yearned for it to be his. He thought all those yearnings had dried up long before, but this one was undeniable. The drawing had turned up in a castle in Croatia. It was the kind of place where these things ended up and could explain why it hadn't been surfaced earlier. He moved his magnifying glass to the estimate. US$ 55,000–70,000.

'You say you already have buyers?' Adrian said to Herman.

'Yes. It's a bit like a craze at school. They all want one.'

'I suppose there wouldn't be too much harm in doing it,' Adrian said.

'I could help,' said Herman.

'With what?' said Adrian

'I can help with the catering. I think you could do with a hand there. I know these people, they like good drink and I think we should give them a dinner afterwards.'

'A dinner?'

Adrian traditionally threw everyone out of his gallery openings by eight and was back in bed in his pyjamas flicking through a six-kilo catalogue raisonné by nine.

'Don't worry, I'll arrange it all,' said Herman. 'I actually like doing that sort of thing. I'll leave the art to you.'

Thus were the arrangements put in place. Martino's art arrived in pine flight cases, whose numerous brass screws were drilled out by a team of studio assistants who Martino had sent in advance. Adrian hated the pictures; they gave off an uncomfortable static. Martino had sent a scale model of the gallery and the hang, which his minions adhered to, though Adrian would have done it differently.

The term for the vernissage was 'rammed', though Adrian would not have used it. The Mont Cervin bar crowd had turned out in numbers. Even Roman was there. Ludo ushered in a large party of pals from Monaco who were in riotous good cheer, shouting and laughing with their backs to the paintings. Ludo had just won a seat in the UK Parliament and was on top form. Adrian got pinned to the far wall of the gallery, both unable and unwilling to get through the squeeze. He was appalled to see Gianni, dressed as a doctor, running his stethoscope over the female guests, apparently for a laugh.

Occasionally, Herman dragged someone through the crowd and said, 'Adrian, he wants to buy that one over there. Over to you!' and then left. Otherwise, he happily moved amongst the guests with trays of champagne glasses and wooden boards of canapés. At around eight o'clock Herman called for silence and, for a terrible moment, Adrian thought he was going to talk about the show but he said, 'Right everyone, we're all going to dinner. Come on!'

Soon, Adrian and his dowdy assistant were alone in the empty gallery staring at the unfamiliar dirty glasses. They collected them up, turned off the lights and locked up before going home through the silent Zürich streets.

'How did it go?' Heidi asked when he got home.

'Ugh,' he said.

'Did nothing sell?'

Adrian said, 'Everything sold.'

'That's marvellous,' said Heidi.

'No it's not,' said Adrian. 'It is not at all marvellous,' he wearily took off his jacket. 'I'm sorry darling, I'm in a bit of a grump. Ignore me.'

As he was buttoning up his flannelette pyjamas, she said, 'What's wrong, Adrian? Please tell me.'

He sighed and said, 'I had a horrible evening tonight. It was ghastly. Noisy, brash and vulgar. All that I hate. If this is what it takes to run a successful gallery, I don't think I can do it anymore. If this is the future, I want no part in it. I think I'd be much happier with a job at the university or the National Gallery.'

With the lights off he closed his eyes and indulged in a naughty fantasy: he imagined he worked at the Prado

27

in Madrid, and was promoted to the top job. He was sitting at his desk when the big door opened and a young woman came in with a portfolio of never-seen-before Michelangelo cartoons. Forty of them. Adrian shuddered with pleasure in the dark.

7

In the restaurant the long table rang with conversation and laughter. Martino sat at one end like an Easter Island statue, his gleaming skull and bulbous eyes not showing active displeasure, which Herman thought about the best he was ever going to get from him. At the other end, Marie looked at Herman passing around the dishes and thought how wonderful it was to see him so happy. Martino sent away all his food and solemnly ate an apple.

Then he stood up and said, 'I will not thank you for coming. It is your pleasure, not mine. Though I have experienced worse evenings.'

Herman was thinking what a rude man he was, but nodded and smiled like everyone else.

'I never talk about my art, as you know,' Martino stated. 'The work says everything that needs to be said better than any person could. And sometimes it is silent. But tonight I will toast to Herman!'

'Herman!' they all stood and laughed.

Martino did a small bow in Herman's direction and said, 'Now Herman will speak.'

Herman stood up. The room swam. He gulped. Marie gave him an encouraging smile.

Herman looked at his audience and thought *what on earth can I say about Martino's pictures?* The main but not sole problem was that Herman had really not actually looked at them, despite selling most of them. Before the guests turned up he had been too busy arranging the Wallisser teller on the special beechwood boards he had found, and more concerned with getting the proportion of sausage to cheese and gherkin correct. People tended to put too many gherkins on their teller.

'When I look at Martino's pictures,' Herman started, 'and I think when other people look at them,' he looked at the suntanned faces staring at him, and thought – *that's it, that's what they want to hear*: 'I cannot but help believe that they make us all ski a little bit faster and a little bit better.'

There was a cheer, and Herman saw a smile swim like a crocodile onto Martino's greedy gob. A few people clapped, a few yodelled and Gianni leapt onto the table, as was his wont, and mimed slaloming while the guests shouted, 'hup hup hup hup'.

Herman swallowed and thought at least Gianni hadn't dropped his pants.

Ludo yelled, 'That's so bloody true. It's incredible!'

Martino nodded wisely, thinking *he's good, this guy, he's really good.*

That night, back at home, Herman brought Marie's chamomile tea up to the bedroom and placed it on her bedside table. 'I really enjoyed tonight,' he said.

'I did too. You were so sweet, and everyone loved it.'

'Do you think so?' Herman asked.

'Yes. And you sold all the paintings.'

'I know. Rather odd. Well, Georgio was so useful. He told everyone they were a good investment, and everyone listens to Georgio about money.'

In the morning, Herman rose with a bounce in his step because he had realised that if there was going to be another opening he would be able to organise the eats again and needed, therefore, to track down some really exciting wooden tellers he had seen and was in a hurry to go and buy them in case they sold out. While he dressed he looked out on the silver lake. Pure discretion. Silence. Calmness. Swiss assurance. He took the car into town to check the tellers were there – they were – and hurried to the gallery to discuss numbers for the next vernissage, his mind churning with difficulties and possibilities of having two different teller designs at one function.

Adrian was standing at the desk, his hand over his domed head.

'That was rather good, last night, didn't you think?' said Herman.

Adrian sighed. 'In a way, but it wasn't my thing, to be honest.'

'Didn't you like the ham? Not the sausage?'

'It wasn't the food,' Adrian said. 'It was the whole thing. It was far too noisy and crowded for me. I've never had that many people in the gallery. It's not designed for that. A picture could have been damaged. And now I have to do all these transactions and send out all these invoices. I hate having to deal with the bank and money.'

'I'm sorry.'

'It's not really your fault. There's nothing we can do.' Adrian's forehead wrinkled with pain. 'It's the way things are heading. Those people didn't know anything,' he said. 'They're imbeciles. I'm sorry. I know they're your friends. But I can't deal with them. Honestly, it's not worth it.'

He walked into the back office where a little old lady sat in front of a screen, basically running the gallery.

When he returned, Herman was in the gallery trying to look at the pictures but actually crouching down picking up a toothpick.

He looked up to see Adrian staring at him.

'Next time I want to use a longer toothpick. Talking of which, when is our next opening?'

'Herman,' Adrian said. 'I've decided to close the gallery.'

'Oh.'

'I want a job in an institution or a public gallery. A position without having to make sales. To be honest I find sales rather common. I'm sorry,' he said. When he saw Herman's dismay he added, 'Maybe you can get a job at another gallery?'

'I can't see that happening,' said Herman. 'I don't know a thing about art.'

'Well, I'm sorry.'

Herman drove along the magisterial Zürichsee, but his heart was heavy. The telepathic gates swung open and, with an opulent crunch of gravel, he drew up at his sumptuous home. Inside was a wife whom he loved and who loved him dearly. But Herman knew he wanted more. He could no longer deny it. He needed to serve finger food to rich folk.

He spoke to Marie about Adrian's news.

'It's okay,' he told her, 'I'm not that upset. I mean, I always knew it wasn't going to last. Of course it wouldn't. I know nothing about art. But I liked giving that dinner and seeing the people enjoying my menu.'

'I saw how pleased you were,' Marie said.

'You know what I thought about it? For the first time in a long while I felt really useful. It was like having our own little *stubbe*. With the cosy tables all close to each other and the felt curtain over the door to keep out the draught? Like that.'

Uh-oh, thought Marie, *he's not back on that one, is he?*

Alone, Herman rowed out onto the lake and listened to the sound of the blades dipping into the water and the drips falling from them as he leant back to take another pull. He stared at the wooded shore, the paved gardens, the steeple in the village, the terraced vineyards on the hill. The castle's flagpole was a white needle against the dark mountain. Herman was swallowing the pain of not buying the teller boards. The ones made of beech. He was going to leave that pain out on the water, so when he tied the boat at the jetty he would return to Marie without any resentment.

In the sitting-room, Marie paused from sewing some tapestry to watch him walk back to the house.

The next day Marie rang Frederic, her old and feeble financial advisor. He was short, with a horseshoe of white hair around a mottled skull. In the thirty years she had known him she had never seen any expression on his face more committed than patient kindness.

She said, 'I'm thinking of buying a gallery in Zürich.'

'An art gallery?' he said.

'Yes.'

'Ooh, I'm afraid I cannot advise that,' he said.

'Yes, I know it won't make any money, but Herman is working there and it might be closing down and I don't want him to lose his job.'

'I can't recommend it, I'm afraid,' said Frederic.

'Will you look into it?'

'Are you quite sure? I have had a few clients who started art galleries. It never goes well.'

'Find out how much the owner wants for it.'

'I have to counsel against it.'

'If you could look into it I would be grateful.'

'Yes, of course.'

A couple of days later Frederic rang back.

'I spoke to Herr Krietman at the gallery,' he said. 'I am afraid it is not good news,' Frederic successfully hid his glee.

'Is he not interested in selling it?' Marie asked. 'Oh.'

'No. Not precisely, but in as many words.'

'What did he say?'

'He said he was prepared to sell, but the problem is one of valuation. He informed me that the gallery had a large inventory of paintings, the value of which I think is unrealistic.'

'Like what?'

'The gallery possesses some Picassos and Matisses, and their value is I think unrealistically high. They are very likely, in my opinion, to be worth a great deal less in twenty or thirty years than they are now. And the property itself has a most unsatisfactory lease of only 864 years, which is too insecure for your requirements. I have to advise against the purchase.'

Later, Marie found Herman happily lining up the shoes in the boot room and removing grit from the soles with a special needle he had driven to town to get. He held it up smiling. 'See. Perfect implement. And stainless of course so it will last forever. Now, where do we store it, in the shoe care drawer or the needlework pouch? Decisions, decisions.'

'That was Frederic calling back. Adrian says the gallery is for sale.'

'What did he say?' he asked.

'Adrian wants eighteen million Swiss francs for the inventory, the gallery and the business. Frederic says it's a bit steep.'

'Eighteen million?' said Herman. 'Golly. I guess that's that then.'

'It's a lot of money,' Marie said. It was a hell of a lot of money. It took her three weeks to earn that much. 'But I can see how happy you were at the opening, and I enjoyed it too, and think I should buy it and if we don't like it we can always get Frederic to sell it. It will be fun, and give you and I something to do together. We might have to learn about contemporary art, though.'

Herman said, 'I have a hunch it's not as difficult as it sometimes sounds.'

8

As Herman adjusted his cuffs he gazed out of the window and admired the upgrade on the boathouse. He had recently bought a new motor launch with white calfskin upholstery and pink piping, which required an appropriate mooring. His days of pulling oars were behind him.

Herman had got rather good at selling art. He still knew little about it, but that actually helped, because he couldn't judge it and so never knew if it wasn't any good.

He turned in profile to the mirror to admire his signature look – the Nehru jacket and white trousers – and pulled his tummy in.

Then he said to himself, 'It's only six hundred and fifty thousand. Swiss francs. Dollars. Pounds. That? It's fabulous isn't it? And only three-quarter of a million pounds.'

Herman had refined the skill of putting the word *only* in front of almost any sum of money, however large. But it took practice. At first he found it hard to say, 'only twenty thousand dollars,' of a piece of art, but now, 'only a million,' tripped off his tongue lightly and gaily.

about to be fashionable. This one was a small, nervous American called Sarah Absolom. Herman couldn't make head nor tail of her stuff, but was confident that everything would go well. It certainly had for the last three years. He had worked out that the key to selling art was not so much what it looked like, but about how many houses the customer had. Luckily every man and his dog who could afford it was investing in property, as Herman was looking for people not so much with a discerning eye as empty walls.

Georgio had helped with the guest list too. Along with Roman from the bar at the Mont Cervin. They always packed the place out with people who knew how to enjoy themselves. The problem Herman now had was weeding out the people who couldn't afford the art. It was getting harder for Herman to know who to talk to because he really didn't want to waste his time on the wrong guests.

What Herman needed was a device that could tell him exactly how rich people were when he met them. To the nearest ten mill. Some kind of electric contraption attached discreetly to his right hand that sensed the figure when palm to palm contact was made and triggered something in his pocket that vibrated like the new mobile phones when the net worth of the individual exceeded ten million US dollars. Maybe a modification could be attached that separated assets from cash. A beep. Cash was the important thing. Until that device was invented, Herman would just have to continue to be jovial to everyone.

There were some customers who needed to talk about the art, so Herman picked up a few phrases which always got him by. One favourite was to say that the work interrogated the space. Nobody ever argued with that and it pretty well worked with anything, though of course he had to be careful not to repeat it too often about different pictures in case someone noticed, though to be honest he didn't think they were listening that closely. He decided that he had to work up a second remark, so was keeping his ears open for a good one.

The main thing the collectors wanted from the exhibition was to have a good time and to feel special, which was what they got in return for buying Herman's art. He made sure of that.

In the restaurant later that night, as he sat down after making his speech about Sarah's work (Herman had noticed how many short men were in the room, so had made the well received remark that Sarah's art made everyone feel a little bit taller), he looked down the long table at Marie, glowing in the candlelight, and thought how much this was like the little stubbe he had imagined, full of happy customers, enjoying his Walisser teller and happily chattering to each other. He patted his tummy and looked for the raclette amongst the candles and glasses. He didn't need anything more.

Well, he wanted one thing more. He wanted to hear, no, he wanted to overhear, someone saying, 'Marie Stoop married so very well. Herman's not rich, but he's clever and his business is growing very well. He really is a success.'

Back at Delincourt at the end of the evening, they sat together on a sofa drinking champagne, flushed with the success and fun of the evening. A fire of pine logs crackled in the grate, pinging sparks at the guard under a painting of an Alpine scene bought by Marie's grandfather, in the first waterfall of money in the 1930s. A child led a horse loaded with firewood through the snow towards a hamlet where a single dim light glowed in a chalet window. It was touching and romantic, like most of the other paintings in the sumptuous panelled room.

Marie's mother's collection, much of it inherited from her parents, featured many pictures of the Alps, including the shepherds in summer, the summits in winter, the high lakes, the dramatic weather, the plunging cliffs, and of course, the chamois on the rocks.

'I was thinking,' said Herman, 'that a Collishaw would look very good up there. These pictures are, are, not quite right now, are they?'

Marie thought, this has gone a bit too far. I'm not moving these pictures. She secretly loved them more than any of the new stuff Herman showed in the gallery.

'Or maybe a Sarah Absolom?' Herman offered.

But Marie had a better idea. She would buy Herman another house, one with a lot of walls, so he could do it there.

9

In the summer of 1991, Herman got wind of a new art movement which had swaggered into London. At its head was a group of bold young artists, flanked by gallerists, critics and curators, and drawing along in its slipstream art advisors, social climbers, flunkeys, fixers, dilettanti and flaneurs, all having a gay old time.

Herman hurried to London to see if he could achieve his long-held ambition of serving a first-class Walliser teller to the English. To do this he had to open a gallery, but it turned out that selling art in London was even easier than in Zürich. The ratio of empty-wall-space to rich people was nothing short of spectacular. And somehow the rich had got the notion firmly in their heads that buying Herman's paintings made them look clever. It was, to Herman, the most brilliant misreading of the actual situation, though he obviously didn't explain that to any of them. Instead he smiled blithely, sold lots of pictures and sourced crisper and thinner gherkins.

Business was so brisk that Marie found a house in the English county of Somerset where she and Herman could entertain customers on weekends.

Called the Highworth Estate, it comprised a ten-bedroom Georgian house, various outbuildings, staff accommodation and two and a half thousand acres of mature woodland and arable farmland. Ludo Daventry, now a close friend of Herman and Marie, was quick to rename it the Highnetworth Estate.

After completing the redecoration of the house, Herman stuffed it with art. He wanted to give his clients the idea that an empty wall meant an empty mind. When a Zachman painting called *Pocket Rocket* was lifted from its customised pine box by a couple of men in white gloves from the art transport company, it turned out to be too big for the space Herman had assigned for it on the sweeping staircase. They offered to put it up in another couple of places, but Herman decreed they weren't right either.

'It's not interrogating the space,' Herman said.

One of the art handlers, a young blond man called Jim who was keen to make his way in the trade, nodded, and made a note to remember the phrase. He often wanted to know what to say about art.

Despite suspecting that Martino would disapprove, Herman sent *Pocket Rocket* to be sold at auction. It was meant to be Herman's job as Zachman's gallerist to place Martino's work in the most prestigious private and public collections, so that the man's place in the history of art would be secured. He certainly was not authorised to put it under the hammer where it could fall into anybody's hands. Martino definitely did not want his work reappearing on the open market where it risked dulling his gallery prices.

Two months later *Pocket Rocket*, for which Herman had paid Martino £86,000, was sold in London for £221,000.

Herman hardly noticed; money was by now pouring into the gallery. This was London in the 90s, a place that

44

farted credit and belched cash. But it was something else Herman was after. He hankered after a certain kind of compliment so much that he considered adopting a disguise, just to hear someone say *Herman Gertsch's a bloody clever man. He's not just a shit-hot dealer, he serves the best frigging finger food in the whole art world.* But, poor Herman, it was not that he heard. When he lurked, one quiet sunny afternoon in the London gallery, eavesdropping on some random visitors, he heard words that drained the blood from his face. *Apparently it's all his wife's money.*

That hurt.

As a salve, Herman started secretly purchasing, with cash that some Russian friends of Georgio always insisted on paying with, a private collection of his own paintings which would have nothing to do with Marie.

This anxiety aside, things were going Herman's way. His galleries enjoyed a triumphant decade following his arrival in London. The programmes at his galleries were critically acclaimed, the openings and dinners were famous, and the profits positively volcanic, shooting into the sky and forming a hot lava that immolated anything that got in their way, whether it was competition, criticism or regulation. And to make the picture perfect, Marie had two children, a boy, Walter, and a girl, Polly. They made Highworth a happy family home.

Herman always imagined that getting rich would make him more content, but he was wrong: the more money he had, the more things annoyed him, particularly very small things. At Highworth it started with one of the pink-bricked chimneys being three inches taller than the other – nobody else noticed but it spoilt the entire front elevation for Herman, who had the lower one heightened, and then wished he had the other one shortened. Then he found that the hinges didn't exactly match on the back door, and from then on every time he went there he found something to irritate him. He had a growing sense that there was something tatty about Somerset. For instance, if he stood right in the corner of his dressing room he could see what he suspected was a caravan about three miles away. The grey dot was tiny on the landscape, and actually only visible at all in the winter months because foliage obscured it from May onwards, but Herman knew it to be there, and if he looked really carefully, through binoculars for instance, he could still make it out in July.

Things improved when Herman discovered that not only had the Somerset locals never heard of Rauschenberg, but better, they had never seen a raclette. He immediately commissioned a top American architect to convert the outbuildings at the old farmyard into a suite of ambitious exhibition spaces, and hired a team of curators to programme some openings.

In the old milking parlour, now transformed into a slate-floored office with thick white shelves, Herman brought the subject of the caravan up when he was having a meeting with Marie.

She said, 'Why don't we just plant some trees at the bottom of that field? Then you won't be able to see it. Ask Mark to organise it.'

'But what about in the winter?'

'Plant spruce, or leylandia.'

'You know I cannot tolerate non-indigenous species,' Herman very nearly spluttered.

'I'll put a curtain up. How about that? You won't see through that. That's if I can possibly find a material you can tolerate,' she smiled.

Herman's cheeks burned. He realised he had made a bit of an ass of himself. He hoped the matter would not be mentioned again. But when, at the end of the meeting, Marie was out of earshot, Herman's assistant said, 'If you want, I could find out about that caravan. It's most likely a hippy's static. There's a lot of them hippies down there on the levels. My dad told me. He works for the council. He's always trying to serve notices on them.'

'Really?' said Herman.

'Yeah.' This assistant was a newly employed girl called Sharon Pratt, who had feathered hair, thighs that touched when she stood with her feet apart, as she often did, and fake tan, all of which Herman was going to fire her for as soon as he found a legal way of doing it, though now he thought it might be worth fixing the defects rather than replacing the item.

'Well, let me show it to you. Later,' said Herman. When he heard Marie drive off to the supermarket he led Sharon across the newly cobbled yard and into the house.

In the house, Herman noticed to his satisfaction the look of open wonder on Sharon's simple face at the art, lighting, floors, rugs, furniture, paint finishes; everything, basically.

In a truly weak moment even by Herman's new standards, he said, 'What do you think of what we've done?'

Her face notched up a few more watts of wonder. 'It's amazing, Mister Gertsch. Everyone in the village loves what you done round here.'

'Come on, I'll show you where you can see the caravan and you can have a look around upstairs at the same time.'

10

To open a five thousand square foot gallery near the Meatpacking District of New York, Herman departed Somerset for two months, leaving Marie and the children at home. He had signed a couple of blue chip American artists, and brought – or rather bought – the best directors and saleswomen and men from other galleries which didn't have pockets as deep as Marie.

When he returned to Highworth, he just caught the bent, dried-up stems of the five thousand crocuses he had had planted up the drive. He walked in the woods with his children and he looked at the new fencing, at the saplings in their plastic socks, at the gates, the styles and the signs. It was all as he and Marie had decreed. In the house, the hinges on the back door had been changed to match, and the other chimney had been shortened to be level with the lower one. Everything was perfect.

In the office, Sharon said, 'I spoke to my dad about that caravan. It doesn't have planning permission.'

Herman instantly knew what she was talking about.

'Oh yes?'

'It's an illegal static. He is a hippy.'

'What exactly does your father do?'

'He's the chief enforcement officer on the council.'

'Is he?'

'Yeah.'

'If it's illegal, then surely it's just a question of removal?'

'On paper, yeah. In theory. But it's Brother.'

'What do you mean?'

'Brother? He's a bit of a local folk hero on the quiet. My dad can't stand him, cos Brother gives him the run-around. My dad says he's the slipperiest man in South Somerset and therefore the Western Hemisphere. He's hard to track down and even harder to winkle out, my dad says. You see that's the Levels down there. They're not like yourself, they're a bunch of pirates what live there.'

'But surely they must conform to the laws of the land like any other citizen?'

'Like I say, in theory. But they operate a bit under the radar.'

Herman tutted.

He hired the biggest planning consultancy firm in the world, based in London, to look into the case. It was cut and dried. The caravan was there without consent. The council had tried to get it removed on many occasions, but for one reason or another – mainly a lack of backbone, Herman concluded – the job had not been done.

'I will soon run him to ground,' he said to Sharon. 'Easy. By the way, Sharon, do you have a middle name? I've been meaning to ask you.'

'Celia. I am Sharon Celia Pratt.'

'I think Celia would be better in the office. It just sounds more us, if you see what I mean. Do you mind if I use it? And Pratt ...'

'Yeah?'

'May I ask what your mother's maiden name was?'

'Somerton. Louise Somerton.'

'Don't you think Somerton sounds better? The art world is so silly about these things, but if you want to get on, I think Celia Somerton sounds more like a woman with a top job at a gallery than Sharon Pratt.'

'Celia Somerton. I don't mind that. Sounds good.'

'And one more piece of advice. Black clothes. No prints or stripes. They don't help either.'

Zigott Olins, the planning consultancy, tried to serve a notice on Brother. It was returned unserved six times. The last processor they sent down to try to find the man came back a week later and handed in his notice. Mostly they couldn't find the offender, but when they did he tricked them either into serving it on someone else or just disappeared into the reeds and bulrushes that grew up around his caravan. The problem was that you had to drive a mile-long track, giving Brother plenty of time to take evasive action. The police wouldn't have anything to do with the case. The Chief Constable said they had already wasted far too much time on the man and he wasn't actively harmful so it was best to leave him alone.

After a year of no success Herman sued for peace, sending round a handwritten letter suggesting Brother come to discuss it over dinner. He would charm the ruffian with simple fare: Bernese Oberland sausage and wafer-thin slices of Swiss gruyere, an irresistible combination. The man turned up and listened politely to Herman's argument, agreeing with everything. But at the end of the meal he announced he wasn't actually Brother and, lifting a bottle of wine off the table, departed.

Herman turned his guns on the council but their eyes glazed over as soon as Brother's name was mentioned. Brother had been evading court orders for over twenty years. He was unarrestable on some ground or other. If only he had been violent, but the police could never get him to attack them. He just disappeared in a wisp of air.

'I know just the thing,' said Herman, in a private jet on his way from Zürich to London. 'Art. I have not yet tried art on him.'

'What do you mean?' Marie said.

'I mean that eye-sore caravan man.'

'Not that again.'

'Listen to this. You'll like it. I'm going to ask one of our artists, Martino maybe, to go round and camouflage it, so it disappears into the background. Then that will be that. It's a perfect solution. Art conquers all. Of course!'

Martino didn't want to do it, and while Herman thought of who to ask next, Marie hung a curtain over the offending window.

'Now you can't see it,' she said.

'I know, but that's not the point, is it? It's the principle of the thing. He's making a fool of me.'

'He is not. You are doing that very well yourself. Stop this silly obsession. There are far more important things for you to be thinking about. Like the children.'

'Yes. Of course,' Herman stood up. 'Where are they?'

'Walter's been waiting to play football with you for hours.'

'Of course. Let me change my trousers.'

'I'll come and play too. Come on, it's a lovely afternoon. We might all go for a walk. We haven't been for a walk for too long. You know I love them.'

Herman decided that Marie was right. She always was. And didn't give the caravan another thought. It receded in his reality to the size it actually was in the landscape. Barely noticeable. The rest of the landscape of his life returned. He got it in perspective, as Marie had told him to.

He had a lot to do, as the empire was multiplying. Herman, in his desire to throw a decent cocktail party, had found himself gatekeeper of the places which introduced the wealthy to social success, and the artists to riches. He was the giver of dreams.

He became very good at judging artists, and he didn't do it like other people, poring over books or going to look at shows. He had a simple test: to discover if an artist was going to make it, you watched how they were with a collector's children. Cranston Brakes, the cantankerous American painter, professed to loathe kids in private, but the way he got down on the floor with the spoilt, fat offspring of Trudi and Kim Kitsplinger, the voracious Texan collectors, and played plasticine for hours with the brat after lunch, was breathtaking. Herman signed Cranston up for a show pretty well on the spot. That was the kind of artist he wanted.

All this time Herman was secretly acquiring works of art, building his personal collection. He bought only the best, and quietly savoured the idea of one day revealing them as his own achievement. It would be worth a fortune by then. It was already worth a fortune. He had bought the cream of the cream. Marie would be bowled over. And that crusty financial adviser of hers who always eyed him with ill-concealed suspicion would have to admit he had been wrong.

II

Walter was growing into a kind and gentle young man with a round face and thick brown hair. Herman was determined that his son do something more ambitious than follow him into the art world. On Walter's thirteenth birthday, he had opened his presents in the morning and, after a birthday lunch, had found Herman alone in his study.

'Did you like your present?' Herman asked.

'Dad. Why would you give me a knife and a chopping board?' Walter asked.

'It's not a chopping board. Didn't you notice the contours? It's a teller. A special board for mountain saus–'

'Dad, I know what a teller is. For God's sake.'

'Did you like the sausage?'

'I'm a vegetarian, Dad.'

'I thought that might be a phase.'

'No. It's not. In fact I am thinking of going vegan.'

'Vegan?' Herman swallowed. 'But that's dairy too! Do you think you could still lay out, I don't mean eat, I mean prepare, a Walliser teller even if you were a vegan?'

'For Pete's sake, Dad, I have no interest in dried sausage, gherkins or, for that matter, any Swiss hors d'oeuvres. Please, get it out of your head. I'm not interested in a career in catering or hospitality. I'm sorry. I know it's a disappointment. I'm not that kind of son. I've tried, but I can't be.'

'You mean when you asked me to teach you to carve ham on the bone?'

'I did try, Dad. But … it's just not me. I thought you knew by now.'

Herman felt a hammer strike his DNA.

Walter said, 'Why didn't you give me the de Kooning book that I asked for? That's what I really wanted. It's art I love, Dad, not cured mountain sausage. I'm just sorry.'

'Art? Everyone loves art. It's such an easy option, Walter, it's such a well-worn path. Whereas Swiss mountain cuisine, particularly the Walliser teller, is so misunderstood and overlooked. The field is open for a total renaissance. You could make such a difference there …'

Herman and Marie sent Walter to Wellfield House, a boarding school near Highworth that was renowned for the prowess of its sporting teams and the wealth of its students. Herman thought it might be a good place to pick up some clients, but didn't mention that to Marie or Walter. He encouraged Walter to befriend Khaled's son, in what Walter suspected of being a roundabout business move, though Walter was happy to find Ali as allergic to hard work and rules as he was and the two of them became firm friends. Herman and Marie dropped Walter off at school in his oversize uniform on his first day, a hot September afternoon. Framed photographs of illustrious students, a few of whom were internationally famous, lined the corridor they walked along to Walter's study. Herman stopped at a portrait.

'Look,' he said.

'That's the only one I don't recognize,' Marie said.

'Renzo Matti. Wow, he went here. That's really something to be proud of, Walter,' Herman said.

'Who is he?' Marie asked.

'A really interesting Italian chef,' Herman said.

Walter opened the door and faced the narrow bed, pine desk and flimsy wardrobe of his school study for the first time. He could hear his father banging on to his housemaster about the chef. He shook his head and smiled before starting to unpack.

With Walter at school, Herman and Marie flew to Zürich for a show by an English artist called Dave Bell, who Ludo had overheard being discussed by some curators when his plane was delayed in St Kitts in the spring. The show had gone well. Herman had looked at the fresh, aspirational faces at the dinner and said in his speech that owning the paintings made people more sexy. It worked a treat. And while in the toilet booth, a place he often used for eavesdropping, he hadn't heard any men say anything about Marie being rich. What joy. Just Gianni telling a story about being pulled off the bed by his ankles while having sex.

Back upstairs, bidding his guests farewell, Herman's phone rang.

'Gertsch?'

'Yes.'

'Martino here. Where are you?'

'In Zürich. What can I do for you?'

'You should count yourself lucky I am not there too, because if I was I would walk round and punch your stupid fat Swiss face.'

'Martino!'

'Do not ever buy my work and sell it for a profit.'

'What are you talking about?' Herman said.

'*Pocket Rocket*. I sold it to you in 2000. I have just seen it in the auctions in New York. Are you selling it?'

'No.'

'Well who owns it?'

'I don't know. Look, I must have forgotten to tell you that I did put it in an auction shortly after I bought it. I should have mentioned it.'

'You what?'

'I bought it for Highworth but it didn't fit on the staircase. So I sold it. I didn't make any profit. Or hardly any.'

'You are meant to be my dealer, not bloodsucker.'

'I am sorry, Martino, I was going to keep it but it was too big.'

Martino said nothing.

'I didn't plan to do it. I will not do it again.' He grimaced as he thought about two more pictures he had bought and paid for and not admitted to Martino were in his personal collection.

'Who bought those two red pictures in my New York show? Was it you?' Martino said.

'No!' lied Herman, wincing.

'Who was it?'

'An anonymous collector.'

'Tell me his name.'

'I am afraid I am not at liberty to do that.' Herman tried to hide in pomposity. He was mouthing and waving goodbye to departing guests. 'He's asked to remain anonymous. Could we have this conversation another time? I'm just in a dinner.'

'No. Who is he?'

'I can tell you this: he has the best taste.'

'What. Is. His. Name?'

'He doesn't want his name known by the public.'

'I'm not the public. I'm the artist.'

Herman closed his eyes and rocked slowly forward on his toes.

'He paid in full,' Herman said as a diversion. 'No discount. Or very little.'

'Tell me, you knob.'

'We refer to him as Herr X at the gallery.'

'And what is his real name?'

'I'm afraid I can't reveal that.'

'Why not?'

'He specifically asked not to be named, or …'

'Or what?'

'Or he wouldn't buy your work. I will definitely lose him as a client if I reveal his name.'

'You fucking liar. It's you, isn't it?'

Herman blushed. He actually felt himself blushing. 'Of course it's not.'

'He better not sell them, whoever it is.'

'He's an established, reputable collector, not a seller.'

'Really?' Martino brightened. 'He's a proper collector?'

'Yes. Would I sell your work to anyone else?'

'What else is in his collection?'

Herman said, 'I cannot talk about his collection.'

'Why?'

'He's very discreet. To the point of paranoia, between you and me. I don't want to break his confidence.'

On the drive along the lake back to Delincourt, Herman felt for Marie's hand and held it. He thought, *the sooner I get shot of these pictures the better.*

The next morning was spent at Adrian's old leather desk thinking about what to do. Dave Bell came into the gallery glowing with his first a sold-out show. He asked Herman who had bought all the works, and Herman ran through the list, explaining client Herr X had bought two.

'The best two!' Dave had said. 'And who the hell is Herr X, God bless his cotton socks?'

'Herr X is a top client. I managed to get away with only giving him five per cent discount.'

Herman got the happy Englishman on his way, and sat back down heavily. He worked out he had forty-five secret paintings. There were some he could probably sell privately and quietly, which wouldn't attract much attention, but others, particularly Martino's (though Sarah Absolom's as well, now she had got so famous) would cause real problems for him if they suddenly appeared in public. Questions would be asked and Herman would be exposed as a … as a what, exactly? A greedy dissembler at best, a lying cheat at worst. It was significant enough to dent his reputation and knock the gallery down a few notches. So he would have to keep the collection, and basically never mention it, or Herr X, again. Ever.

He wanted to talk to Marie about it, but that would mean explaining what he had done, and something made him hesitate. It was a stupid mess to have got into, and he didn't want her to know. He wasn't proud of himself.

A couple of days later Dave Bell was back in London. He stood at an ATM staring at his bank balance, soaking up the thrilling and confusing sensation of finding something euphoric that was usually so painful. He calculated that he could now pay back all tax, all overdue rent on flat and studio, and release himself from some horrible commercial and personal loans. But something took precedence: a bender. It was good to get the priorities right. Soon he was striding into the Groucho Club, a place whose doors had been closed to the artist for a good few months. He drew himself up in front of the receptionists, who were looking at him warily and said, 'Ladies, I believe I have an outstanding account to settle,' before flourishing his cheque book.

'What's happened? A rich aunt died?' said a gravelly voice behind him.

'No, my dear Jim,' said Bell to his ursine comrade. 'I have harvested the fruits of my own labour. A sold-out show. Zürich. Krietman Stoop.'

'Oh I've heard about them. Any good? Or total shits like all other dealers?'

'Excellent. Epic party, and stinking rich clients. Very well connected. Herman is a gent.'

'Who did you sell to?'

'The best works, two of them, went before the show opened to Herman's top client.'

'What's their name?'

'I would tell you, Jim, but I can't,' said Dave. 'Well, Herman Gertsch wouldn't tell me. It's secret. The man likes anonymity. But he paid up. Top dollar. Which is why I propose we repair to the bar for a beverage. Will you be so good as to join me?'

A woman opened a glass door and the two artists entered the cool calm of the downstairs bar in its early afternoon mood. Dave called for champagne.

'See if you can find out who he is,' Jim said. 'I've got a show coming up; collectors who like your work often like mine.'

'They call him Herr X. Salut!' Bell raised his flute.

'Herr X? That's Harvey Brice. The property developer. Tall dude with the floppy hair. That's what everyone says. And I don't think he's denying it. He bought two big pieces of Martino's.'

Over the next nine glorious roller-coaster hours, during which the murmurings of the tea-time clientele transitioned to animated chatter at drinks time and then into the shrieking squawks of the club at full throttle, Dave stood resolute in the downstairs bar, handing out, spading out largesse. At 3am, with the job of making everyone in range comprehensively drunk fully completed, the young artist was to be found alone on the Soho pavement beaming broadly in a stained white suit, barefoot, with a bleeding nose. He decided to call Herman.

'I just want to say for a Swiss fucker you are a beautiful person. I don't care if you are a Nazi, which I am sure you are not. Or if your dad hid their gold. I do not care! I just think you are a fucking amazing guy. You gave me my first sellout show! I'd give you a tonguer if you were with me. I might even tit you up.'

'Thank you,' said Herman.

'And as for your mystery collector Herr X. You send him my love and tell him I am looking forward to seeing him soon. A little dicky bird told me his real name. So his secret is out. I want him to come to my mate's show. Jim Firth. Great artist.'

'Who did they say it was?'

'Harvey Brice.'

'Harvey Brice?' The cheek of the man, thought Herman. Harvey Brice was a two-bit hustler; his collection, if you could give it that name, was a random bunch of cast-offs masquerading as a cogent selection. He was best known amongst dealers for not paying. He was probably hinting at being Herr X to get to good parties. 'It's not Harvey Brice. I can tell you that,' Herman said.

'Well can you tell the real Herr X about Jim's show, will you?'

'Of course I'll let him know, but he rarely ventures out,' said Herman. Then he thought *why didn't I take the opportunity to say Herr X had decided to stop collecting?*

'I've got to go,' said Dave Bell. 'Thanks for ringing. It's a bit inconvenient to talk right now.'

Herman turned off his phone and wondered about going further and actually killing Herr X. Perversely the thought hurt. How would he do it? A car crash. But people would ask for details. Careful. A mountain road in Peru. Far away from the media. What was he doing in Peru? Family holiday. They all perished. Wouldn't want to leave a widow behind, artists would sense the commercial promise of a rich grieving woman and start searching for her. It would mean a funeral. It could be a small one, in view of the tragedy. Close family only. Artists would definitely start asking about what was happening to their pictures. They could be sold by his estate. Herman could tell them there was nothing he could do to stop it.

12

Herman cast his expert eye over his staff as he wafted through the office at Highworth. Celia had lost three stone but still looked too fat. Nevertheless, it was a start. It sounded tough but she was the one who wanted to work in the art world. Her hair was cut to one length and made a straight line across her shoulders. So that was a relief.

'Pardon me,' she said to Herman, 'only what it is, the accountant's been on the phone, wanting some information about your Herr X.'

'Leave it with me. I'll call him.'

From the safety of his study in the house, Herman dialled his London office, gently kicking the door to as he heard the ring tone.

'I just had a message from Celia about Herr X,' he said, as casually as possible.

'Yes. New money laundering regulations mean we have to give the Inland Revenue the names of buyers and sellers, and, err, I've had a look, but I don't seem to have one on file. Can you let me know who it is?'

'That could be a problem,' Herman said. 'You see I sold him works on the understanding his name would remain secret. He's a very private man.'

'HMRC won't let us take payments over a million without full verification.'

'How much has he spent?'

'Two point four million, and it's all in cash, which is unusual. They just want to know who he is.'

'I'm going to need to talk to him about this. What precisely do you need?'

'Name, obviously, country of domicile, tax number, address, email.'

'I'll get back to you.'

Herman had a think. If he didn't come up with something, or rather someone, he would have to account for the cash he had bought the pictures with. Georgio's Russian friends were unlikely to be happy to be dragged into this, and frankly they were a bit scary even before anything went wrong. He dismissed the idea of putting up a fake name. It would start unravelling straight away. He needed a person, not just a name.

There were other reasons for giving Herr X a name. For a start, it seemed suspicious for him not to have one. Second, since he heard about Harvey Brice, various other collectors in the art world were rumoured to be Herr X, and although some denied it, others like Brice traded on it, if only socially, and Herman didn't like that. He wanted Herr X to be under his control. He was, after all, Herman's creation. If he could just find him a name it would solve all these problems, but for that he needed a commodity not readily available in the art world: a person he could really trust.

Later that day, in a meeting called to discuss menus with the directors, the staff started talking about the forthcoming programme of shows and Herman's mind started wandering. He realised that there was absolutely no possibility he could rely on anyone to pretend to be Herr X without word getting out. The works of art in his name were worth millions. Instead, what he needed was a real person who would never find out he was being used by Herman in this way. Someone like a hermit, or a tramp, but one with an address and a national insurance number.

Then he had one of his brilliant ideas. On a level with when he pickled and then lightly fried the shallots before placing them on the teller. Caramelisation. That had been a turning point, and so would this moment prove to be.

When the office had thinned out after the meeting, he went to the filing cabinet.

'Can I help?' Celia said behind him.

'No no no, thank you. You carry on.' He held his hands in the drawer and smiled so she wouldn't notice which file he was pulling out. He took it under his arm over to the house and, with the door wide open so he could hear Marie coming, opened it. It was Mendip Council's file on the man who lived in the caravan. Celia had been responsible for obtaining it. It contained all Brother's planning violations over the years. Celia's father had had it at home and he had asked Celia to make an illegal copy during the time they had been trying to move the caravan.

He turned a few pages and stopped. John Sparkler Burn. NI TS 5379342. Brother's real name and national insurance number. The man who could never be found. The slipperiest man in South Somerset and therefore the Western hemisphere.

Herman took out his phone and photographed the page. Along with a newly created email address, JSB777@hotmail.com, he gave the information to the accountants. The London gallery was nominated as John Sparkler Burn's forwarding address.

The next show in London was for the American wunderkind Sean6, a young man who habitually wore combat fatigues and high heels. In the queue that went round the block on the first night, Herman spotted two billionaires, whom he enjoyed pulling out and taking past the bouncers.

During the party, Sean6 found Herman and said, 'Hey, has Herr X bought anything?'

'No. And now everything is spoken for.'

'But I have to have something in his collection. He's got Martinos and Dave Bells. What the fuck's wrong with my work?'

'He told me he was buying less.'

'That makes it more important he buys me, right? Look: get me into the collection. Okay?'

'I'll ring him and see what I can do. Actually, he has a name. John Burn.'

'So it's not that weird dude Brice?'

'Definitely not.'

'John Burn. Okay. You talk him into it.'

'If anyone can, I can,' said Herman, at last truthfully. He decided to make an advance party to go to the dinner venue – an ex-borstal in one of London's last convincing slums – where a kitchen had been set up and a retinue of uniformed staff was standing by. He calmed himself by inspecting the food preparation, adjusting the knives and forks. Why they lined the knives up from the top and not the bottom of their handles Herman would never understand. He went down the long trestles adjusting each one.

When a thousand candles were lit and the electric lights turned off, Marie found Herman staring at the set-up and said, 'It's so clever how you make things look so good. You are my shining star. Sean should be very grateful.'

'Thank you. I went for the brown paper tablecloth in the end ...' He smiled as Celia went down the table turning the wine bottles to face the same direction. She understood. She had lost two more stone and so was allowed to come to London to help. If she could do that last ten pounds she could go to New York.

'I don't mean this,' Marie said, indicating the table, 'I meant the show, in the gallery. That looked amazing.'

'Oh yes, that. Did it? Good. Now, let's have a look at these starters ... '

'Before you go, who's John Burn?'

'Why do you ask?'

'Three people have asked to meet him tonight.'

'Who asked that?'

'Sean. Dora Bandell and Zac Murano.'

Dora was a big collector, and Zac an up-and-coming artist whom Herman admired because of his precocious talent at getting himself into the right social circles.

'John Burn is Herr X. That's his real name.'

'I thought he was Swiss.'

'Why?'

'Because of the Herr.'

'That was to put people off the scent. He's a very private man.'

'Is he here tonight?'

'God no.'

'Well I look forward to meeting him. Dora said he was one of your biggest clients. He's got some amazing Martinos, yes?'

'Yes. He has a strong collection.'

Over the next few months they went from Zürich to Highworth via Hong Kong, Los Angeles and the Pole. There was a rehang going on in the hall when they entered the house, dropped their bags and called for Walter and Polly. Marie glanced at the new painting on the staircase and said, 'Hey, isn't that the Fryer you said John Burn had bought?'

'Yes,' said Herman. 'How observant of you.'

'What's it doing here?'

'He loaned it to me. Well, he knew I loved it. He doesn't have too much space at home at the moment.'

'Why?'

I shouldn't have said that, Herman thought.

'He's between houses. Not exactly sure where. He plays his cards pretty close to his chest.'

'That's so kind of him to lend it,' Marie hung up her coat. 'I actually love that picture. He's got a good eye. You never said what he does. How did he make his money?'

'The usual,' Herman said. 'City stuff,' then thought, *careful, that's so easy to check up on.* 'Now he's mainly in mining. Out in the field. He likes the tough stuff. Drilling.' *Woah boy,* he shouted inside his head, *that's quite enough.*

'What does he mine?'

'I have no idea,' Herman said, congratulating himself on at last not saying something stupid.

'Well we must have him over. He sounds intriguing. Rugged, with an appreciation of good art,' Marie smiled. 'Is he married?'

'Yes.' *Woah!!!* 'No. He was. Not anymore. I think, that's what he hinted.' *What?*

'He could be perfect for Rosa.'

Rosa was Marie's adorable but not incredibly pretty cousin.

Herman wanted to try and quash this. 'I've heard people say he'll try anything to bed a woman. Totally without scruples.'

'They're probably jealous,' Marie said. 'He's a free agent.'

Herman needed to ram the point home. 'I also heard a rumour that he wasn't a very nice husband,' he said. 'He was a bit of a shit.'

'What are you talking about?'

'You know …' Herman said. He certainly didn't.

'You mean violent?'

'I'm afraid so.'

'Yuk,' said Marie.

'Yes,' said Herman, relieved to have struck this miserable, and, he hoped, concluding, note.

'Still, we're not marrying him,' Marie said, 'so let's invite him round and see what account he makes of himself. You never know, rumours are often wrong.'

Herman gave a sceptical grunt and got out of the room as fast as possible. He decided the next day to go straight to London, via Frankfurt, Milan, Basle and Moscow. He returned a week later with some cash from his Moscow clients in an envelope, which he gave to the accountant, a small man with frizzy brown hair who sat behind a desk in the old milking parlour.

'That's for those two Derrings I bought for a client last week in Milan,' Herman said.

The accountant took a biro and said, 'In the name of?'

'Burn. The man we used to call Herr X,' Herman said.

'Oh yes, I read. John Sparkler Burn,' the accountant said.

'Yes. John Sparkler Burn,' said Herman quietly. 'But that is highly secret information. Please do not share it with anyone but HMRC, do you understand? No-one in the gallery must know.'

'Of course.'

While Herman made a mental note to fire the accountant as soon as possible, he sensed someone standing behind him. He turned to see Celia. Herman tried to calculate if she had heard, as he walked out past her. It wasn't long before Celia put her face around his door.

'Herman, pardon me for disturbing you, only didn't I hear you say back there John Sparkler Burn?' she said.

'Yes,' said Herman. 'That's my client Herr X's real name.'

'But isn't that … isn't that Brother's name?'

A yawning silence opened and closed. Herman stared at her. As he saw it he had two options: to trust her, or to kill her. So it looked like murder.

'Isn't it?' she said again. 'Only how can it be Brother? It's not Brother, is it?'

Herman stood up, said, 'Come in, Celia,' and closed the door. This was no time to become a killer. He started to explain to Celia what he had done.

'But why not use your name?' she said.

'Because the artists don't like me buying their work for myself. You know what they can be like. They always think I'm trying to rip them off somehow.'

'And they want their work to end up in collections that won't sell it, don't they?'

'You know,' smiled Herman.

'Places like the Flint,' Celia said.

'Exactly,' said Herman. 'So I pretended someone else was buying them.'

'But why Brother?'

'I needed a real person who could never be found. I knew how elusive he was, so I thought he'd be perfect.'

'Well,' said Celia. 'I sort of see.'

Herman looked at her and wondered how he would kill her if he had to.

'You look worried, Herman,' Celia said. 'Are you scared I might tell?'

Strangulation, he decided.

'You don't have to worry,' she said. 'Look at me, a girl from the sticks. This job has been my big opportunity, right? I don't want to stay in this dump. I want to see the world and meet people. I want to go to cities and beautiful places. I love my job.'

Herman was nodding, thinking what was she going to demand for her silence?

'I've tried hard to fit in and do my best, Herman.'

'Yes, I have noticed that. You're very important to the gallery.'

'I've studied books on art, I've watched videos and I have been to all the talks, but for all that I don't think you quite think I fit in, do you?'

'What? Of course I do Celia. You're indispensable. Indispensable. Were you thinking that you might want to move to London?'

'I'm thinking I just want to help you, Herman, in any way I can.'

'And, err, what is it that you want?'

The question seemed to hurt her. 'I want you to trust me, Herman. I rate you as a boss. You are world famous in the art world. I don't think everyone realises how brilliant you are, sometimes. And I want you to rely on me. So I can be part of your team. That's what I want.'

'Is it?' Herman felt relief, happiness, suspicion and guilt all dragging him in different directions. Tears glistened in his eyes. 'Really?'

'Are you all right, Herman?' Celia said. 'Can I get you a tea or coffee?'

He nodded and felt for his handkerchief. When she returned he said, 'Thank you, Celia. Thank you, you are kind. I really appreciate you. I really do.'

'Your secret is safe with Celia,' she said. There was something so soft and kind in her tone it made him feel suddenly lonely. She seemed like the only person who would understand.

'Yes,' he said. 'Thank you.' Herman inhaled for what seemed like the first time in about twenty minutes. 'Why I'm doing it,' he said, just wanting to admit it out loud now he had found another human being who might not condemn him, 'why I'm doing it is because I want to create a collection that stands alone outside the gallery. On its own merits. As you know, Marie owns most of the business.'

'Yeah,' said Celia. 'I must say I have heard people saying it's her what wears the trousers.'

Herman smiled weakly. 'Do they?' he swallowed.

'Yeah. They say she's the one with the money.'

'Yes,' murmured Herman. 'You see that's why I need to have a personal project that's just mine, Celia.'

'To show people you can stand on your own two feet, in your own right,' Celia said.

'Yes,' said Herman.

'Which you can. Of course you can,' she said. 'I get it,' she said. 'I get it.'

'Thank you, Celia,' he said quietly.

Celia realised that the high door to the temple of art was opening, for once, rather than being slammed in her face by some of the bitches who worked for Herman in London, and always kept her off the party lists. And not only was it opening, Herman himself was standing beside it, beckoning her in.

'It's not going to go on for that long,' Herman said fluttering his hand. 'Just till I have around a hundred works, then I'll go public. No more than four more years. But I don't want anyone to find out before then. You see, it could be a problem if they did.'

'You're not doing anything wrong,' Celia said. 'You're doing something clever, if you ask me.'

'So I can trust you?' Herman asked.

Celia took a short breath. To be trusted with a secret this big was a sign she had arrived in the art world. Finally. 'Herman,' she lowered her voice. 'Of course you can trust me, I ain't going to tell anyone.'

She saw the anxiety drain from his face and his boyish smile return.

'Really?' he said.

'No one will ever find out. Not from me.'

'Do you want to do something that helps me even more?' Herman said.

'Of course. What?'

Herman opened a drawer, removed a file, and glanced through it until he found a piece of paper. He placed it on the desk in front of Celia. It was headed DEED OF POWER OF AUTHORITY. 'You see, this makes it legal for me to buy work in his name,' Herman said. 'I need you to witness Brother's signature.'

'Did he sign it?'

'No. I did,' said Herman with a catch in his throat. He coughed. 'I copied it off a letter in this file, which you got off your father for when we were trying to move on that caravan.'

'Oh yeah, I remember,' she said.

'If you could just sign and put your name and address here.'

She took the biro and signed. She passed the biro back, now firmly in Herman's inner circle.

'I really think you must come and join the team in London next time we have a show there,' Herman said. 'I'm sure you'd be a great help.'

'Is there anything I should know about him?' Celia asked.

'About who?'

'Your John Burn. If I'm going to protect you I need to know what you've told people. We better get our stories straight, right?'

'Oh yes, of course. He's in mining. He's often abroad, working. He works in out of the way places like the Amazon and the Congo jungle. He was married but isn't now. No one knows where he lives. I have an email for him, and his post comes to the gallery for forwarding.'

'May I make a suggestion?'

'Of course.'

'We put that file somewhere where no one will find it. Would you like me to do that?'

'Would you? Thank you Celia. Thank you very much.'

13

At the art storage facility, a huge warehouse with wooden partitions rising to the roof, the John Burn section grew steadily longer and taller as Herman went about his business.

Khaled rang Herman.

'I have news, my old friend. I have been made king.'

'Have you? How did that happen?'

'My great uncle killed my cousin, who was the king, and the council have chosen me to succeed him.'

'That's very clever of the council if I may say. Well done. Congratulations. I should keep an eye on that great uncle of yours!'

'Don't worry. I am having him executed next week after a fair trial.'

'Does this mean we won't see you at the Mont Cervin anymore?'

'I am afraid it does, so I have thought of another way for us to meet. Everyone tells me I must modernise the kingdom. Erena insists I need a museum of modern art. Will you help me create and fill it?'

'Your Highness, it would of course be a great honour. Thank you.'

He dashed through to the kitchen where Marie was cooking dinner, and told her the news.

'But that's fantastic. Imagine the budget!'

'But there will be challenges,' said Herman.

'Of course. They have very conservative tastes.'

Herman was lost in thought.

'You will cope with it, my love,' said Marie.

'Imagine the opening parties. Everyone will come.' His brow furrowed.

'What's wrong?' Marie said.

'Pork, Marie. Pork. Absolutely verboten. Yet ...' He scratched his chin, and put a finger in the air. 'That's what makes it such an interesting challenge. It means I will have to design a teller with no pork. Impossible, you would think. But if I pull it off it, it will be incredible.'

'You are silly, Herman, saying something like that. How can you joke?'

'Because I am happy. This is a wonderful thing for Khaled to ask me to do.'

News of the appointment reached the art world. Now Herman Gertsch of Krietman Stoop was by Royal command. Power went to his head. He ordered more Nehru jackets, got into the habit of clicking his fingers at staff (even though Marie always said quietly *Don't do that darling*) and, when a bit drunk, started peeing inaccurately, saying to himself, sometimes out loud, *I am courted by kings, and I can piss where I frigging want.* Power even went to his bottom, which expanded in a rather self-satisfied way.

Lots of acquaintances told Marie how clever Herman was. It wasn't something she had been expecting when she had married him, though she had worked out that, to people in the art world, the word clever meant something different to those outside it.

In the short gaps between cutting deals and planning parties, Herman marched round the farm at Highworth looking for things to change. When every barn, wall, gate, fence and stile had been done up, straightened, tightened, painted and signaged, his eyes cast further afield. He reroofed a bemused neighbour's barn in slate and lead because it annoyed Herman to see asbestos. He had a bridge heightened to get a monumental sculpture through. He went to Paris and back twice in one day. Finally, Marie got him to go skiing.

When they arrived at the Mont Cervin Hotel, the manager rushed out from behind the bar to say hello in a happy torrent of laughter, and when Herman and Marie came down to dinner Roman swept the reserved sign from the best table. People lined up to pay court until it was time for a hearty, not in the medical sense, Swiss dinner.

At dinner, Marie said 'Herman, my darling. You're working far too hard.'

He knew he was. He had doubled the load since reading on an art-world website that Marie was the driving force behind the gallery.

'There's a lot to do,' Herman replied. 'Thank goodness I have Celia to help, she makes it easier.' He seemed to have finished the cheese board, so signalled to the waiter. Celia had abandoned her last patterned garment and shed the weight that had banned her from New York and LA, where Herman had had to open a gallery to scotch rumours that the business was a vanity project.

'More cheese please,' he said.

Marie said, 'Are you sure? Too much dairy can kill you, you know?'

'Nonsense. I'm Swiss. Dairy is health food for us.'

After thirty-six hours of skiing, Herman left Marie in Zermatt and got on his way to a Dave Bell retrospective at the Hamburger Bahnhoff in Berlin. Dave Bell was now a polished, slim, fit and excessively, even tediously, sober middle-aged man. When Herman found himself hyperventilating on his private jet he beckoned the hostess for a drink and could hardly get the glass to his mouth he was shaking so much. He kept hearing someone he thought might be God say, 'You have 125 employees in sixteen countries; you need to make 7 million in sales each week before you break even, and any one of your artists or collectors could abandon you at any time.'

Herman made it to the Bahnhof dinner. Of course he did. You crawled on broken legs to get to an art dinner with Sir Benjamin Minto, the most important man in the world – not the real world, the one that mattered: the art world. Minto was the head of the Flint Galleries in Britain, the temples inside of which the nation's contemporary art was stored and exhibited. You left your mother's death bed if a chance to sit next to him came up. On Herman's other side was the German Minister of Culture, a virtual nobody compared to Minto.

Herman ate the food: a crevette salad and then a lean lamb chop and pickled cabbage. Far too light. He slipped away as soon as he thought everyone had properly seen where he had been seated.

After Herman had departed, the Minister of Culture turned to the woman on his right and said, 'There's a very fine line between being a genius and an idiot. Herman is so amazing the way he keeps himself so open to that. He doesn't care. Brilliant.'

'He is uber intelligent,' the bony middle-aged giantess agreed. 'Even on a totally random subject, like Tyrolean sausage making, he is absolutely fascinating and so engaged. He spoke to me about the grain on a chopping board for ten minutes. Incredible. Imagine bringing that level of attention to detail to your whole life.'

Herman reboarded his plane and touched down in Zürich at 10 p.m. He had to be on the same plane at 6 a.m. to go to Milan. It was hardly worth getting off. As it taxied bumpily to a halt by the airport dumpsters, he picked a newspaper out of the rack. He later thought about this moment so many times, trying to work out what exactly had happened. He found himself staring at a page of classified ads. Personal. Vacancies. For Sale. Properties to Let. He looked down the columns and an unboxed advert of just a few lines leapt from the page and tore out his eyes.

TEMPORARY CHEF required.
Must have experience of and love for traditional Swiss cuisine. Raclette, Fondue, Walliser teller. 346 7682.

Herman felt his heart hammer in his chest. As though sleepwalking, he took out his phone, closed a couple of emails from collectors wanting to spend 500,000 US dollars between them, and dialled the number.

'Der Whimper Stubbe, guten Tag,' piped a jolly Swiss lady.

'I am inquiring about the job.'

'Very good. You have experience of traditional Tyrolean cooking?'

'I do,' he said with a dry mouth.

'I must be clear from outset, we are not interested in any vegan, Asian fusion or Californian cuisine. Just good old mountain hut food served in a traditional Alpine style.'

To be talked to like this after all these years propelled Herman into a swoon. With tears in his eyes, he dreamily

But most of Herman's energy in the gallery was spent positioning the gherkins on the Walliser teller board. That very night he had had some special ham sent from the Bernese Oberland and was feeling confident enough to include quails' eggs, not normally associated with the Swiss mountain dish, but something which Herman felt could make an interesting variation.

He padded across the thickly carpeted floor to Marie's dressing room where she was sitting in an armchair engrossed in a book. On the table beside her was Seamus Heaney's recent translation of the Aeneid and in her hands was P.G. Wodehouse's *Pigs Have Wings*. She looked up, startled.

'My god! Is it that late? ' she said. 'Fix me a drink, I'll be down as fast as I can.'

'Let's have Negronis,' Herman said.

'Great idea,' said Marie.

Pouring the vermouth and then gin into his cocktail shaker, he mused on how lucky he was, but, oh, what was this? The top of the vermouth had not been screwed back on tight. It was just resting on the bottle. He tutted. Who had done that? There were worse things, he supposed, but still it wasn't nice. Had one of the servants been at it? Had Marie forgotten to put the top back on properly? He wouldn't want to mention it to her. He would remember to tell Margaret to check the tops were all screwed on. And also remind her to stand the bottles on the drinks tray with their labels facing the same direction. But which direction?

Herman sipped his cocktail until it was the same size as his wife's, then put it on the table and waited for her. Georgio had found the artist whose show it was at the gallery that night. By listening to ski clients chatting about the art scene, he often came up with names who were agreed to go to the restaurant to discuss the job. After the call, with just a tenth of his mind on the task, he trotted out some replies to the collectors about how pleased he was they had bought their pictures, and then got down to the real business.

Job interviews were about preparation and commitment. He had to look right. Herman typed the generic term for traditional Alpine costume into Google: *trachten*. Then he clicked the images icon. The screen populated with a multiplicity of extreme Tyrolean and Bavarian garment porn. Merry men in leather shorts and felt trilbies with a feather in the band smiled winsomely at Herman. His hungry eyes lit into the detail of their embroidered shirts and leather braces with cross pieces. He rattled some more words into the keyboard, struck ENTER and was faced with a screen of knee-length white socks. A bomb could have gone off behind him and he wouldn't have turned his head. Nothing could break the spell. Actually, one thing would. Marie, behind him, saying *What are you doing?* But Marie was miles away. Herman admired the wanderers' hose. In Herman's book, the attractiveness of Swiss men was determined not by the narrowness of their waist but the width of their calfs, and Herman could see some on show that had clearly trod the mountain paths in summer and skied the pistes in winter.

Herman cancelled the Milan meeting. It was only with the city mayor who wanted to art-wash his suburbs with an installation by one or other of the gallery's artists. Usually Herman would have happily spent a few hours tickling a million euros out of the man, but he just felt too stressed, and he could only think of one way of easing it.

At 11.30am, as agreed, Herman Gertsch, in hiking boots, long white socks, leather shorts, white blouse, red braces and natty little jacket stood outside the Whimper

Stubbe in Zuog. His Tyrolean costume was set off by a bushy moustache that came down either side of his mouth which he had glued on an hour earlier. A long way from the fashionable skiing slopes, the town of Zuog was a community that lived behind heavy net curtains. The restaurant was on the corner of a deserted square. Herman went down a couple of steps and opened the door into a cosy room with crowded tables, its aertex walls dotted with hunting trophies, and photographs of old alpine scenes.

Frau Bettleheim was a red-cheeked young woman in a voluminous skirt.

Herman put out his hand. 'My name is Otto Schmidt. I have come about the job.'

'Julianne,' she said. 'Shall we sit?'

He really liked her down-to-earth questions: *Did you walk from the station?* Quite unlike the ones he was used to answering, like *What did you think of Martino's show?* And she asked, *Did you bring an umbrella?* Not, *What did you make of Sao Paulo?* It was such a relief for poor exhausted Herman, run ragged having to produce an interesting opinion all day long. Frau Bettleheim explained that her husband, Hugo, was the main chef. As she was soon to have a baby, they needed a relief chef to fill in some gaps in the rota. Herman proposed that he joined in lunch service so Hugo and she could see if he was right for the post.

Hugo showed Herman how he liked things done, and the service, just twelve covers, went smoothly. When the last profiterole went out with the cheese board, Julianne stood behind the bar and tapped off steins of lager for Herman and Hugo. Herman was in ecstasy, standing in the little basement bar talking, at last unapologetically, about cured Swiss sausage. But then he looked at his watch. Three o'clock. He had to be at Highworth for dinner.

Frau Bettleheim and Hugo praised Herman and hoped he would consider their offer of a part-time job. It had been Herman's idea to say that the appointment wasn't right for him and turn it down. Accepting it would be madness. Utter insanity. But as the car raced towards his Bombardier twelve-seater twin engine private jet, parked at the airstrip below St Moritz, he knew that somehow he was going to do some shifts in that kitchen, if they were the last things he ever did.

14

He was able to combine his two careers successfully because it turned out that cooking in the stubbe made Herman a better art dealer.

He opened new galleries in Los Angeles, Rome and Hong Kong. It was insane not to, they were all so profitable. Rich people in their thousands had all come to the realisation that it wasn't enough, spiritually speaking, to live only on the envy of the poor. They needed art in their lives to get the more effective envy of the rich. The galleries provided one opening after another at which Herman could experiment with finger food he had worked on with Hugo in the stubbe. The collectors trusted him, the public curators came to him for advice, the artists adored him. Herman gave guidance to everyone.

As a rule, when Herman was with Hugo and Frau Bettleheim he never answered his phone but one day he saw three missed calls from Walter in quick succession. Herman found being a father as easy as everything else in his life, and enjoyed an excellent relationship with his son, though he was a little disappointed Walter had not taken up Herman's offer when he left school, to start a chain of Swiss restaurants.

'In London you can eat Ethiopian, Latvian, Brazilian and Jamaican, Walter, but there is still not a single Swiss restaurant. It's a disgrace, true, but what an opportunity!'

Herman had laid out his vision to his son in a conversation while waiting to depart on a flight to New York: 'You can recreate an alpine stubbe in the very heart of London. A cosy room with pine-panelled walls and photos of early mountaineers and chamois. Waitresses in Swiss national costume. Fondue. Raclette. Walliser teller with extra sausage and gherkins. It's a winning formula. Are you still there?'

Walter had not been receptive. But maybe now the lad was ready to talk. Walter called him back and listened as he carried on with the service.

'Dad, I've got a bit of a situation here.'

'Okay. What's happened?'

'Well I was driving into a festival with Ali and some friends and the security pulled us and searched our van and found some mushrooms.'

Herman's heart gladdened.

'What were you going to do with them?' he asked.

'Hand them out to the crowd.'

'I'm so pleased. What were your serving ideas? A la Grecque with garlic and olive oil is chic and simple. Plus you can use tooth picks. What's your cost point?'

'We weren't going to sell them. And they're magic mushrooms. We were going to give them away. That's what you do with magic mushrooms.'

'Who paid for them?'

'Ali and I bought them.'

'What? But why? They're illegal.'

'For fun.'

'You're the only drug dealers I've heard of who give drugs away,' laughed Herman. 'Lucky you got busted. Imagine if you were successful!'

'That's not the point, Dad. The point is this random guy just took the rap for me. He drove the bus through security and we all got out and got away.'

'You weren't caught? Thank god. One veal chop, one wurst.'

'Dad. He got arrested.'

'Who is he?'

'Like, a guy we know.'

'So not a close friend. Do I know his parents?'

'No. We got the mushrooms off him. Not a friend but he's good peeps. Wise, like a shaman, but without the bullshit. Well, look what he did for us.'

'He's a drug dealer, Walter. Correct? He deserves all he gets.' Herman looked at the bit of paper Julianne had just slid across the polished steel.

'He's not really a drug dealer. He's more like a man of medicine'.

Herman looked out of the pavement level window. No one walked by.

'I want to help him,' Walter said. 'Can I call David Ashton?'

'Walk away, Walter. This man could blackmail you. He'd blackmail Ali if he knew who he was.'

'He knows who Ali is.'

'You told a drug dealer who Ali is? Have you gone mad?'

'No, he's cool. He said he thought more royalty should take magic mushrooms.'

'Drop this, Walter. Count yourself lucky you weren't in the van.'

'I was in the van. That's what I told you.'

'My advice is get as far away from him as possible. Didn't you say you wanted to take a trip to the Amazon?'

'Iquitos, yes.'

'Maybe you should do that for a few months to let this blow over.'

'I'll give it a thought,' said Walter.

'That's two rosti for table six. One with egg,' said Herman.

'Dad, where are you?'

'In an important meeting. Please don't call a lawyer. You could stir things up.'

It was good to give his son sound advice.

When Herman was back at Highworth he talked to Walter about the incident. Herman was sitting in his car answering a text from Khaled, who was inviting Herman and John Burn to lunch in London. Herman wrote: *I would love to attend, but unfortunately John is detained in the Amazon.*

He pressed send and looked up to see Walter getting out of his car by the garages.

'Did you sort out that festival thing?' he called.

Walter stopped, and turned. 'Oh that. Ali dealt with it. Yeah, I think it was all okay in the end,' he said.

'Good job,' Herman said. But he felt a gap opening up between them.

Herman was right. His son had not told him the truth. The man who drove the van had got a suspended sentence and a big fine. Walter and Ali both felt guilty about him, but hadn't gone to say sorry, or offer to pay his fine. The guilt appeared in waves to young Walter late at night, and sometimes at odd times of the day. He eyed his father walking towards him with arms full of art books and papers and wondered whether he should tell him about it, but then Herman's phone started ringing.

'The King,' he said. Before he answered he said, 'Walter, you know you said you were interested in going to the Amazon? What were you going to do there?'

'Buy a ton of DMT, Dad,' Walter said sarcastically.

'What's DMT?' asked Herman.

'It's a jungle medicine that cures depression,' said Walter over his shoulder as he walked back to the house. 'You should try some.'

'Your Highness!' said Herman into his phone. 'How good to speak to you. I know, such a pity, but he's doing important humanitarian work sourcing medicine in the Amazon. It's fascinating, I'll tell you all about it at lunch.'

When he finished the conversation Herman looked around for Walter but couldn't see him. He knew he should be spending more time at home. And yet he was just about to green-light another gallery in Madrid, mopping up the few rich people who were too lazy to get to Basle or London.

He went to his office, closed the door and sat down to take himself through his workaholic protocol, as he promised he would do when he was stressed to the point of his heart fluttering like a moth.

He got out the list.

THINGS TO DO TO MAKE LIFE BALANCED SUSTAINABLE AND HEALTHY

1. Close Hong Kong
2. Close Miami
3. Stop doing shifts at the Whimper Stubbe
4. Take family on hiking vacation to Jungfrau (leave phone at gallery)
5. Don't use phone at home after 7 p.m.
6. Therapy/Meditation

That last one made him wince. He sat back deep in the buttoned leather chair, chin down, bottom lip out. Grumpy.

He stared at the Dave Bell over the chimney piece and smiled. It was going up in value so fast, if he tried to say what it was worth, it was wrong by the time he got to the end of the sentence. The picture smiled back and said, *that's more like it, cock.* Or rather he imagined it did. Herman remembered his super-power: he was a dealer of contemporary art. Nothing could beat him. Over there was a photograph of Herman with the President of the French Republic, and a couple more with European royalty trying to lick his ass.

He picked up the paper and slipped it back in the drawer. He got out his phone and green-lighted Madrid. The difficult feeling eased momentarily.

He felt for his moustache in the back of the drawer, stuffed it in his pocket and stood up.

In the sitting room his family were watching tennis.

'I'm afraid I've got to go to Zürich.'

'It's Polly's sports day,' Marie said. 'You said you'd go.'

'You'll have to do it without me. I'm sorry.'

'I'll come with you, Mum,' said Walter from an armchair. He was putting his hair in a ponytail. He was on his year off. 'The first of many, I hope,' he said.

'I didn't see you there,' said Herman. 'How are you?'

Walter nodded.

'Thank you, darling,' said Marie.

'I've been summoned, I'm afraid.'

'John Burn?' Marie said.

''Fraid so.'

Herman took the Merc at breakneck speed down the back lane through a manure-splattered farmyard to get to his lunch shift. Not far from his house, a pub with a 'for sale' sign flashed past. The Crossed Keys. Herman knew the place. It had the hallmarks of what Herman called *old* Somerset: it was a rotting building in a damp hollow, the interior redolent of drugs, booze and chaos. But a pub! He could buy it. Of course he could buy it, he could buy anything. But his own pub. Up the road. He should put his lawyer and some Swiss architects on it in the morning. Clean it up and create a traditional stubbe. Here, in Somerset. It could save him from this madness. He grabbed his phone and scrolled for the lawyer.

Herman was thinking: *This is a chance to showcase Swiss humour as well as Swiss food: I could change the name from the Crossed Keys to the Crossed Skis,* when the side window smacked his head, the steering wheel punched his neck and the dashboard pulverized his nose.

The milk truck, an eighteen-wheel, thirty-two ton, articulated vehicle, with 25,000 litres of warm milk slopping and slurping around its stainless steel tank, smashed into the door of his Merc, carted it fifty metres up the road and squashed it and Herman against an old oak. It was all over for Herman. Marie had been right, in the end it was dairy that did it for him.

15

It took two years for Marie even to begin to emerge from the shock and the grief. During that time, she wandered subterranean tunnels dripping their pain, with only Walter and Polly staggering at her side. Even when she found her way out, it was only into a grey and joyless world. Some of her friends urged her to rejoin the scene, but she didn't want to.

With absolutely nobody raising an eyebrow, a grieving widow could have a gin at 11 a.m., go to bed before supper, play jazz at top volume, burst into tears at nothing, and ask everyone to leave or make everyone stay. It was a lifestyle Marie grew content, or at least familiar, with. She resigned from all the committees and boards of museum directors Herman had worked so hard to get them onto, had herself removed from all the many mailing lists and, in time, even her friends stopped sending invitations.

She left the art world, a planet that she was happy to see recede below her. She sold Highworth and moved back to Switzerland, where little had changed except the arrival of some forbidding entrance gates. Walter and Polly both lived with her, though came and went. All of them were still recovering, and always would be.

It was a cold, but still day; a thick line of grey cloud hung low over the dark lake, slicing off the mountain peaks. Marie stood in the drawing room, her back to a crackling pine fire, staring at the bumps and nodules of the garden under snow.

She was waiting for David Ashton, Herman's London lawyer, to arrive with the last legal documents for her to sign to wind up Krietman Stoop. She had closed the gallery down, and sold all the assets. Because everyone knew the exceptional circumstances, the markets were not spooked. She actually had a reason to sell art, which people agreed was not because she had lost faith in the investments. When the stock in hand had been auctioned at Christie's one humid and hot autumn afternoon, Marie had earned a fortune, yes, another. She had not been present. That kind of thing had always depressed her. But she had heard the news soon enough, and was put in a bad mood by it, because the receipt of 120 million Swiss francs meant she could not avoid a meeting with her financial advisor.

He arrived at the door in black coat and homburg, stamping his feet. At seventy-three years of age, David Ashton was by far the youngest of Marie's advisors. She liked his solidity and impeccable desk-side manner.

She sat in the drawing room as he stood beside her, laying documents on the desk, pointing at them, murmuring, 'Here and here.'

'This is for the lease transfer in Los Angeles,' he said. 'Here and here. Don't date it. This is for the sale of Zürich …'

When the sheaf had been dealt with he said, 'Now all we have outstanding is the sale of the warehouse in Spitalfields.'

'Is there a problem with it?' she said.

'I think we're finally getting there. We were held up trying to get hold of John Burn. We have finally, I'm glad to say, located him, and we're asking him to move his collection to another storage facility.'

Ashton picked up the papers, carefully slipped them into folders and stored them in his briefcase.

Marie wanted to change the subject but she couldn't think of anything she wanted to say, so stood up and shepherded Ashton to the door. He was thinking: *Having come all the way from London, you'd think a guest would be offered a cup of tea.* She wanted to avoid talking about John Burn. In bitter moments, she blamed the man for Herman's death: after all, it was he who had summoned Herman at such short notice and made him hurry on the road. And the creep hadn't turned up to the funeral or written a letter of condolence.

'It turns out he has an address in Somerset, not far from Highworth,' Ashton said. 'After extensive inquiries and a search of the gallery we finally dug it out. A file about him was hidden in a box in the stationery cupboard. He must have asked Herman to keep it secret. He certainly knew how to cover his tracks, that man. I'm going to see him next week.'

'Goodbye, David. I am sure we will see each other soon,' Marie said, hoping the precise opposite, not because she disliked Ashton, in fact she liked him more than most people, which meant she wasn't actively allergic to him, but she didn't want to have any more conversations about Krietman Stoop – they reminded her too much of Herman.

She watched the car disappear into the fog and saw a red glow as he stopped for the gates to open ponderously before closing again. Marie turned and walked into the house, retreating deeper into the kind of anonymity that only the really rich and really poor can reach.

16

Brother's Yard, on the Somerset Levels, was a strip of land
between two old peat pits which had flooded to create
lakes. Originally home to a single caravan where peat
diggers drank tea between shifts, it was now a huddled
collection of vans, buses, static caravans and tourers, many
sprouting awnings, corrugated lean-tos and imaginatively
angled plywood extensions. Parked up alongside these
abodes were the residents' vehicles: a converted ambulance,
a heavily panniered bicycle, a scarred van, a lopsided
pick-up and a couple of good old-fashioned bangers. This
was why the pristine black Mercedes which drove onto
the yard that icy winter morning stood out.

Brother, a lean, middle-aged man with thick, spiky
greying hair, sharp sideburns and a tweed cap pulled low
over his blue eyes, had noticed the car the moment it came
onto the yard. He observed it nosing past the old fridge
mail box, rocking slowly over potholes and drawing up
by a faded gas bottle. To him, the car had the unfamiliar
look of a vehicle with an MOT, more than three quid's
worth of gas in its tank, tread on all four tyres and valid

insurance. He flicked the contents of the ashtray into his wood-burner, stashed his nugget under a cushion, and then returned to watch. His first thought was that it was someone from Mendip District Council, but the car was too expensive for the Head of Enforcement, who usually drove a Mondeo, no doubt charging the tax payers 80p a mile while he made Brother's life a misery. It wasn't a bailiff; Brother knew all the local bailiffs, and it wasn't the police; the police drove onto the yard like they owned the place.

It was a tall, elderly man who emerged from the car, with grey hair swept back onto his collar. Brother admired his woollen pinstripe suit, and the black alpaca coat he pulled over it. Brother himself was attired that morning in a vintage Savile Row herringbone tweed that had the date 1979 on a label in the inside pocket.

The stranger headed towards Planet Geoff's pitch, perhaps drawn by the thick white smoke that drifted from his chimney into the icy stillness of the January morning. Planet Geoff was an inventor who had the firm, perhaps too firm, belief that with a minor modification the internal combustion engine could run on water. The man knocked on Planet Geoff's door, which the unshaven wild-eyed inventor opened a crack. Brother strained his ears to hear the conversation but Planet Geoff's caravan was too far away and Brother could only hear the calls of coots and moorhens in the rushes, the distant clanking of diggers and the beeping of reversing lorries carrying away the peat.

The conversation went on for a good ten minutes, as it tended to when you said hello to Planet Geoff, but ended when the man nodded a few times, waved gently, dragged himself from Planet Geoff's powerful gravitational pull, and walked between a shattered puddle of ice and a tyre draped in dead weeds towards Brother. Brother withdrew into the space between the kitchen and the bedroom; he didn't want to be served any court order. But the knock on the door was polite and soft, so he called, 'Who's that?'

'Good morning,' the man said, in a gentle, patrician voice that was neither aggressive nor defensive and which Brother decided it was safe to open the door to. 'Are you John Sparkler Burn?'

'No,' answered Brother, whose names were John Sparkler Burn. Sparkler was a gift from his mother, who gave birth to him in a painted gypsy caravan in the hills of central Wales during a slanting rain storm in the autumn of 1965.

'Do you know where I can find him?'

'Mr Burn,' said Brother, 'is currently' away. I cannot say precisely where. He keeps his plans to himself. But he did mention he might be unreachable for a fair time. That much I know. Plus he gave no forwarding address. May I tell him who was asking for him, and why?'

Ashton smiled politely. 'I come on private business, as a legal representative of Krietman Stoop, the art gallery.' Brother opened the door, inspected the gentleman. 'It is a great honour to meet you,' Ashton said quietly, holding out an elegant hand. Brother got the strong impression that the man respected him to the point of being deferential, which was somewhat unusual.

'John Burn's not in trouble again?' Brother asked with a tut and theatrical sigh.

'Absolutely not. I simply have a package to deliver to him. Perhaps if I left it with you, you could pass it on to him. If, of course, you see him any time soon.' The lawyer flashed a collusive smile, and looked into Brother's eyes as he handed over a fat A4 manila envelope as if he were trying to convey a secret message.

'Happy days,' said Brother. 'I'll hand it on as soon as I see him. If I see him.'

'Good. I must return now to London.' As he shook Brother's hand he said, 'Very good to meet you, friend of John Burn. Keep well. Goodbye.'

Brother watched the car leave, closed the door, sat down and placed the envelope on his lap. It was expensive thick paper which, when slit open with the Opinel knife Brother kept about him, yielded a book-shaped object neatly encased in bubble wrap, and a letter on heavy watermarked paper. He read the letter:

6 February 2015
Dear Mr Burn,

You will no doubt have heard the news of the death of Herman Gertsch, of Krietman Stoop gallery. It was decided by the executors of his estate to wind up Krietman Stoop and sell its various divisions to make a cash distribution amongst his heirs. This means that the works of art belonging to you and known collectively as the John Burn Collection, currently stored by the gallery at its facility in London, must now revert to your sole care. Please will you let us have, at your earliest convenience, instructions as to where you wish your Collection to be sent? We enclose an up-to-date manifest of the works for your information.

As anonymity has thus far been so important to you, I assure you that we will commission any orders you give us with the utmost discretion.

I look forward to hearing your instructions.
Yours sincerely,
David Ashton

Brother peeled the tape off the bubble wrap but, seeing it stretch the plastic, carefully slit around the tape so he could reuse the wrap. He revealed a ring binder with a dark blue cover and about a hundred leaves, each displaying one or two small reproductions of artworks. Brother perused about ten pages, stopping occasionally to look at an image. He recognized the works to be what he called modern art, and not the sort of thing he liked.

Brother's tastes in art ran to figurative, preferably narrative, oil painting. *Derby Day* by Frank Wright was a favourite: a huge canvas teeming with stories which he could look at for hours, especially after a spliff of good black.

Something twitching the reeds caught his attention: a water vole Brother knew well was padding across his pitch to sniff about amongst the plates' and pans' scraps of food. Brother's hands went loose on the clip file.

Planet Geoff, in a fur hat with ear flaps, poked his head around the door. 'Who was that?' he asked, twirling a lock of his wispy brown beard around his blackened index finger.

'Said he was a lawyer,' Brother said. Geoff winced. 'And he left me this.'

Jan put her head round the door, and then Anna joined them as they squeezed into the caravan. They looked at the book and then the letter.

'That'll be a premium rate number,' said Anna, a ruined beauty, her voice also scarred by years of smoking and boozing.

'No it's not. It's a London land line,' said Jan.

'You ring up – they deliver the pictures and then say you have to pay for them,' said Anna.

Paul opened the door, his face tightened by booze, like a bear under a bulky layer of clothes. 'What's going on?'

he wheezed. Paul had only recently arrived on the yard and still from time to time reverted to his old homeless lifestyle on the streets of Glastonbury, clad in greasy clothes and pushing a bicycle loaded with possessions. He'd eked out a living painting the shops, pubs, houses and cafes of the High Street and selling them to the occupants of the buildings or swapping them for booze, food and fags.

As a practising artist, Paul was ceremoniously passed the book. He fell quiet looking at the pictures. 'Not my kind of thing,' he murmured, then looked up with a smile on his defeated face. 'But I am sure there are lots who love it. Good luck to them.' He handed the file back to Brother. 'What's it to do with you?'

'Nothing,' said Brother. 'Far as I know. Dunno what it's about. Man just dropped it off.'

When they had a pot of tea brewed and were sipping at their mugs, Brother said, 'It's a scam, or a mistake. One or the other. The only picture I own is that one there,' he nodded at the oil painting of Tor Kebab in Glastonbury that hung on the cupboard. 'I've owned it for three happy years and when funds permit,' he smiled at Paul, whose work it was, 'I will be paying for it.'

Paul lifted his mug, 'Whenever it suits, that would be very kind, dear chap,' he said.

Various theories about the file were advanced: Jan felt that extra-terrestrials or time travel could well be involved. Anna thought the ring binder could be daubed in poison by Mendip District Council. Mary handed the file back to Brother and, with her bright blue eyes fixed on him said, 'This has come to you for a reason. You will find out soon enough.' But Mary always said there was a reason for everything; it seemed to be her way of softening the hard blows life so often dealt her.

And so the ring file was gently forgotten, first used only to roll spliffs on, then shoved under a cushion in Brother's caravan, and finally stowed in the locker above the window, where it lay squeezed between some books. Brother's attention turned to other things, like the planning appeal, which had something of a medieval quest about the tricky obstacles and cunning opponents which had to be defeated one by one for him to win. Each day also had its off-grid chores for Brother: charging batteries, collecting spring water and splitting kindling, as well as the urgent matter of sitting on the couch, rolling a fat one, sparking it up, lying back on the cushions, drawing smoke into his lungs, and gazing at the reeds in the lake's black water while wisps of memories, feelings and thoughts wafted across his mind.

17

Lily always searched the landscape for her first glimpse of the Glastonbury Tor when she made trips back home. As the coach wheezed down the hill out of Castle Cary she scanned the horizon and located the mysterious hill and its solemn tower rising from the plain. And after passing an orchard where bonfire smoke hung in slithers, she caught the glints of the swollen canals and waterlogged fields of the Somerset Levels in winter.

She alighted by the ruined abbey in Glastonbury town and wandered up the hill to a café where, even before she was inside, she could see her stepdad, cap pulled low over his eyes, rising from a table to greet her.

He wore a tweed jacket with frayed cuffs, leather waistcoat, collarless shirt and moleskin trousers, and smelled of wood smoke, engine oil and tobacco. When he embraced her she felt the body of a man who lived off-grid: lean from fetching wood and water and lugging around twelve-volt batteries. Brother held her away from him, looked into her heart-shaped face and said 'gold rings to you, my girl.'

Lily had been deserted twice in her life: first at birth by her father, a man called Whipper Brandon, who had nipped out of the maternity ward for a celebratory pint and never came back, and then, at four years of age, by her mother, who had to go to Goa and prevent cruelty to animals, leaving Lily temporarily in the care of her then-boyfriend, who happened to be Brother. Lily couldn't have been luckier, because Brother loved, adored and looked after her with great, if sometimes clumsy, care and, by good fortune, her mum was too busy feeding dogs on the beach and her dad too pissed to return and further disrupt their daughter's childhood. Brother bicycled the little girl to and from school down the arrow-straight lanes beside the reed-clogged waterways. He taught her to poach fish and swim in the lakes, to saw and split wood, to cook on an open fire, to tell the truth, and to respect all people and fear none. With his help and encouragement she had first taken and passed GCSEs and then A levels at the local college. On her graduation day, Brother turned out in his three-piece green corduroy suit, spotted cravat and polished brown brogues and had openly cried with happiness and pride.

She had won a place studying history of art at Bristol, changed to business management after her first year, got a degree, applied for seventeen jobs and landed one as an office manager for a stockbroker in the City. With which she was perfectly happy. Her life became, for the first time, relatively risk free. Solid, and comfortably safe. Just as she liked it. Her days of lying to bailiffs and repelling debt collectors, of arguing with council enforcement officers and evading PCSOs were over. She was happy to toe the line, pay her bills, and never fear an envelope or a knock on the door.

A weekend at the yard with her stepdad reminded Lily of how civilised off-grid life could be. Those who lived in over-illuminated houses and under profligate street-lighting never knew the beauty and simplicity of dusk and darkness. As night fell she wandered around the caravans saying hello and catching up on news.

She stood in the thick grasses by the bank of the lake, listening to the wind in the reeds, watching it ruffling moonlight on the water. The solar lights around Anna's door were diminishing as they ran out of juice. She could see Anna's torch moving behind her curtain, and over the other side of the yard a head torch in the darkness moving from Paul's caravan to the compost toilet.

While she wandered back to Brother's caravan she saw his clothes on the line and remembered how he had done all their washing by hand throughout her childhood. He didn't hold with synthetic fibres, and she could see his old winter leggings pegged on the line. And there was no bathroom – she had showered behind the caravan under water warmed by the sun or by a wood fire, looking across the lake as she soaped herself. And Brother had no garbage bin; he never bought anything with plastic packaging, and anything he didn't eat went onto the compost heap.

For Saturday dinner he cooked a pair of road-kill pheasants with potatoes and sprouts from his patch, all perfectly accompanied by Planet Geoff's Special Swirly Cider. Brother's caravan filled with the dark wrinkled faces and wonky smiles of the yard's occupants. Someone had once said to Brother that all of them at the yard were 'on the spectrum', and Brother had replied: 'We are all on the spectrum, my friend, but not of mental illness, of humanity.' But Anna was well to the end of both spectrums. She had an alarming way of smiling and crying at the same time when certain thoughts or memories flitted across her mind. There had been talk in the little tribe of Brother's Yard of getting rid of Anna because of her screams in the night, dubious taste in men and frequent fights, but Brother had insisted she stay. 'One for all, and all for one – that's the politics on this yard,' he had announced, before returning to his caravan and hoping the uprising against Anna would die down. It did, and now she was sitting amongst them passing her flask of booze to Lily, who tried not to glance at the top before she took a sip. Anna looked a bit grimy, it was true, but after the pale, moisturised, made-up visages of London, all the faces in the candlelight seemed rich to Lily.

At dawn on Sunday morning Lily left her caravan for a pee by the reeds. She loved the absence of drains and sewers, flushing toilets, air freshener, bleach and a door that had to be locked. She stood up, shivered and listened to a clutch of coots fanning their wings in the water, followed by a smart quack from a mallard in the rushes. But by the afternoon, Lily was itching to get back to all the things she found so wasteful and wrong earlier in the day: the traffic, the crowds, the dirt, the noise and the artifice of London and its people.

Brother went to rinse the kettle in the lake so they could have a brew before they set off. While he was on his haunches by the water, Lily took a look at the bookshelf she had known since she was a child. She saw *The Book of Tribes*, from which without opening she could summon almost every page and every photograph. Rumi's *Spiritual Couplets*, and beside it, *Holistic Herbal Cures*, and *Indoor Marijuana Horticulture*, marking the year Brother first went into growing dope; a lost year in which he managed to smoke the profits, estimated at £12,000, almost single-handedly. The second year he turned to magic mushroom picking and managed to get busted on his first outing. He landed a three year suspended sentence for that.

Battered copies of *A Practical Approach To Planning Law, Telling & Duxbury's Planning Law and Procedure,* and *On Your Feet – The Magistrates' Court* all related to the war of attrition against eviction. The shelf continued with *Tapping on a Budget, Understanding Star Signs, The Beatles Lyrics* and *The Art of Changing.* Lily smiled – changing was an art Brother had not mastered, but she was okay with him exactly as he was; then *The Book of British Birds,* and what was this? Something new. Her hand reached up to an unfamiliar blue ring binder and pulled it from the shelf. She opened it up and immediately identified a small colour reproduction of an early Callum Smith and a very early Ryan Young.

As she turned the pages she recognised two more early Dave Bell, pre his first show, and two even earlier, maybe 1990, Sean6 sculptures. Without taking her eyes off the folder she slowly sat down and turned page after page of the most panoramic, all encompassing, exquisitely selected selection of the very best of the most important British and later European and American art of the last twenty-five years, with one or two key pieces, (she glimpsed some Janson and Kings), from the seventies and eighties.

The door swung open. 'I'm really going to miss you, Lily,' Brother said, kicking off his boots, placing the kettle on the burner, opening the burner door and chucking on some especially dry oak he had set aside for her visit.

'What's this?' she asked.

'I meant to show that to you,' he said. 'A stranger came by a couple of months ago and gave it me. Claimed it was mine. Not sure of the angle. Thought you might be able to shed some light on it. Anyway, he never came back.'

'Did you do anything about it?'

'No. It felt like some kind of scam, or a trap. There's a letter somewhere. It was to do with Krietman Stoop, that gallery near Shepton. What happened to that?' Brother said.

'The owner died,' said Lily.

'Was he called Herman something? He said my caravan ruined his view. Cunt. Sorry, Lil. But really. I never met him. He didn't get anywhere. He gave up the fight.' Brother smiled and held out his hands. 'They're never gonna move me, are they? He actually asked me to dinner one night to try to schmooze me. I sent Kevin. He came back with a bottle of very palatable claret.'

Brother rooted around the back of the shelf and passed Lily a worn piece of paper with half-inch strips torn off the bottom. Lily carefully read it.

'Have you rung them?' she asked, glancing at the folder again.

'I don't want to get entangled, love. In my position, you know? Sugar or honey?'

'This is an amazing collection of art. Honey, please.'

'They must be copies or fakes or something,' Brother said.

'I recognise some of them,' Lily said.

'I thought you'd know about them. It's your kind of art, isn't it?'

Lily looked up from the book and smiled. They had long argued about what he termed 'her kind of art'. Lily turned another page. She jumped.

'This one was in my A level textbook. I love this one. I wrote an essay about it.' She set the folder down, pulled on her shoes and walked across to the little Piper caravan that used to be her bedroom. Its interior was as she had left it when she set off for uni: eternally young pop stars looked down at the patient soft toys on the bed, both not wanting to admit it was basically all over for them. People often wanted to borrow the Piper for festivals but Brother kept it on the yard in case Lily came back. She went to the locker and found her old college books, pulling out a doodled copy of Grant Pooke's *Contemporary British Art* and flicked through it till she came to an image of a Joachim Muller net that matched the one in the folder. With her finger to mark the page in the book, she returned to Brother's caravan and opened it beside the folder. The images were identical.

'Oh my god, Dad, look at this …'

Below the glossy reproduction in Grant Pooke's *Contemporary British Art* was in tiny print the acknowledgment, something Lily, who had studied the page hundreds of times, had never before noticed. It read: *Collection of John Burn.*

Brother located his spectacles, bent over and read the words by Lily's index finger.

'Mistaken identity,' he said. 'It's someone else. Same name, that's all.'

'That must be it,' Lily said. 'This,' she held up the file, 'must belong to him, whoever he is. Mystery solved. Shall I go and give it back to the lawyer, explain what has happened? We don't want anyone to think you're claiming it.'

'Would you?'

'I'll do it next week.'

Lily left work at five, hurried to the Underground, rode the tube to Piccadilly, and walked up the brass-nosed stairs through an incoming tide of commuters borne on a warm stale wind. She found the lawyer's building and spoke to a security guard on the ground floor.

'Hello. I have come to see David Ashton. My name is Lily Brandon.'

The man looked at his list and said, 'Take the elevator to the third floor.'

Lily emerged from the lift and stood facing a wide desk behind which sat two receptionists wearing headsets. She was directed to a speckled sofa and was just enjoying the view of an illuminated Buckingham Palace, lightly obscured by the leafless trees of Green Park, when a door flew open and an elegant, patrician man sailed towards her proffering his hand.

'Forgive me. David Ashton.'

'How do you do? I am Lily Brandon. I'm John Burn's stepdaughter. Well, not your John Burn, another John Burn. And I need to talk to someone.'

The lawyer hesitated, stared at Lily and said, 'Shall we go into my office? What's the time? Tea? Coffee? Water? A glass of champagne?'

Not champagne. She didn't really drink alcohol. Plus she already felt that she and Brother were too far in as it was without building up a bar tab. She didn't want to look like she was trying to take advantage. She wanted to do the right thing. 'Nothing, thank you,' she said. She wanted to clear it up as soon as possible, so her stepdad didn't get into any trouble, and then leave.

'Very good. Liz, can you in your usual marvellous way conjure me up a glass of sparkling water?'

The receptionist ghosted into action while Lily was led into a modern panelled office and took a seat in front of Mr Ashton's leather-topped desk. She reached into her bag and took out the folder and the letter.

'Someone has made some kind of mistake.'

The lawyer looked at Lily and then at the folder and letter on the desk.

'It's nothing to do with my stepdad. I'm sure it's no surprise,' Lily said, 'I've no idea why you went to his yard, but the John Burn who lives there isn't the one you want. And I'm sure the real one'll want to know his collection is safe.'

Ashton said, 'Of course. Thank you.' He slid a compliment slip across the desk, and lowered his voice. 'Would you please write on this piece of paper where you would like the Collection sent?'

Lily frowned. 'It's nothing to do with my stepdad, or me. That's what I'm telling you. I'm worried he'll get into trouble. That's why I'm here.'

'Of course,' said Ashton, and then added with exaggerated diction in a whisper, 'So just write down what you want doing with it.'

'What's going on?' Lily said.

'I have been dealing with your stepfather for over twenty-five years, Miss Brandon. I know how he likes to do things.' He pointed at the compliment slip and nodded.

'But you've never met him,' said Lily.

'Exactly,' said the lawyer.

'Apart from when you dropped this off,' she touched the folder.

'So it was him? I knew it.' The lawyer brought his palms together in front of his mouth and almost teared up with excitement. 'John Burn himself. After all these years …'

'John Burn, yes. But not the art collector John Burn.'

'Your father is the collector,' Ashton smiled.

'Okay,' said Lily. 'What did he tell you? Because he does like to tell stories sometimes. And I am very sorry if he in any way misled you. But he has no claim whatever on any of these artworks. I want to make that very clear.'

The lawyer now looked hard at Lily.

'You don't know?' he said.

'Yes I do know. This is nothing to do with him.'

'You honestly don't know?' Ashton said.

Lily was getting annoyed. 'What are you talking about?'

'So he hasn't told you either?' The lawyer laughed quietly to himself. 'Your father is the most extraordinary man.'

'I know,' said Lily. 'But he did not assemble this collection of art.'

'He did. Did he ask you to come and see me?'

'Yes,' said Lily. 'I don't want my stepdad to get in trouble over someone else's mistake.'

'He must think it's time you knew.'

'What?'

'Let me explain. Do you know who Herman Gertsch was?'

'The art dealer? Yes.'

'He passed away two years ago in an accident.'

'I read about it.'

The lawyer leant back in his seat. 'I worked for Herman from 1991 right up to his death,' he said. That explained the Jane Tabor sculpture on the wall to the right of his desk, Lily thought. 'And as the executor of his will I am still looking after his estate,' Ashton continued. 'Herman had many illustrious collectors buying from his gallery, but your stepfather was always his favourite.'

Lily smiled and shook her head. 'I have told you; not my stepdad, somebody else.'

The lawyer looked at her. 'Your father is a very secretive man.'

'Not this secretive,' Lily smiled. 'I can assure you.'

The lawyer slowly shook his head. 'He has decided it's time you know the truth. And I am very pleased you appreciate his collection – not everyone would. You obviously have his eye.'

'So ...' said Lily, wanting to put a stop to this nonsense, 'how exactly do you think my dad bought all these paintings and sculptures?'

'As far as I know, Herman spoke on the phone and had occasional private meetings with your stepfather when they discussed the buying policy and individual works.' He paused. 'I know your stepfather often used to go around shows late at night the night before they opened.'

'How do you know?'

'Herman told me; everyone knew.'

'Did you ever see him?'

'No.'

'Did anyone else?'

'I don't think so; your stepfather, as you know, is an enigma. He knows all there is to know about the art market, but he never wanted to be acknowledged, never went to galleries during the day, never attended parties, and was never seen in public. He even kept up the façade to you, and it is obvious why: had you known he could never have kept it secret for so long.'

'It is not a façade. He is not involved. It's not his collection,' Lily said.

Mr Ashton smiled, rather patronisingly and annoyingly, Lily thought. 'He didn't sell one single piece,' Ashton continued, 'even when prices were moving up with astonishing rapidity. You should be very impressed by him.'

'I am impressed by him, but not for that reason.' Lily said. 'Look, how many times do I have to tell you, it may have been *a* John Burn who bought all this work, but it wasn't my stepdad. You've got the wrong person. All right. What's his middle name?'

'Sparkler,' replied Ashton, without hesitation. 'John Sparkler Burn. I cannot imagine there are too many of them.'

Lily's forehead furrowed. She said, 'I don't understand this.'

She felt reality wobble and tilt underneath her, in a scary and not unfamiliar way. It had happened quite a lot in her childhood. It felt like a tremor, and she wasn't good at earthquakes. She tended to fall into the cracks. That's why she now chose to live on solid ground.

The lawyer picked up the phone on his desk. 'Liz,' he said, 'can you bring me through the John Burn file? Thank you.'

The receptionist came in, carrying some papers wrapped in a red ribbon, which Ashton proceeded to untie. He riffled through the bundle and passed a document to Lily. She took it and looked at it. Written across the top was *Deed of Power of Authority*. Underneath it said:

I, John Sparkler Burn, of Brother's Yard, Glastonbury, Somerset, (hereafter called the owner), do grant permission to Herman Gunter Gretsch (hereafter called the dealer) to choose, purchase and store any works of art that the dealer deems fit for selection. The owner will provide all funds for payment of works of art as they fall due.

Signed John Sparkler Brother.

'That is his signature?'

'It looks like it.'

'Witnessed on January 10 1992, at Brother's Yard, Glastonbury, in the county of Somerset,' Ashton said, pointing to a second signature.

Lily sat back and said, 'May I have some water please?'

The secretary said, 'Still or sparkling?'

'From the tap's fine,' Lily replied.

'We only have bottled water,' the woman said.

'Still, then, please.'

'Here is a schedule of financial transactions,' said Ashton looking down at the file as he passed her a second sheet.

Lily looked through a four-page document which itemised the purchase price and date for each of the works in the folder. There were about 120 transactions dating from the first in April 1991, a painting by Martino Zachman bought in Switzerland. The prices ranged between £2,000 and £360,000. The figure was totalled on the third page: £6,235,500. Then a second list itemized values as of October 2017. Its total was £31,675,000.

'He's done quite well,' Ashton remarked drily. 'Actually, that figure's three months out of date, it's probably nearer thirty-five million now.'

Lily felt light headed. She stood up and walked round the room. 'So where did the money come from? Whose account?'

'It was always delivered in cash directly to Herman Gertsch. You will have to ask your stepfather where he got it.'

Lily thought about her childhood. She remembered combing second-hand shops for school uniforms and text books, she remembered the many times Brother had to drive the van at twenty miles an hour to eke out fuel. She remembered adventures and escapades, most of which were fun and some of which were frankly dangerous, but she could not remember a single occasion on which Brother had any cash to spare. She would probably have noticed if he had had six million quid to throw at cutting-edge contemporary art.

'So,' the lawyer said. 'Now we have established where we are, so to speak, let us discuss the future. What do you want doing with the Collection? There are a lot of decisions that have to be made that cannot be put off any longer. Herman Gertsch and the gallery took care of all your stepfather's correspondence. We were under strict instructions never to send anything to Mr Burn at his Somerset address.'

The lawyer took a sheaf of invitations and letters and passed them to Lily, who started reading them. There were scores of them, inviting Burn to openings all over the world, to dinners at museums, to weekend symposia, to art fairs, festivals and other cultural events. There were requests for Burn to join the boards of art galleries, museums and commercial companies, and letters asking for the loan of particular works and permission to reproduce images of works in books and in advertising campaigns.

'That is from the last few months,' said Ashton. 'We have to reply to them, particularly the request for loans. Herman was generous but judicious in his loan policy for the John Burn Collection. It's one of the reasons it enjoys such a good reputation.'

Lily looked up from the pile of cards and letters.

'First things first,' she said, 'can I have a copy of that Deed of Authority?'

'Of course.' Ashton paused.

'Good. I think before anything else, I need to speak to the woman who witnessed this.'

'Celia Somerton. She was Herman's PA.'

'Yes,' said Lily, 'do you have her phone number?'

'I will see if we have it somewhere for you,' said Ashton, calling 'Liz!'

Four days later Lily returned by coach to Glastonbury, but this time she didn't notice the view. Brother was waiting with the engine running because the starter was giving trouble. Lily climbed up, threw her bag in the back and gave him a kiss.

'What's wrong?' Brother said, urging the van on as it toiled out of town, 'has something happened?'

Lily scrutinized her stepfather. He clicked a Zippo under a flattened spliff and adjusted his cap as they nosed out onto the Levels.

'Did you ever tell someone you're the John Burn who's the art collector?'

'No,' said Brother. 'I never even heard of this other guy.' After a tussle with the gearstick, Brother dropped the van into second to slow down for one of the five humpback bridges between Glastonbury and the yard.

'You never met Herman Gertsch?'

'No.'

'Never?'

'No. What's this all about?' He revved the engine, brightening the headlights, and then slowed to negotiate a raised drain-cover which the road had sunk around.

'And you never signed a contract to buy art with him?'

'What?'

'You say "what" like that, Dad, looking innocent, but they've got a contract with your signature on it. I've got a copy in my bag.'

'A contract? To buy art? It's a forgery. It's a scam.'

'It's witnessed.'

'You know I sign nothing. It's me motto. Sign nothing, ever. And to buy art? You're having a laugh.' He wiggled the gear stick, revved and turned the van onto the pitted drive. Soon the headlights were panning across caravans, jerry cans and items of disabled furniture.

Walking from the van around the obstacles Lily repeated, 'So you never met Herman Gertsch? You never went to his art gallery and you never signed anything with him?'

Brother sighed, 'I said, I didn't know the man.'

In the static, with their shoes kicked off, Brother lit a candle, riddled the burner and chucked some split ash onto the embers while Lily rummaged for the Deed in her knapsack. She passed it to him, and he took his spectacles out of the incense burner on the sideboard. He didn't like to wear them because they reminded him of his weakening powers. The light of the candle caught Brother's cheek-bones as he studied the document. Lily passingly thought how no-one in London knew how brightly a single candle burned.

'How old is this?' he asked.

'It's dated 1991,' Lily said.

'That's twenty-five years ago. I'm not that sharp on last Wednesday.' He mumbled to himself and said, 'It does look like my moniker. But I don't remember signing it. Why would I sign this? I never had any money. You know that. It just never seemed to be in my path, whatever I did, more's the pity.'

'It's witnessed by a woman called Celia Somerton. Does that mean anything to you?'

'No.'

'I've tried to find her, through the lawyers, on Google and FB, but I can't track her down.'

'Celia Somerton? Nope. Don't mean a thing to me.'

'Sit down,' Lily said. She took his hand in hers and looked into his eyes. 'This could be very serious, okay? I want you to tell me the truth. It may not be too late to get you out of it, whatever you've promised to anyone else. Remember. You have a suspended sentence. You don't want to go to jail.'

'I'm not going to,' Brother said. 'Because I ain't done nothing wrong. I don't know what this is, okay? I swear Lily, I don't.'

'You haven't been handling money, dodgy money, and giving it to someone in London to buy art for someone else?'

'I told you …'

'This isn't anything to do with Kev?' Lily asked.

Kev was a dreadlocked pal of Brother's who also lived on the yard but was away in India.

'I don't see how it could be,' Brother said. 'Not that I know of, anyway.'

'Well I don't know what's going on,' Lily said. 'This man John Burn exists, okay. But as far as I can tell from the internet and talking to his lawyer, he's an obsessively private person. Even his lawyer has never met him. There are loads of mentions of him on the internet but not a single photo.'

'Does it say where he lives? Where he's from?'

'No, and no. Actually, correct that. He lives here, in your yard, according to his lawyer, and his middle name is Sparkler.'

Brother spooned and stirred three sugars into his tea.

'Just run that past me again, Lily. You know how thick I am,' he said.

'Somebody, for the last twenty-five years,' she said, 'has been buying a lot of amazing art in your name. Your full name. And there appears to be the paperwork that says you own them.'

'With my signature?' Brother repeated. 'So are they legally mine? And nobody is challenging it?'

Lily said, 'No, Dad. Not yet. But it's obviously a mistake or a scam or something. The other John Burn, the one who paid for it all, who actually is the owner, will turn up. From what I can make out he's not a man who's used to being messed around with. You want the pictures to be exactly as he left them. You never know, you might get a reward for being straight. But whatever happens, you must not touch them.'

'You mean sell them?'

'Well, yes. I suppose that is what we are talking about.'

'Are they valuable?'

'That's not important. It's irrelevant,' Lily said. 'If you take one of those pictures and try and sell it, it will immediately be recognised and you'll get done for theft, and we both know what will happen then.'

Brother was giving serious consideration to a course of action he often took when faced with a mind bendingly complex situation: dropping a tab of acid. He was imagining how this would all seem tripping off his tits. Often, but not always, he had to admit, it made things clearer. He decided not to mention the plan to Lily, who frowned on that method of problem solving.

As Lily lay in her childhood bed in her little caravan across the pitch from Brother, listening to the familiar nocturnal sounds of the yard, the fluttering of grebes settling on the water, the flicking ticking of insects beating on the windows, she thought about the John Burn Collection, and why it had come into her life. Lily was no great mystic; she knew that life was mostly fairly unmagical. She stared at the stars through the window opened on its cantilevered aluminium fitting and heard Jan, across the yard, opening and closing her caravan door, and then the muffled sound of Terry, her ten-year-old son, telling her to settle down and get into bed.

The next morning was warm across the Levels. The winter was retreating north and the westerly breeze was gently blowing in a soft early spring day, bringing the willows at the water's edge into leaf, and drawing the rushes up thickly from the brown depths. Lily and Brother sat outside on a naily bench watching the sun burn through the last of the mist and reveal the view of the Tor, which looked from this point like a silhouette of someone lying on their side. From the road to Bath, to the north, the Tor had the symmetry of a Japanese volcano, and from the east, coming from the 303, it had the curves of a dolphin's head.

Lily opened the file, and turned the pages again. 'The more I see it, the more I see how fantastic it is.'

'So what's it all worth?' Brother asked. 'There's one or two in there I think I recognise ...' On seeing Lily's face he held up his hands. 'All right, all right. I know I can't sell them.'

On top of the certainty that Brother would go to jail if he sold a picture, Lily was also terrified of what would happen to Brother if he got his hands on even a tiny percentage of what the Collection was worth. She could never forget what happened when his mum had died and Brother had inherited nine grand. After six months he was a drunken, out of it, shambles. The caravan looked like a pit, the pitch overgrown, the van written off, and Brother was hollow-eyed and barking mad. Money did not suit Brother; even he admitted it.

But she couldn't lie to her stepdad, so went to her bag, delved into it and handed him the valuation that Ashton had given her. Brother put his spectacles on, and bent towards the print.

'Holy Mary mother of god, holy shit, Lily. Holy shit! Have you seen this?'

She nodded. 'But they're not yours, Dad.'

'I know they're not mine,' said Brother. 'But are they really this valuable? I mean, I don't want to be rude, but to be honest they don't look worth this, not by a long chalk, speaking as a layman. Thirty-two million quid. Woah.'

Lily stared at him.

'But I don't own them,' Brother repeated. 'I know. And I can't sell them.' He also knew that without any question Lily would inform on him if he tried to sell them, and she would no doubt say it was for his own good. And he knew something else. He wasn't a thief and he wasn't a criminal. He had never stolen anything in his life, and he wasn't about to start with the crime of the century. But a man could dream.

'We've got to get this sorted out.' Lily said.

18

A day or two after Lily had gone, Brother kicked off his boots, lay on his couch, crossed his ankles and bent his head forward to spark up the spliff between his orange-tipped fingers. He inhaled, held the smoke in his lungs and then let go. He was thinking of spending, no, blowing, no, spunking, thirty-two million quid.

Where to start?

Get Geoff's water-powered engine into production. Hire all the backup he needed. All the top know-how. Beat big oil at their own game.

And get Jan some childcare.

And Anna a holiday and a bit of counselling.

He'd hire Mary a carer and buy her a house on grid. She was too frail to be off grid. She could keep her caravan, of course, for days out by the lake in the summer, but he'd splash out for a bungalow, with a few bedrooms for her friends. He'd put a chef on stand-by for her, a round-the-clock masseur, a song and dance man for entertainment, a doctor on call 24/7, and a team of nurses, good ones, who cared.

He'd publish Kev the Poet's poems. In calfskin editions, tooled in gold. And distribute them freely.

He'd save the yard, of course. Win the appeal. He'd hire top counsel. Silks. QCs. A major legal team to blow away Councillor Eric Pratt and all the others who were trying to evict them from land he owned.

Then it would be eco houses all round. Brother's with a lofty banqueting hall of oak and glass. Employing all his mates as labourers and joiners, on thirty quid an hour. No, make it fifty. Plus eight weeks paid holiday during festival season. There would be a carved minstrels' gallery. The Alabama Three in residency. A party every weekend. No expense spared. The best wines from Bordeaux. Tequila from Mexico, fresh lemons from Spain. A barrel of MDMA, delivered direct from the lab. A bale of ganja flown in first class from Jamaica. A bushel of coke from the Andes. All free at the point of use. Courtesy of John Burn esquire, art collector and philanthropist.

Brother patted his chest where a bit of burnt hash had fallen, and then started coughing, so swung round his legs and sat up, his eyes watering.

He was picturing his other houses. Antigua. He had never been to Antigua but imagined a pale clapboard house on a white sand beach. A blonde on the veranda. And his yacht, *The Lily*, moored at his private jetty. Where else? Goa? Why not? An Indian palace amongst the palm groves and rice paddies in earshot of the surf breaking on Arambol beach. Cute hippy chicks cross-legged on Kashmiri rugs lolling about his balcony. Where else? This was getting exhausting, and he still had millions left.

A string of racehorses. Arabs. Why not? On the flat, of course. Sport of Kings. Brother liked a flutter. He would kit himself out for Royal Ascot on Savile Row. Bespoke morning suit. Silk topper. Handmade shoes from Lobb.

Voile shirts courtesy of Turnbull and Asser. He would show the tailor, *his* tailor, exactly how the sleeve should fall and the cuffs button. Nothing too fancy at the collar. Just classic. Five or six suits. He could drop a hundred grand on clothes. A hundred grand. Mere bagatelle.

There was a knock on the door and it opened.

'How you diddling, Brother?' said a neat, handsome man with dark, seductive eyes and dreadlocks coiled on his head.

'Kev, man. You're back.'

Kev the Poet flashed a smile. 'What's going down?'

'All good. How are you?' Brother said.

They embraced, and while Brother skinned up a spliff, Kev flopped onto the couch, making the ashtray jump, and gave a brief account of his winter in India. The blast of hot, scented Delhi air stepping off the airplane. The rented Enfield Bullet. The two accidents, both from which he walked away miraculously unharmed. The girl from Stockholm, the one from Sydney, bumping into an old lover from Brighton at the night market in Arpora. Vulgar Russians, aggressive Israelis. The ghat at Varanasi by candlelight. The trip to the mountains. The wooden shack with the view of the Himalayas. The sticky black hash. The attempted robbery. The opium. The dream about his father. The hassles at Heathrow customs.

'Good to have you back,' Brother said, patting Kev on the knee, his eyes a little watery with joy.

'Feels great to be on the yard again,' Kev said. 'Anything been going on while I was away?'

Brother remembered the last thing Lily saying to him, as she boarded the bus: 'Promise me you won't tell anyone about the collection, will you? Not until we've got it sorted out.' Brother had given her his promise. The coach doors had hissed and banged shut.

'Everyone's ok,' he said to Kev. 'Mary's had a bad chest, Anna her ups and downs. You know how it is …'

Kev nodded.

'Jan and Terry, ok. Geoff very close to a breakthrough. No news on the appeal.'

'Life as usual on the yard,' Kev said.

'There has been one other thing,' Brother said. 'While you were away I became a major art collector.' He brushed the baccy and twigs off the file and passed it to Kev. 'Take a look at my collection.'

Kev leafed through the images and said, 'Have you inherited this lot? Who the hell from?'

'It's time you were told the truth, dear Kev,' Brother tossed him a lighter. 'As you have been my trusted mate for near on twenty years. I am not a penniless hazel weaver, willow whittler and amateur mechanic, I am the wealthy owner of a warehouse full of prestigious contemporary art. I am J.S. Burn esquire, collector extraordinaire, and top philanthropist.'

'Bollocks.'

'Look …' Brother shoved the page of Lily's A Level art textbook, and pointed to his name under the photo. 'See. Collection of John Burn. Moi. A man of distinction and taste. In the tradition of Kenneth Clark of *Civilisation* fame. Charles Saatchi. Gloria Vanderbilt. Carnegie.'

'You did not buy these paintings,' Kev said.

'I may have,' said Brother.

'You didn't.'

'I could of. I could've been bidding at Sotheby's when Lily was at school and you were asleep.'

'You weren't bidding at Sotheby's. You were getting stoned off your tits in your caravan.'

'All right.'

Kev said, 'What's going on?'

'Well,' said Brother, 'to me, it looks like I'm the victim of a case of mistaken identity. I share my name with this big art collector and somehow people have got us confused. They think I'm him, or he's me, whichever way round it is. How long more for, is anybody's guess.'

'But these are fab, man,' said Kev the Poet. 'I mean, that's a Callum Smith, isn't it? And that Muller. It's a beaut.' He put the book down. 'You know these are worth a fortune?'

'I know. But I can't nick them. There's no way I would get away with it. I really do not want to spend my next five years in prison.'

Kevin nodded. 'Yeah … I guess they are easily traceable.'

'All the paperwork has to be in place for a sale. People don't buy art off the back of a lorry. Plus, it must only be a matter of time before the owner turns up. And he sounds sketchy. Every time I walk out of the caravan I feel a pair a cross-hairs on my neck like a sniper's got me in his sights.'

'That's the weed talking,' said Kev.

'Even if I found some fence to take a picture, I may get a few quid for it but I am not gonna have my freedom to enjoy it in. Realistically.'

Kev nodded. 'It's a bitch. But I see it.'

'And you know me. Art heists aren't my gig, to be honest. I like a quiet life. It is funny though.'

Brother told Kev about Ashton's visit, and Lily's meeting with him. Kev thought for a moment and said, 'So you have gone back to this lawyer guy and said the collection's not yours?'

'Definitely,' said Brother, 'Like I said, Lily went and tried to give it back. They wouldn't accept it.'

'You've given your number to the lawyer and said if anyone inquires tell them to ring it?'

'Yes,' said Brother. 'In a nutshell.'

Kev spread his hands and smiled, 'So you are in the clear, my son. And while you are waiting for the owner to get in touch, because he surely will, there's nothing that says you can't enjoy the art.'

'What do you mean?'

'These are great paintings, Brother. Some of them are classics, even I recognise them. So why not bring them to the people while they're in your care?'

'What do you mean?'

'I mean get some here.'

'What, on the yard? In my caravan?'

'Why not? And maybe in your friend Kev's caravan ...'

Brother said, 'Kev, you can't nick them.'

'I know, I know, I know.'

'Really. I'm not selling any. It don't make sense to do it.'

'I understand, my friend. On my honour. No sales. But we'd just be just keeping them safe for the owner. On loan.'

'He'll be well pissed off.'

'He'll be cool when he sees you've got them all safe and sound. He took his eye off the ball. We're just looking at them as we look after them.'

'What if they get damaged? What if they get nicked?'

'That's not gonna happen. No one on the yard will know what they are, for a start.'

'Paul will.'

'I'll talk to him, he'll understand.'

'He's a bit low at the moment, had a stint in the hospital with the drinking.'

'And we'll just be careful to make sure nothing gets damaged.'

Brother's brow knitted with anxiety.

'You got to risk it for the biscuit,' Kev said.

Brother smiled. 'Damned right,' he said.

Kev turned the pages of the file until he paused on a bold green, blue, yellow and grey image, by the British painter Ryan Young. He whistled and swivelled it to Brother.

'Come on,' he said. 'That's a blinder. Ryan Young, on top form. I can't believe this!' Then he stopped at another one, with swirly black marks on a silver background. 'This would look good in Lily's Piper. It could be a surprise when she next came to the yard.'

'It would certainly be that,' said Brother. 'I'd have to break it to her gently. Probably best not to mention it for the time being.'

'Now,' murmured Kev, 'something for me ...'

An hour later he had made his choice. Brother rolled another fat one, luxuriated, and then sat up and dialled the number on the letterhead with Kev watching him closely.

'Hello,' he said. 'This is John Burn here ...'

'Good afternoon, would you like to speak to Mister Ashton?'

The tone and content of the secretary's question was reassuring. Mister David Ashton, top lawyer in London's West End, would take Brother's call. Brother's own lawyer in Shepton Mallet sometimes took three weeks to get back to him. So, this was what it felt like to be an art collector and to be rich. Brother thought little good could come of talking to the lawyer, so said, 'I don't have time for that. I want to order some of my pictures out of storage.'

'One moment please.' The phone went quiet as Brother happily imagined the scene in the office as they scurried round at the beck and call of their important client. 'I'm so sorry to keep you waiting,' a new voice obligingly said, after what Brother had thought was a pleasingly short pause, 'can I give you the number of the art storage company, and our contact there? He is expecting your call.'

After writing the information on a Rizla Brother said, 'Thank you. Please give David my cordial wishes and say that he must accompany me on the shooting field one of these days.'

Brother clicked off the call with a flourish of his wrist. He was enjoying himself. 'Drive it like you nicked it,' he said.

Brother went to the basin, poured some water from the jug into the kettle and placed it on the wood-burner, then poured more water into the basin to wash up the cups. While he listened to the kettle vibrate to the boil he watched Terry dragging jerry cans of water he and Jan had filled at the spring in Coxley to their caravan.

With the brew made, he took a deep breath, dialled Artmove, and spoke to a man called Lawrence.

'What can we do for you, Mister Burn?'

'Well, I am just back from wintering in Antigua, and wish to freshen up my summer residence here in Somerset with a couple of new paintings.'

'Of course. We have the collection here in storage. What do you want and when do you want them?'

19

A fluffy mist lay across the Somerset Levels like a goose down duvet, as if it were giving the whole county a warm lie-in. It was the kind of day when the Tor floated on a sea of cloud and a lot of amateur photographers took cheesy photographs. The climate on the Levels was soft and slow; warm springs, hot summers and long, mellow autumns: a climate for ripening cider apples, fattening cattle and encouraging the humans to laze around doing as little as possible in the most enjoyable way. Just as a low blurry sun faded in and out of the fog at Brother's Yard, a spectral white van came through the gently rolling wisps of mist and appeared round the overflowing dustbins. This was the art transportation company, and the van was driven by Mike Chambers and Jim Ring, two employees of Artmove.

The men from the art handling companies were the chorus in the opera that was contemporary art. They were on stage for many of the important moments of the drama: they were the first people outside the artist's inner circle to see new work, when they picked it up from the studio to convey it to the gallery, and they were the ones who took the sold work from the gallery to hang in the collector's house. And of course they were also present when the unsold works were returned from the gallery to the studio. During all of these tender moments, the art handlers supported the main players by taking elaborate and exaggerated care of all artworks, treating every item as if it were phenomenally important, even if it had failed to make the grade. To survive in the art handling business you needed a strong back, a firm grip, steady hands, a pair of white gloves and the ability to keep a straight face whatever you were thinking.

Jim drove the van, a chisel-jawed boy in his late twenties with curly blond hair, eyes too close together and a firm belief in his own good looks. Beside him slouched Mike, a podgy, sleepy-faced man of thirty-five who was, or had been, an artist. He didn't know what tense to put it in any more. His last show was four years ago and hadn't sold; he seemed to have gone from up-and-coming to has-been without anything in between. To earn money he'd done some fabricating for a friend who was mining a rich seam of success. But after a year of painting pictures on twenty quid an hour that were sold by his mate for two hundred grand, he quit the job before it ruined his friendship. Mike liked to get into his own studio when he could, but he could spend all day painting and end up with less of a picture than he started with. He took a job with Artmove to make ends meet. On one job, Mike had delivered a painting by his friend that Mike had actually painted. He had derived pleasure when the new owner was so pleased with it. Mike permitted himself a comment: 'that paint is beautifully applied'. There was always a chance you could be pulled from the chorus and given a starring role. Callum Smith had painted figurines for Stanley Kench before hitting the big time.

They pulled up in Brother's Yard, and the chief lurched towards them in a drover's coat with bootstraps flapping.

'This can't be the right place,' said Jim. 'Who's this loony?'

'Welcome friends!' Brother called. 'You delivering paintings?'

'Delivery from,' Mike said, glancing at the paperwork, 'the John Burn Collection. Are you the curator?'

'They're for me,' Brother said, offering a spliff.

Mike declined. 'Where are we to hang them?'

'Right here,' Brother led them round an abandoned sofa and along the track to his pitch.

Jim said, 'I'll stay with the van.' He didn't want anything nicked.

Brother swung open Lily's caravan door, and put his head into its warm plastic scented interior. 'Somewhere in here if you can find a good spot,' he said.

Mike was used to surprises in this job. He had once been flown to the Isle of Man to move a Patrick Jegg light box six inches to the right. Now everyone and his dog had a private museum – why shouldn't there be a show in some caravans? He walked back to the van where Jim was sitting in the cab with the door locked while Terry circled him on a bicycle. Mike and Jim opened up the back and used the lift to bring the three pictures, which were all around twenty-four inches square, to ground level; they didn't need to, but curators liked it.

Mike had once used the tail-lift on a piece of art the size and weight of a disposable lighter. He hoped it made it look like the thing was so heavy with meaning and significance it couldn't be picked up by a man on his own. They trolleyed the pictures, which were in wooden flight cases, down the track. Mike took the drill to the twenty-four counter-sunk screws and lifted out the first work, a Thea Ardilles: ethereal black swirls on a silver background. He knew it, and loved it. But everything in the John Burn Collection was great.

Brother was admiring the flight case.

'Are you doing anything with this?' he asked.

'It belongs to the John Burn Collection,' Mike said.

'That's mine. So can you leave it? It could come in very handy.'

Mike came to the door of the caravan. 'You're John Burn?'

'Yup. Pleased to meet you, young man.'

'I'm Mike Chambers.' Mike had sold a work to John Burn at his first show, fourteen years ago – the one that everyone said showed so much promise. The news of the sale had made Mike euphoric. He thought it was a sign that he had made the step up into the big leagues. But John Burn didn't even recognise his name now.

An hour later, Mike found Brother by the water's edge tying a hook on a line. 'I got the picture up between the book case and the window,' Mike said. 'If you want to check it.'

Brother stepped into the caravan, and looked at the picture. 'That looks great,' he said. 'Wicked, yeah?'

'It's a beautiful piece,' Mike said. 'The best small Ardilles I've ever seen.'

'It's for my stepdaughter,' Brother said. 'A surprise.'

With the second picture, an early Ryan Young, hanging in the lounge of Brother's caravan, Mike found Brother round the back of the pitch nailing up a length of guttering.

'Okay?' Brother said, adding, 'what you laughing about?'

'Just that I thought you would have someone to do that sort of thing for you.'

Brother answered, 'Unfortunately, my butler is ill-disposed today.'

'That's that one done. Before I went I wanted to say thanks for buying a picture of mine. It was back in 2004. Mike Chambers,' Mike repeated. 'It actually changed my career, got me lots of shows. So thank you. It went a bit tits up later,' Mike smiled, 'hence, this …'

'Don't give up on your art, mate. You must never do that. If it's your dream.'

Mike looked urgently at Brother. 'Do you really mean that?'

'What?' Brother asked.

'That you consider it worth me continuing to produce work?'

'Course I do, man, you must!' Brother said. It was exciting how seriously Mike took his opinion. Brother loved putting a smile on his rather hangdog features.

'Thanks, that means so much to me. It really does. So much.'

With the third picture up in Kev's lean-to, Mike returned to Brother. He said, 'Can you sign here please?' and pointed to the delivery note. Brother took the pen and obliged.

'Hey,' Brother said, 'I tell you what, seeing as you've let me have the packing case, would you and your mate like to stay for a bite to eat? I caught three trout this morning and was going to grill them over the fire. I don't know how you're placed vis-à-vis your boss but I've got some mushrooms we could do after. You're welcome to crash here and go back tomorrow morning.'

'That's a kind offer, but we have to get back to the depot,' Mike said.

'Next time,' said Brother.

Mike returned to the back of the van and checked that the tapes, rugs and bubble wrap were secure. He rattled down the shutter and climbed into the passenger seat. As Jim started the engine, Mike studied the delivery note. The name of the receiver was indeed John Burn, and the signature confirmed it.

Brother went into his caravan for something but forgot what it was so lay down on the banquette and lit his spliff, creating a strato-nimbus of smoke while he shook out the match and threw it with a twist that made it spiral into the burner. He gazed out of the window at the sky and the land that swelled at the Tor. Willow fluff wafted through the air and floated on the water among the cells of pondweed. His eyes moved to the Ryan Young: a dandelion head being blown on a sun-drenched day in four flat colours. He stared at it for a quarter of an hour before slipping into sleep, enjoying the feeling of all being well, in every detail, washing around inside him.

When Jim turned the van onto the Glastonbury bypass he said, 'Phew. Back to civilisation.'

'That was one of the strangest encounters I've ever had,' Mike said. 'Do you realise who that was we were talking to?'

'Some skanky pikey.'

'That was John Burn.'

'Who's he when he's at home?'

'He's one of the greatest collectors of modern times. He owns an amazing set of Sarah Absoloms, three incredible Martino Zachmans, Kings, loads of early Callum Smiths, some seminal early Justin Jansons, loads and loads ...'

'What? That old crusty?'

'That old crusty.' Mike chuckled, shaking his head. 'He's notoriously secretive. He probably owns all that land down there and just lives really simply in the caravan. Pretty cool.'

'What a div,' Jim opined.

By the time they drew into the depot in Vauxhall, Mike had decided not to say anything about who they had met. He didn't want to be the one to disturb John Burn's peace. The meeting was all the more special if he told nobody about it. They parked the van, and Mike delivered the note to the girl at the desk who filed it without a second glance. He then hurried back to his flat, determined to get the studio cleared of all the junk that had accumulated in it and get back to work now John Burn had said he should.

20

Rachel Baker, a short, middle-aged woman with abundant black curls and a rich mouth was picking her wardrobe for the Venice Biennale from the illuminated cupboards in her Kensington flat, while talking to her PA at her gallery in London. She said, 'What time's my flight to New York tonight?' as she laid three silk dresses on the sofa beside six packs of black stockings.

'Eleven o'clock; the car picks you up from Flint Britain at nine o'clock, you fly from Heathrow Terminal 5. BA flight.'

'Have you ordered my car to get me to the Flint?' Rachel said.

'Yes. It should be with you in an hour.'

Rachel was on her way to a party at the Flint, ostensibly to celebrate the opening of a show by Ella Ng, one of her artists, but actually to make sure no dealers sniffed around Ella now she was moving up to the next level of her career. Rachel spent most of her time going from place to place, not having meetings but preventing meetings. Other crucial encounters that needed to be stamped on were the ones she was flying to New York that night to prevent: between her artist Joachim Muller, who had a show opening at MOMA, and any other European dealers who might be in his vicinity. Joachim had joined her from the defunct Krietman Stoop, and his star was also on the rise, which meant he would need watching all night. At the same time there might be one or two of Joachim's collectors at his show and they would also have to be kept away from both any dealers at the party, and any artists who weren't controlled by Rachel. She kept all her collectors on a strict diet of her artists, with no snacking elsewhere. Some dealers liked to make, rather than prevent, introductions, but they never lasted long.

Rachel would spend Tuesday in New York. She had a lunch scheduled with a collector called Gail Hepburn, a woman who had rung Rachel on the morning of 9/11 to complain her doctor couldn't make a house call to her Upper East Side apartment to look at her corns.

'When am I going to Atlanta?'

'Wednesday morning after Joachim's show. You leave JFK at 10 a.m. I've ordered a limousine from your hotel. In Atlanta, I have booked a suite at Loews Midtown.'

'Is there a car picking me up at Atlanta airport?'

'Yes, I'll put the taxi number on your schedule.'

The trip to Atlanta was for a collectors' dinner. Rachel often found it was easier to meet artists and start their seduction and subsequent theft from another dealer in out-of-the-way places like Atlanta. A little sophisticated flattery went a long way in a far-away place like that. She was after an American artist called Geary Stern, who, though seventy, was having a resurgence of interest in his work, particularly amongst young artists. She was going to meet him at the house of some collectors called Heidi and Fritz Geller, which she had had no intention

now it was both of them. Surely she could get a sale out of this.

Rachel's sex life had to be kept under wraps to give any credibility to the idea that someone in the art world might one day get to shag her.

The sound of the key in the front door heralded the arrival of her secret lover. It was Jim, the driver of the art van. He was stupid and boring but he could open a bottle wine, fix a dripping tap and have sex whenever she wanted. She put her hand over the receiver. 'Shoes!' she pointed furiously to the mat where she made him leave his working footwear. 'Have a shower. I'm leaving in ten minutes for the Flint.'

'Can't I come?'

'No. Of course not.' She sometimes wondered if she could take him out in public, but knew it was impossible. All he could ever say about a piece of art was that it interrogated the space.

'Lauren?' Rachel said.

'Yes,' said her PA. Lauren was used to waiting while her boss talked to someone at her end.

'I come back from Atlanta on Thursday evening, yes?'

'Leaving Atlanta at ten at night, arrive Heathrow 6 a.m. Friday. Car to the gallery, arrive 8 a.m. At 2 p.m. you have a car to City Airport for a flight to Venice at 4 p.m. Arrive Marco Polo Airport 7.30 p.m. I have booked a water taxi to take you to the Gritti Palace.'

'Make sure I have the room I always have, overlooking the canal. They may try to bump me out. Don't let them.'

'Okay,' said Lauren.

'Have you booked dinner for five people at ten o'clock at Harry's Bar?' That was for her and two of her artists and their freeloading partners.

'Yes. And I have you booked on a plane returning to Heathrow on Monday night.'

'And on Wednesday I go to Frankfurt.' The Frankfurt trip was ostensibly to go to the opening of some piffling group show one of her artists was in, but its real purpose was to bump into Nick Speller, another ex-Herman Gertsch artist who had a one-man show at the Kunsthalle opening the same night. She had found out which hotel he was at and got Lauren to book her a room there. Ever since Herman had died, there had been a feeding frenzy on his artists. Herman's funeral had been one of the hottest tickets in town, with every dealer on the globe wanting to thieve his artists on the pretext of mourning him.

Rachel never got jet lag – jet lag was for tourists – but she had fallen asleep in the taxi on the way to Herman's funeral, and dreamt that she had to plant a bomb to kill Hitler, but just before she left it under the Führer's desk he told her he wanted to buy a picture. She awoke fumbling to defuse the bomb. She had touched up her make up as the dealers filed into the church. At least none of them had had to change clothes for the funeral. She thought momentarily how good it would be if some appalling accident befell the lot of them, in the way she often hoped a 747 with full fuel tanks would plough into the Basel Art Fair while she was out to lunch.

'All right, I'll just double confirm all that, put it on a schedule and email it to you before I go tonight,' Lauren said.

Rachel finished the call in her usual manner. 'Losing signal. Sorry. Got to go,' and flicked it off.

'Hurry up,' she called to Jim as she scattered her clothes over the bedroom floorboards.

After sex, for which she marked Jim six out of ten, she was about to say, 'Do you mind, can you go, I'm busy,' but remembered the plodding rules of romance.

Getting him off her was like removing an airline luggage tag. 'That was nice,' she said. 'You are nice. How was your day?'

She was not listening when he answered, but something somewhere in the back of her mind alerted her to something he said. 'Where did you say you were?' she said.

'Miles away. Right out in the sticks. Some manky place in darkest Somerset. Delivering to a collector.'

A list of contacts scrolled in Rachel's head. She didn't know a single collector in Somerset. She stroked his tummy. 'What was his name?' she asked.

'John Burn,' Jim said. 'Right wally he was.'

'John Burn?' Rachel said.

'He was a weird guy. He lived in a caravan in a kind of junkyard. Most unsavoury. He looked like a flipping hippy.'

'And you are certain he was called John Burn?'

'Yeah. Mike said he was a big collector.'

Rachel sat up. She had at last squeezed something useful out of Jim apart from sex. When she had got him the job at Artmove she had vaguely hoped he might pick up a bit of useful intel here and there, but this surpassed anything even she could have dreamt up.

'You definitely know it was John Burn?'

'Mike saw it in the paperwork. Why?'

Rachel waved away his question as she processed this information. That bastard Herman Gertsch had never shared John Burn with other dealers. But now Rachel knew where he was. Her first impulse was to kill Jim in case he talked, and kidnap John Burn. She could feel her heart pumping at the thought of all the work she could sell him now Herman was out of the picture. She speculated on the closeness of the connection she was to forge with

John Burn, developing in her mind the partnership they were to enjoy growing his collection. Rachel had looked so hard for John Burn over the years; even once going to the Amazon because Herman told her John Burn had a place there. Even told her the name of the town. And where had he been all the time? Somerset. Not Brazil, Switzerland, Bechistan or Moscow as people had often claimed. Rachel hated the countryside, but had heard that Somerset was where the rich people were going now. As soon as she was back from Atlanta she'd be on her way down there. She started hyperventilating at the thought.

'What's the big deal?' Jim asked.

Rachel paused. 'Nothing, really, nothing important at all. Tell me, could you find this caravan again? Or,' she corrected herself, 'tell me how to find it?' She wasn't taking Jim down there, she wouldn't want another man hanging around when she met John Burn.

'I've got it on the sat nav in the van.'

'Good. Text it to me tomorrow. And then delete it off the sat nav and your phone. Will you do that? And I want you to do me one last favour. It's important.'

'What?' Jim liked the idea of doing something important.

'Don't ever tell anyone, and I mean anyone, that you have met John Burn, or that you even know where he lives.'

'Why would I?'

'Well, just don't, okay?'

'Why?' Jim asked.

'Don't ask so many questions. It's boring.'

Jim put his hands between her legs. Rachel flicked it away.

'I'm busy,' she said. 'Go and get dressed.' She looked at his back and bottom and then picked up her phone. 'Lauren. I need to change my schedule. Between New York and Venice on Thursday, I have to fit in a trip to Somerset.'

21

A light fall of summer rain, like a blessing, removed the shine from the surface of the lake, speckled the windows of Brother's caravan, then blew gently on its benevolent way across the Levels. Brother was having one of his good long stares out of the window while the paperwork for the planning appeal hung limp in his hand. Sunshine followed the clouds, and the grasses and leaves glistened. A roll of vapour rose through the reeds and evaporated in the sunlight.

He was thinking about what to do about something important which had slipped his mind when he heard Mary across the yard say, 'Wrong place, love. There's no-one here called John Burn. Try Shipham.'

He put his head round his door to see a glamorous woman with ringlets in a silky dress standing in high heels by Mary's caravan.

'Ello ello,' he said to himself, launching himself off his caravan. And to the woman he called, 'Hello gorgeous!'

She was, indeed, gorgeous, with beguiling dark eyes, olive skin and a ripe mouth.

'I hope I'm not intruding,' she said.

'Intrusions are not necessarily bad,' said Brother, 'how can I help you?

'My name is Rachel Baker, and as I happened to be passing by ...' In fact Rachel had just got off the plane from America, got in a taxi at Heathrow and driven straight to Brother's Yard where she now had an hour before having to return to Heathrow for her flight to Italy. 'I just wanted to come by and say hello to John Burn as I was in the area.'

'Why did you want to see him?' asked Brother.

'I am an art dealer, and I wanted to introduce myself.'

Brother smiled broadly, squaring his shoulders. 'I am said John Burn, esquire, art collector,' he said and touched his cap with his forefinger and shook her hand. He looked her up and down in a way he wouldn't usually have dared to as Brother, but as John Burn the art collector it seemed almost required of him. 'My friends protect my privacy,' he explained.

'Of course,' said Rachel. 'Do you have ten minutes?' she asked in such a way that Brother thought, it looks like being a major art collector radically, hugely, massively, and completely alters my chances with women.

'My schedule is tight, I will admit,' Brother said, 'but I think I can find time to sit with you. Quick cuppa? Or is it time for a cheeky cider and a fat one?'

'Tea would be so kind,' Rachel said as Brother led her to his pitch.

Brother put the kettle on the hob and rooted around for a cleanish mug. Rachel glanced into Lily's Piper, and was comforted when she saw the Thea Ardilles. She was in the right place. Weird as it was. She reasoned this was some kind of philanthropic project, in which John Burn was trying to transform the lives of some of the strange people she had seen lurking around the trailer park, by exposure to art.

She watched Brother dart across to the washing up area, pluck a teaspoon out of a pan and nip back to his caravan. He was whistling happily, and flashed her a smile. Brother's love-life had been slow since, since, well since about the mid-90s when Lily's mum had left him with a badly broken heart. He had never quite found the courage and the confidence to get back out there, the way Kev did. But, he was just thinking as he watched Rachel try and find a nail-free spot on the bench, *maybe I can score as a collector of art.*

Used to being received by collectors in slick palaces of one sort or another, Rachel was taken aback. Most collectors wanted to impress her, either with their wealth, or knowledge, or taste. That wasn't John Burn's style: she hadn't seen anything like him.

Rachel remembered when she had first heard the name John Burn, way back in '91. Here he was now, holding two mugs of tea with what looked like a joint in his mouth. She had to catch her breath, it was so extraordinary to be in his presence, so legendary was the man. John Burn had not been the revolution in art in the early nineties – that honour belonged to the artists. Nor had he been the ringmaster – that had been the handful of young art dealers around at the time including, of course, Herman Gertsch. But John Burn had been the spark that made it all catch fire, take off, and tear around the art world. He had bought the new art when others had hesitated. Rachel was then a young gallerist just starting out, and she had been close enough to the revolution to know its history. It had not started with money, though money had been needed and John Burn was one of its suppliers, but it had been fuelled by something more important than cash: excitement, unpredictability, danger, courage, thrills. John Burn exemplified them all.

Rachel said, 'Do you know Thea?'

'Thea? Thea who?'

Rachel nodded at the picture visible through the window of Lily's Piper. 'Thea Ardilles.'

'Who's she?'

Rachel smiled at Burn's classic English deadpan humour. Being American, she always had a soft spot for that, though usually it came with men who were losers: in this case John Burn ticked every box. Rich, modest, and ruggedly handsome. Thank goodness I don't have a boyfriend, she told herself, and then remembered Jim, and then forgot him.

She watched Brother light up what indeed was clearly marijuana, raise his eyebrows and draw in a lungful. She felt glum. He hadn't lost his sense of fun – she had. She excused herself with the fact that it was okay for John Burn, he had all that money – she had to work, or be eaten up by galleries snapping at her heels. Her working day seemed to consist of being chased by sharks onto a beach full of crocodiles. Which reminded her. She had so much she would have liked to ask John Burn, but she had a job to do.

'I wanted to show you this,' she said, settling carefully back on the bench, and reaching for her iPad. She tapped it and turned the screen to Brother. 'I thought you'd like it.'

Brother examined the screen. To Rachel, it was an image of infinite teasing ambiguity that intertwined kitsch, conventional notions of ugliness and the perversion of numerous art references, and, more importantly, was an object she could sell for at least sixty thousand dollars. To

Brother it looked like a delivery of sand with a bucket and tow rope.

'Amazing, eh?'

'Are you building something?'

'What an intriguing response,' said Rachel. 'Yes!' her eyes lit up.

When Brother leant forward for another look at the screen he felt Rachel's forearm touch his. Usually, women like her – hot, sophisticated and obviously desirable – didn't actually notice Brother, but if he touched them, flinched.

'Would you like it?'

Brother smiled at her. She loved that he hadn't had his teeth fixed like the other rich people.

'What is it?' Brother asked.

'It's by Zac Manillo, you know him?'

'No,' said Brother.

'You will soon. He is absolutely about to be the hottest young artist on either side of the Atlantic. If you want in, I can give you first refusal on some selected pieces, but this is the one you need in the Collection. It is absolutely seminal. Can I put you down for it?' Her brown eyes, full of innocence and filth, bore into Brother's. He really couldn't think of anything to say except yes.

'Why, great!' said Rachel, 'that's' fantastic. I know Zac will be so proud to have a piece in the John Burn Collection.'

'Hold on a moment,' John Burn the Collector laid his hand confidently on Rachel's. Her skin was quite unlike any he had ever touched in Glastonbury. Legally, he owned a lot of paintings, but he was still skint, and Brother didn't lie about money. 'There's no way I can buy anything for at least a month,' he said.

'Why is that?' said Rachel.

He wasn't stupid, Brother. He knew that rich people said they were broke just as often as the poor. He proceeded on the basis that the rich and poor said exactly the same thing about cash – the difference being that only the poor meant it.

'I'm brassic!' Brother laughed. 'I can't even afford to get the van on the road.' It was more fun to tell the truth. Anyway, what was the alternative? It was all going to come out in the end. 'I would buy it now if I could. No – I will buy it just as soon as I get clear of a few debts.' That, he thought, he was totally safe saying, adding, 'How much is it?'

'Seventy-five thousand US dollars.'

'What's that in sheckles?'

'Say, with discount, fifty thousand pounds sterling.'

Brother chuckled. 'You're having a laugh, darlin'.'

As Rachel couldn't discount any more without looking stupid she took another tack. 'Look, you don't have to pay me right now, seriously, I'll send you an invoice but don't worry about paying it. How's that?'

'What are you saying? I don't have to pay?'

'I just want you to have it, I know you're going to love it so much. Okay?' Her lips promised so much if he just went along with her.

'If I don't have to pay it seems more than reasonable,' Brother laughed. 'Okay. Deal.'

'C'est fait,' Rachel said as she slid the iPad back into her bag.

Rachel looked across the water to the Tor and the Mendip Hills. 'It's such a beautiful place you have here,' she said.

'Yeah. It's not bad on the yard. No place like the Levels at this time of year. Someone once said when I die I want to go to May. And I say, I hope I've been good enough when I die to go to the Levels in May. But I doubt that,' he winked at her.

'So, tell me,' Rachel said, 'what is it that most interests you? What are your passions?'

'Well, what I am really hassled about right now, and have been for the last twenty ... well, no ... near on thirty years, is the planning laws of this country as they relate to low-impact eco housing. Look at these people here on the yard. They're all under threat of eviction. Me included. Why? I own this land, I bought it and planned for everyone to live out their days on it, but will the council let us?'

Here we go, thought Rachel, the rich man and his charitable foundation. John Burn's housing project. It was a current fad. Hadn't Brad Pitt got one in New Orleans? It wouldn't be long before John Burn asked her for a contribution. It made Rachel sick the number of times she had been asked for money from billionaires for their do-gooding hobby horse.

'... I mean the council want us to live in little brick boxes in housing estates built by their mates who make millions out it. These people here just want to live on their chosen land, is that too much to ask? It is Britain after all, not North Korea.'

'Yes, it's scandalous,' Rachel said, on automatic, 'truly dreadful. Well they are really lucky to have a man like you to highlight their plight.' Before he tried to sell her a table at a fundraising dinner at $500 a plate, she moved the conversation on. 'But tell me, which artists are you loving at the moment?'

Brother knew that as Burn The Collector he should be able to answer this, but he scratched his head searching for a name. 'You need to ask my daughter, Lily, about new artists,' he said, 'I don't know any.'

His irony was beginning to grate on Rachel, but she smiled. If he didn't want to talk about plans for the collection, so be it. 'Well, another time I would love you to tell me what's caught your discerning eye recently.'

'Hang about,' he said, and bounded into the caravan to a plastic barrel of cider standing on the counter, from which he tapped off a couple of glasses. 'If you really want to know what I'm into the moment, it's this!' he laughed. 'Drink it, it's from Heck's, a little family-run cider farm I found in Street.'

Rachel looked at it and wondered how many calories it held and then severely reprimanded herself: for god's sake woman, have the courage to live. She downed it. 'Wow,' she said.

The sun was burning the last whips of mist off the lake, and the heat was rising. It was developing slowly and promisingly into a shimmering hot, languorous summer's day.

'You know what else I fancy?' Brother said. 'Take off your shoes and come with me.' He took her hand firmly. He couldn't believe he'd done it. He'd needed that quick extra hit of cider he'd sneaked in the caravan. He led this exquisite, sexy woman barefoot over the thick grass, between the hip-high stalks of cow parsley, as far as the gap in the rushes at the waterside.

'It's a fine morning,' Brother said, 'fancy a dip? Come on.'

He stripped off his clothes, and launched himself naked into the jolting water. Rachel stood on the soft bank thinking, *my thighs, my tummy, my hair, my make-up and I am fifty years old.* Then thought again, *oh for god's sake. Just dive in.* Sun, cider, Somerset and John Burn had loosened something inside her that had been coiled a little too tight for a little too long.

Brother loved to swim. He was good at swimming, the way he wasn't good at much else. His school and subsequent career proved that. But in water, he was literally in his element. He felt his triceps flex as he closed his fingers and pulled both arms back in a purposeful breaststroke. He loved the gorgeous silver lip on the bow wave that curled in front of him, and the scoops of spoon-shaped reflections, blue, green, black and white, dancing on the surface. As he swam out to the middle he heard the heart-breaking splash which signified that Rachel had dived in before he had had a chance to turn and see her with no clothes on. He cheered himself up with the thought that there would be another chance when she got out.

After a ten-minute swim, Brother manfully climbed out first, soft mud squidging through his toes, picked up his clothes and moved a little down the bank to give Rachel some privacy. Yes – it hurt, but he was landed with being a decent bloke, so tried not to think too hard about what he missed out on in life, generally, and in this case, specifically, seeing Rachel naked.

When she appeared down the path, she had slipped her dress on and coiled her wet hair on her head.

'That was fantastic!' she gasped. She adored his informal coolness – something that money usually squashed out of people. Most collectors' 'spontaneous' swim would involve a changing hut, a jetty, a tray of drinks, garden furniture, towels and a flunky to carry it all out and put it all away. John travelled so light.

'Are you going to be in Venice?' Rachel asked.

'Why?' Brother replied. That summed it up for Rachel. The detachment, the simplicity, the elegance of his life. Venice? Why?

As she picked up her bag she said, 'Zac opens in my London gallery later this month. If you feel like coming to an opening.' She took an invitation from her bag and gave the card to Brother.

'A party?' Brother said. 'What's a ticket cost?'

Rachel smiled. 'John, I'm not like Herman; when you come to my gallery you come to enjoy the show. You are under no pressure to buy. That's how I work. It may mean I don't have his sales, but I have happy collectors.'

Brother thought about it. He wanted to go to a party, but transport was always a problem. Seeing his brow knit, Rachel said, 'You're worried about being seen, right? I could take you round the show the night before on your own when nobody was around. I know you will really respond to Zac's work. And I know you don't usually attend public functions, but if you feel like a change, come on Thursday; it will be a good party.'

'I'd like to but I honestly don't have the diesel,' Brother said.

Rachel smiled, thinking: these stupid games rich people play. 'How about if I send a car?'

'What do you mean?'

'A taxi.'

'To London?'

'And back of course.'

'That'll set you back a fortune.'

'Have it as a gift from me,' Rachel said trying not to be angry about how cheap he was.

'Wicked. In that case, count me in. I look forward to it. I haven't been to a party in London for well on twenty years.'

'I heard that.'

'Did you? How did you hear that?'

'You are famous for being a recluse,' Rachel said.

'Of course I am,' said Brother. 'Well, it's time for a change. Let's start with your party.'

'You're a long way out here,' Rachel said. 'I suppose you've got a chopper?'

'Actually I've got two choppers,' he said, looking at his axes on the chopping block by the caravan wheel.

Rachel nodded.

'A big one and one small one. Well, life's impossible out here without at least one,' he said with a twinkle in his eye.

'Quite,' Rachel said, thinking: *and he wants a free taxi.*

'I will get the car here at four,' she said.

Brother took her to her waiting driver and spent too long, far too long giving the man instructions. He said to Rachel, 'It's good you're going on the A303. It's powerful. On a lot of lay lines. You could well feel it.'

As she pulled away she waved from the back.

Brother thought, *I could get into having an art collection.*

Rachel thought, *why shouldn't something good happen to me, for once?'*

22

The Rachel Baker Gallery stood on the corner of some of the most expensive real estate in the world. Rachel had to sell relentlessly to cover the rent. But if she moved somewhere cheaper the art world would smell blood. Huge plate glass windows with brushed steel frames gave onto ten thousand square feet of shimmering concrete floors and pristine white walls. It was dusk, and the Mayfair street was jammed with long black cars, their brake lights oozing on and off as they deposited passengers into the glow from the gallery. A crowd pressed at the door as guests filtered through security. Inside, people shook off their anxiety about not being admitted and wandered around the show looking, before it got too crowded, with fevered interest at what the other guests were wearing.

Rachel stood with her back to the far wall reading the crowd's dynamic; she could judge a show from the shape and the sound of the opening. She watched the cluster around a tall, mop-haired young man, the artist Zac Manillo, whose show it was, and was pleased to see it gather in size. Many years of openings had taught Rachel that an artist standing for five minutes talking to his mum and distant cousin meant you might as well close the show down then and there.

There was something special in the air: Callum Smith was in the room. And there was Herb Waters, the American superstar sculptor, coming through the door with his last-wife-but-one and his English lawyer. And talking to Herb Waters and Callum Smith were Joachim Muller and Ella Ng, making a constellation of blindingly bright stars that were rarely seen together in the same night sky.

Scattered around the room were some significant collectors, with more coming in. Lisa and Barry Ogden, both wiry thin, both in black, both with skin stretched to breaking point over their cheekbones. And over there was Edmond Peckover, ten billion dollars standing right there in trainers with his floppy belly hanging over the waist of a crumpled suit. Rachel exchanged a smile with him. No one else was worth expending the energy on, though she could see Celia Minoprio, the ancient, wrinkled shipping heiress, giving her coat to a waitress, so walked over to welcome her. As Rachel put an orange juice into Celia's quivering hand, she felt her phone vibrate. She looked at the screen; it was from her assistant: *John Burn's car here.*

Out on the pavement, Rachel spotted the homeless folk from the art project in Somerset spilling from the car, and she thought for one ghastly moment that John Burn had sent them in his place, but lo, there he was, the man himself, stretching his limbs and turning toward the gallery, smiling nervously and patting his waistcoat pocket. Rachel rushed towards him.

'Hello! Welcome, thank you all for coming,' she said, grabbing Brother's hand. She wished she could clap him in handcuffs there and then. To the doorman, she said, 'All these people are good.'

of going to until Heidi had mentioned that Stern would be there. A quarter of the way round the world for two courses, a coffee and a ten-minute chat. Rachel wondered if she was going to have to plant in Stern's mind the idea that there might be a possibility of sleeping with her if he did the right things. Not that she would actually sleep with him. Rachel had worked out that you only got anything out of men by not sleeping with them. She had tried sleeping with them, but that strategy had ended one summer night in the Hamptons when, after a party, she took to bed a man whom she thought was the son of a huge collector, but who turned out to be the son's feckless college friend whose father was not the billionaire owner of one of the world's biggest agri-businesses but a New Jersey limo driver.

She actually liked Heidi Geller and felt a bit sorry for her because the last time she had been at the Geller house she sensed Fritz coming onto her when Heidi was in the kitchen talking to the cook. She was careful to give Fritz nothing back, and made it clear to Heidi by getting up to get a drink when he sat down beside her, and returning to sit by Heidi. She felt Heidi warm to her. Fritz had the money but Heidi was on her side. If Fritz didn't want to buy from Rachel it might look as though it was because Rachel didn't return his advances – Rachel speculated. It was a good situation. Until Rachel felt a hand on her back, or was it her bottom? Right at the bottom of her back just as it curved to her bum her deep-blue silk dress was being pressed onto her skin, in an unequivocally (but deniably) sensual manner. She didn't turn. She thought it was Fritz and did not want to call him on it and open up a chink in their relationship that another dealer would slip through. Then she realised it was Heidi, nut-brown, tight-faced, anxiety-ridden Heidi – making a move on her! So

When Brother, Kev the Poet, Jan, little Terry, Anna, Planet Geoff and Old Mary stepped into the gallery, a frisson like a breeze over water passed through the room. Half the guests had only turned up because John Burn was to make a public appearance for the first time in twenty-five years. Breaking the news that she, Rachel Baker, had found and lured John Burn out of seclusion had been one of the most enjoyable activities of her entire life. The look of agonised envy on the faces of other dealers, none of whom were invited to the opening, obviously, would warm her heart for many years to come.

Callum Smith, Jane Tabor and the collectors Dora Lou Bandel made straight for Brother, parting, or in Dora's case pushing, the crowd as they advanced.

'Am I looking at John Burn?' Callum said. He was a short, thickset man with black curly hair.

'You most certainly are,' said Brother thinking, *uh-oh here comes trouble. Oh well.* He smiled amiably.

Callum Smith stared at him and said, 'It's you! It is actually John Burn. It's really you. I can't believe it! I got to say: respect to you, man. Give me a hug.'

Kev watched Callum Smith embrace Brother. The artist closed his eyes, so sacred a moment did it seem to be. This, thought Kevin, was possibly a very milkable situation.

Brother finally said, 'Cheers, man, you're a gent. Solid gold rings to you as well. What's your name?'

Everyone went quiet. Kev prepared himself for ejection from the gallery and a night in the pub laughing about their adventure. Then Callum guffawed with delight. 'You're a breath of fresh air, you always were and you obviously still are.'

Brother pulled Kev to one side. 'Who is that guy?' he asked. 'Do we know him?'

'Callum fucking Smith.'

'Oh right. Him. Wow. Oh yeah I recognize him now. But he's cool,' Brother leant close to Kev. 'This is a blast.'

Brother had somehow got into this sparkling festival without a wristband. He was deep backstage without a lanyard and a laminate. At any moment he might feel the bouncer's grip. He sailed back towards Herb and Callum. You had to risk it for the biscuit.

To some student girls who had gathered around, Callum Smith said, 'This man here, this one, is responsible for basically getting my career going. Right back at the beginning he always bought my best work. Canny bastard. And I've never met him! This is the first time. It's incredible, man, here, come here, I got to give you another.' He grasped Brother and kissed his cheeks, tearing up. Two of the students gasped to see art history being made. 'It is amazing after all these years.'

To another man, Callum Smith pointed at Brother and said, 'This guy is the greatest art collector in the country. Now, what are you and your posse doing later? You got to come out and eat with me.'

'I'm skint,' said Brother.

'It's on me,' said Callum. 'All of you. Is that your kid?'

'No, that's Jan's; he's Terry.'

'He'll love Greens. We'll get a table at Greens.'

Dora Bandel watched carefully on which works John Burn's eyes lingered. She hissed to Lou, her portly husband, 'Did you see what he was looking at? That one, there. That one. Don't point at it for God's sake,' she sighed theatrically. 'Go and talk to Rachel. Now. No, now. Let's get something before John Burn gets in first, for once.' Over the years, John Burn had many times managed to pip them to the post on the best work. 'Go on,' she stared at Lou until he hurried to Rachel, took her by the arm and led her to the side of the gallery for a conversation.

Sophie Hanley-Smart, a blonde art advisor with a gently turned-up nose and feline eyes, had attached herself to Kev as soon as she realised he knew Brother. She steered him away from the competition. 'If there was a fire in here right now,' she said, trying to get an idea about what she might be able to sell to him and John Burn, 'and you only had time to grab one thing before escaping, what would you chose?' She looked around at the pictures.

You, thought Kev. *You in one hand, and one of those bottles of champagne over there in the other, which we would consume as the building burnt down with all the art in it.* But he found himself stroking his chin and gazing about the gallery. Kevin saw that people had gathered in front of the picture that Dora and Lou had bought. He pointed at it confidently.

'Good call,' said Sophie. 'Dora Bandel said that it was actually John Burn's favourite.'

'He has impeccable taste,' said Kev.

Brother was meanwhile being led by Rachel from one stranger to another, all of whom seemed beguiled by him, which was refreshing. They were the kind of people who didn't usually have much time for Brother. Rich people, basically, and city folk. Occasionally, he wandered off to get a drink, or chat to an interesting looking guest, but Rachel dragged him back to her friends. She even stood outside the loo when he went for a pee. He was her trophy, and she was not going to let him get away. Herman hadn't shared John Burn. Why should she?

Only Dora bore Brother ill will, staring at him icily, a look which Brother failed to thaw even with his I-smoke-ten-spliffs-a-day-and-am-totally-hopeless smile. She was especially pissed off because she had long comforted herself with the hope that the reason John Burn was so reclusive was that he was hideously disfigured, after hearing some rumour to that effect, but there he was: not only handsome, but easy-going and clearly adored by everyone he spoke to. She watched him take a loaded tray of drinks from a waitress who was struggling to stop the glasses slipping.

'Let me take that off you, gorgeous,' he said, and offered the flutes around before handing it back. 'There, you take over now.' It made Dora want to kick in a Leonardo da Vinci drawing.

23

Lily had tried to locate the real, art-owning John Burn, but had no success. Her friend, Laura, an intense, quiet woman who worked in a gallery beyond Hoxton and knew a lot of people in the art world, told Lily that he had a reputation for being a recluse. Laura had spoken to an artist who had worked at Krietman Stoop, who told her that Celia Somerton, who had witnessed the document Brother had signed with Herman Gerstch, had gone mad. A few months after Herman's death, she had had to be led by a paramedic from the gallery to an ambulance, shouting, 'Are you after Frieze tickets? Do you need a hotel in Miami? Herman's not dead, he's just caught in traffic.'

Lily hadn't heard again from David Ashton, couldn't locate Celia Somerton, and so let the matter drop. Brother told her to forget it. It was a storm in a teacup, one of life's mysteries. Behind the scenes, Lily imagined, the art collection had, no doubt, been reunited with its rightful owner and Brother's life was now bumbling along on its way back to overgrown obscurity.

Lily had completed a Data Protection training day at an office on Berkley Square. Her job was sometimes boring. She didn't care; it paid. With her office shoes in her knapsack and her trainers on her feet she weaved, with bowed head, through the pedestrians on her way to the Tube.

On the corner of Hanover Square and Brook Street, Lily saw a crowd on the pavement pressing to get into the Rachel Baker Gallery. It looked like an opening. She crossed the road to see who was getting all the attention.

She looked through the windows and recognised the galvanized buckets, rope and sand which were Zac Manillo's signature materials. When she saw the paintings, she admired how his work had progressed since his last show. Then, the strangest thing: just as Lily turned away to head towards Oxford Circus, she thought she saw Terry, Jan's son from the yard, at the drinks table, stuffing tiny hamburgers in his pocket. The crowd closed in front of the little boy and Lily looked at the rest of the room. She took a breath: there was Callum Smith and Herb Waters. If they were at his opening, it was great for Zac; it meant he had pretty well made it. Those two barely went to their own openings, let alone anyone else's.

Zac Manillo, Herb, Callum, and now Jane Tabor were all listening to a man who looked from behind a bit familiar. That was it: the tight tweed suit and walking boots reminded her of her stepdad. As the man threw his head back, laughing and slapping Herb Waters on the shoulder, Lily's jaw slowly dropped open. It *was* Brother. And now Sir Benjamin Minto, the Chairman and Chief Executive of the Flint Galleries and basically the most important man in contemporary art in Britain, went up to shake Brother's hand. Brother stood back, laughed, stretched out his arms, cupped Sir Benjamin's little face in his hands and kissed him on the cheeks two, no four, no six times, one side and then the other. Lily was recovering from this when Anna, yes, Anna from Brother's Yard, Paranoid Anna, appeared, tapped him on the shoulder and pointed straight at Lily. Brother saw her at the window, waved and beckoned her to come in, shouting something to Herb Waters and Zac Manillo as he marched to the door of the gallery.

Lily was hurried through the airlock of bouncers.

'Dad!' she said, 'what're you doing?… What … what is going on?'

'It's a party, Lily,' he said, tugging her by the arm. 'Come on in and meet everyone. Don't worry. Drinks are free.'

'How did you get here?' Lily said.

'Rachel asked me. She owns the place. She's great. It's a long story. I got one or two of the pictures out of storage and put them up in the yard.'

'You *what*?' said Lily, now hissing. 'You swore you wouldn't.'

'It's okay. They're perfectly safe. Anyway, Rachel saw them.'

'Rachel Baker? What was she doing at the yard?'

'Just passing by, it was pure chance. But she loved the pictures and dug the yard. We went skinny dipping in the lake. Come and meet Herb and Callum. You'll like them.'

'No,' said Lily.

But Brother pulled her proudly towards Herb Waters and Callum Smith.

'Guys, this is Lily, my stepdaughter. She's the art expert in our family. Lily, meet Callum Smith. He's an artist!' Turning to Herb Waters, probably the best-known living American sculptor for the last hundred years, Brother said, 'And what did you say you did?'

Rachel approached, pleased to hear her most important group laughing.

'Rachel, you got to meet my stepdaughter, Lily.' Lily shook Rachel's hand.

'I think we better go now, Dad,' she said. 'Thanks for looking after him.'

Lily pulled Brother to one side. 'Come on, we're going, now.'

'No way, Lily. This is wicked. They're nice peoples. Don't be so shy.'

Rachel adjusted her theories to the new reality of the daughter who was the family art expert. John Burn had possibly suffered some kind of breakdown; he had had trouble dealing with life. It was common in the super-rich: Howard Hughes had lived the second half of his life in a darkened room shuffling around in Kleenex boxes. Getty also had difficulty opening the curtains at one stage. John Burn, after compiling his collection, was victim of some kind of burnout, quite possibly connected with drugs, from the look of his friends. The project of showing art and living among the homeless was probably driven by his daughter in an attempt to rehabilitate him. The daughter was the new power behind the throne.

Rachel took Lily's hand, and said, 'I look forward to hearing what you think of the show…'

'I would love to look,' Lily said. 'But I have to work tomorrow and Dad is coming back with me.' She looked round, but Brother was back with his new best friends, the two most famous artists in the world. Just seeing him in their company brought her out in a sweat.

Rachel said, 'Let Zac show you around,' and suddenly Zac Manillo, the puppy dog enfant adorable of the international art scene, was staring down at her with his soft brown eyes and floppy smile.

'Oh. Well. Really? Are you sure?'

'I am sure,' smiled Zac, thinking, *wow, so cute, and from the urgent look on Rachel's face, Lily obviously has a lot of influence at the John Burn Collection.*

'Well, that would be great, then, ' Lily said.

She was soon locked in conversation with the artist. She passed Kev standing with his head tilted to one side chatting to Sophie Hanley-Smart, while Planet Geoff inspected a canvas at a distance of half an inch.

Later, Zac said to Rachel, 'She's the one with the brains.'

'I'll invite her to dinner,' said Rachel.

Rachel started to tell the invitees it was time to leave. She tugged Brother by the wrist away from some nobodies. A good gallerist could divide a room full of people so one half was already eating its first course at the restaurant before the other realised it had been left behind.

Callum Smith headed for the door holding Terry's hand.

Seeing the photographers on the pavement, Kev flicked open a pair of sunglasses, and handed them to Brother. 'Rock these, man. God knows where this could go. They love you. It's frigging sick.'

'Drive it like you nicked it,' Brother said, then took a deep breath and emerged from the gallery into an explosion of flash bulbs, his arms aloft, and an ain't-life-wild smile spread across his face.

Lily said goodbye to Zac by his limousine. She wasn't going to the restaurant. Greens? The smart Mayfair eaterie? With Herb, Callum, Zac and Brother? Not to forget Anna, Geoff and Terry. Uh-uh.

Zac had never encountered a girl who said no to a gig like this.

'I have to go home,' Lily explained. 'Office tomorrow. Sorry. But it was great to see your new work.'

Zac thought she said such sexy things. Not *you are handsome, or you are going to be so successful and rich, or I love your geeky ways,* the way his other girlfriends did, but *it was so great to see your new work.*

He looked droopy eyed, begging her silently for more.

'It's come on in such an interesting direction,' she said and he felt his soul melt, and, to be honest, his penis harden.

'I know we only met an hour ago, but I've never felt such a connection so strongly with anyone so fast,' he said. He had longed to hear a pretty girl say something coherent about his work. They all just faked it. 'I thought you'd be spoiled and a bit ignorant, being a big collector's daughter, but you are so amazing. A lot of people say they love my work, but they don't get it, like you. The number of idiots who say Hey, Zac, that really interrogates the space. It bugs me. I mean they haven't even looked at it for more than a minute. But you – you even saw my Old Street group show in 2010.'

'And I loved it, apart from the piece with the green cloth in the corner.'

Zac looked bashful, 'Yes, well some things are best forgotten. But tell me, which was your favourite?'

Lily didn't have to hesitate, 'The one with the galvanized bucket diagonal in the pile of sand, it was so spot-on,' she heard his breath shorten with excitement, 'and so full of resonances, and all the right ones…', then she felt him melt into her body, and place his lips on hers.

'What did you think of the one with just the rope and sand?' he murmured.

Lily pulled away. 'I can't. I'm sorry, I just can't. I have to go now. Goodbye, have a good evening, and thank you.'

She waved at Zac as she hurried towards the car whose door was still open, where Rachel sat beside Brother.

'Dad, come home with me,' she said.

'Come with us!' said Rachel, moving along the seat.

But Lily didn't like danger. She didn't want to be there when the penny dropped and the tempers flared. She hated that kind of embarrassing scene; Brother could lope through them, apparently not giving a damn, but not Lily.

'No,' she said. 'Dad. I'll see you later.'

24

'Who's Kevin?' Rachel said in the back of the car after dinner.

'Kev?' said Brother, a nice buzz on from a spectacular dinner and three bottles of claret. 'An advisor of sorts. I run him as a tax loss.'

'That's smart,' said Rachel.

Rachel glanced up at her apartment from the taxi to see if there was a light on. She had texted Jim and told him not to come back but when they got inside she bolted the door so he couldn't get in even if he tried.

While Brother fixed himself a double tequila and sambuca, a combination he always enjoyed if he ever saw the two bottles together with something in them, she checked the bedroom and threw on new sheets.

She had quite a few calls to make so she wanted to get on with sex, but couldn't make it look indecently hurried. She wandered back into the sitting room to find Brother looking at the window, glazing being of major interest to any off-gridder. He had already checked out the bath – an object of delight to anyone living in a caravan – and had cursed himself for not bringing his phone charger when he saw the sockets in the kitchen. It would have been handy to power up the car batteries too, but they were a touch cumbersome and often dripped acid, which pissed off house dwellers.

'Do you like it?' Rachel asked, referring to a spotlit metal sculpture on the terrace.

Brother thought she was asking about the glazing. 'Very neat job. Airtight. Immaculate. And so clear.'

'Wow,' said Rachel. 'What insight.'

Brother turned with a pleased smile. He was about to say *I know my windows* when Rachel said, 'What words to use on that piece of art: *immaculate and airtight. Truly insightful.*'

Deciding not to clear up the misunderstanding, in fact, surfing on it, he lifted his drink. 'Gold rings to you,' he toasted. 'For showing it to me. Solid gold. 64 carat.'

Rachel thought, *the man unquestionably still has genius in him.*

'So tell me,' she said, 'what made you come out of hiding after all these years?'

John Burn the Collector smiled smoothly. 'You, of course, Rachel.'

'Really?' she blushed.

'You came all the way to the yard, you invited me to your party, and you welcomed all me mates. That means a lot. Friends above everything, I say. You're cool.'

'You're an enigma, you know that? I thought you'd be steely and hard, but it turns out you're a bit of a softy,' she said.

Brother, thinking he could finally glean some useful information about John Burn, said, 'So what exactly have you heard about me?'

'Well, I know you have an awful lot of money,' Rachel laughed, 'but I know you also have perfect taste, and I know you are a great collector and every artist you touch becomes successful, and I also know that nobody knows where you live, whether you are married, where you go, even who you are. Everybody thought you'd be at Herman's funeral; the two of you were pretty inseparable as far as I can tell, but I was told you were in Lagos. Herman's PA said you were visiting your mines in Nigeria. What do you mine in Nigeria?'

Brother tried to summon a fact from his schooldays. 'Kryptonite,' he said. And suddenly remembered it was a fictional material. He need not have worried.

'Okay, okay,' said Rachel. 'I get the message. You don't want to tell me. I also know that you give generously to charity and I heard you turned down a knighthood a couple of years ago. You do lots of philanthropy. But your work is always so hush hush.'

Brother was beginning to like himself. 'I've a project going on at the moment to convert the internal combustion engine to run on water,' he said.

'Cars? Running on water? How fascinating!' Rachel said. 'Is that possible?'

'Yes. Geoff, my friend you met tonight, is the chief engineer.'

'Really?' said Rachel.

'H_2O is made up of hydrogen and oxygen. The most explosive combination in nature. Or one of them. You just need to separate the molecule.' He flashed a smile. 'It's not that tricky. Geoff has it sussed. It's the same old story. Big oil and the auto industry have been suppressing the technology.'

'And you've actually got a car to run on water?' asked Rachel.

'Any day now.' He blazed with evangelical certainty. 'And it's gonna revolutionise life on this little planet of ours. Stop global warming in its tracks for starters. Plus, make transport affordable to all. If Geoff's calculations are right, we'll drive at fifty miles an hour for five hours on a pint of water. Incredible, eh? Possibly sixty on sparkling.'

Brother was enjoying being taken seriously on the subject of Geoff's revolutionary propulsion system. It didn't happen often.

'How far are you from a prototype?' she asked. 'I want one!' she laughed.

'That's the thing, very close. There's a few parts left to get and we'll have the baby on the road.'

'Are you selling shares in this invention?'

'It's not to make money, Rachel,' Brother chided. 'We're not corporate breadheads. It's for the people. We're gonna give the technology to anyone who wants to use it. It's way too important to make money out of.'

There was a pause while Rachel stared at Burn.

'I am so glad I met you,' she said.

'And me, you,' he replied. Can I top meself up?' Brother held up his glass.

'Sure, of course.'

This time he mixed a judicious triple Campari, double Sambuca, port and brandy.

Rachel came up behind him and slipped her arm around his tight, muscled stomach.

'Shall we continue this in the bedroom?' she whispered.

Brother had no problem with that suggestion, and soon had her stripped off and on the bed, where he liked to think he shagged her royally. He was used to the confined space of the caravan so made full use of the generous dimensions of Rachel's bedroom.

Usually, while she was having sex, Rachel ran through her to-do list but on this occasion she put it to one side and focused on the job in hand. John Burn wore a nice scent: something manly with a hint of wood-smoke and top notes of hemp. She made a mental note to ask him its name in passing so she could surprise him with a bottle at Christmas. Ah, Christmas. Rachel was often alone at Christmas. To be honest, she wanted a man for Christmas, just as long as he didn't hang around past, say, January the second. But for those five endlessly tedious days when everyone else stopped working, she wanted a man like John Burn. He had a novel body to Rachel – muscled and lean but not all gymed-up. A real man's body, and he knew how to use it. The best surprise was how hungry he was for her. Really rich men, as every female gallerist knew, were no good in bed. But as they weren't there to give pleasure, it was no disappointment. Really rich men had lost their appetite for flesh, and lusted after money, possessions and power. You couldn't get better at sex by being richer – that was the central problem. There was this horrible, non-negotiable fact that poor people could actually have better sex than the rich, a truth that constantly gnawed at the egos of the wealthy. Better to stick to things that were well beyond the reach of the poor, like yachts and houses and, of course, art.

Brother was hungry for sex; the truth was he hadn't had any for months. It had been at the end of the Glastonbury festival, after a ruinous five-day munt. He had lurched around the site seeking shelter from the storm at the point in proceedings known as AOCWD: Any Old Crusty Will Do. Actually, Hetty, whose tent he finally ended up in, sweet Hetty, was a fine woman; crazy-eyed, short of teeth and a little rough round the edges, but she had kept him warm enough under her crocheted rainbow blanket, and he had stumbled out into the beating morning sun, the festival being disassembled around him, with a wide smile on his face and a sweetly pulled muscle in his groin. Rachel was a different proposition: the softness of her skin, the silkiness of her hair, and the crispness of her ironed linen were new territory. Bed sheets full stop were a welcome novelty, actually. He hadn't laid on a bed sheet that fully covered the mattress in years.

He made love to Rachel as though he were never going to get the chance again, which Brother thought really quite likely. He threw in a few cheeky moves which he would never have dared to do as Brother of the Yard but felt natural as John Burn the Great Collector. He feared that at any moment the door might fly open and three coppers would come in and arrest him for impersonating a man of importance so, like a condemned convict with a last meal, he feasted richly on Rachel. When both of them had licked their plates clean of pudding, they lay together on the bed.

Rachel wondered what John Burn usually did for Christmas. Did he remove to a cabin in Aspen for skiing, where the masks and helmet were so useful to hide his identity, or was he to be found on a yacht in the Caribbean anchored off some placid private lagoon? He would surely eschew the high society of the holiday season in St Barts and Mustique.

She rolled over to look into his weather-beaten face. 'Do you ever go to Mustique?' she asked.

'No,' he said. 'Never to Mustique,' as though it were a matter of principal.

'I knew it,' Rachel said, 'it's just not you at all. You are way cooler than that. Then Rachel said, 'I hope you don't mind me asking, but how did you make your money?'

Brother's CV was a little thin; even he would admit it. He had drifted away from school at sixteen and got a job as a mechanic, which had lasted three months, and from then there was something of a gap in his employment record. But they were glorious, cider-filled years, stoned, laughing, lazy, warm and full. To get hold of money, he mended lawn-mowers and cars and laid a few hedges. There was a brief interlude from formal unemployment in 2008 when he had a gig selling hash brownies at festivals, standing with a tray taking fivers off the crowd as it filtered round him. It looked like being an enjoyable way of turning a few quid, until a girl with the munchies ate seven in quick succession and threw a whitey. Her panicking boyfriend led Brother to where she lay sparked out on her back in the lush grass under some guy ropes. After waking her up, it took Brother two hours to talk her round. 'It's okay, you're not dying, you're just stoned out of your mind, my lovely. Hold my hand, come on, there we are… sit up, you'll be okay.' But it was enough of a scare to make him quit the hash brownie industry.

Some people said you were judged by the mark you left on the world, the bigger the better, but Brother believed the opposite: that you should leave as little mark as possible. His life had been gently whiled away, his legacy not in buildings with deep foundations, or other monuments. All Brother would leave behind him was a weedy veg patch, a bunch of loyal friends and many stories of a quiet life lived on the Somerset Levels.

'Would your business have anything to do with hedges?' Rachel asked.

'Funny you should ask that,' Brother said. 'As I definitely can confirm that some of my income derives from hedges. I'm saying no more.'

Rachel glanced at him. He had a hedge fund. Things were really looking up. She nuzzled his lean neck. 'You can't,' she said. 'I understand. I won't inquire any further. Oh. I've been meaning to ask you. What is that divine eau de cologne you're wearing?'

He was a little surprised to be asked this. It wasn't a question that often came his way. He never used any deodorant or scent, washed with just a bar of soap in either lake or rain water, and shaved with a block, badger brush and cut throat razor (for the elegance of it). That was Brother's beauty regime. 'That? Well that's all me,' he said proudly.

Rachel filed the brand away in her meticulously ordered mind: Allmi, for men. She had never heard of it. She would get Lauren to find it. She would gift it to him over the holidays.

On balance, Rachel preferred the Aspen Christmas fantasy to the Caribbean lagoon. There was better cell phone coverage, something she took into account even in romantic fantasies. As he held her in his sinuous brown arms and dropped off to sleep, she reached for her phone and scrolled through her messages, occasionally stopping to study his face in the glow.

Rachel wondered if John Burn might prove to be the cure to her ADS – art dealers' syndrome – the symptoms of which were an inability to appreciate anything about art except its value and saleability, and to be able to socialise only with other humans if they could either purchase or create a situation conducive to the purchase of an artwork. Concomitant symptoms included a lack of interest in anything or anyone outside the art world. Art dealers' blues, they were called, and Rachel had them bad.

John Burn, disinterested in talking about art, or gossiping about the art world, loyal in his friendships, a lover of nature, rude shagger, and capable of generous acts of philanthropy, was maybe the man to save her. With these thoughts in her mind, Rachel eventually dropped off to sleep.

She found herself back in the Hitler dream. She and John Burn were selling the Führer a Gresham figure for the patio at Berchtesgaden. They stood up, shook hands, but then Hitler looked down and saw the bomb. *What is that?* he asked. John told Hitler it was a sculpture by a young up-and-coming artist and it wasn't for sale. Hitler loved the wires and the batteries on it, said he had to have it in his collection, and ordered them to leave it behind when they left. John winked at Rachel. They were a team.

In south London, Zac Manillo was back at his pad, a disused bus station. The bed he lay alone on stood directly on tarmac, and the shower was a fire hose over a metal beam. Various works in different stages of production were scattered over about half an acre of space dominated by a Russian Second World War tank. This was the place where Zac did his big thinking.

Before Lily had got home he had texted her three times. She stared at the last one: COME TO MY PLACE. I NEED YOU IN MY LIFE. YOU ARE MY MUSE.

Lily closed the front door to her little warm first floor flat, rested her mac over the kitchen chair, sat down and wrote a text to Brother: RING ME AS SOON AS YOU GET THIS.

25

Brother was soaking in the bath when Rachel left the apartment that morning. He lay there wallowing in scented joy. He didn't know what he loved most: the sex, being listened to, or the hot water. He hadn't seen more than a kettleful of any of them in fifteen years. He lay back, closed his eyes and waited for the front door to shut before picking up a half smoked spliff and sparking it up. Rachel had given him strict instructions to relax and stay at home till she came back and he was going to follow orders.

Rachel had shut the front door and now stood in the hall and stared too intensely at the keyhole. She so wanted to lock John in, the way she had locked Jim out. It was her ADS, playing up. For her gallery to survive, she HAD to keep John Burn to herself. She had heard in the past rumours that John Burn was a nasty piece of work, but it turned out he was kind, handsome and sexy, which was really fortunate, as she had to marry him. There was simply no other way she could see of keeping him out of the hands of other dealers.

Brother towelled himself down, put on a clean pair of Rachel's knickers and started to get dressed. A four hour wait was never a problem for Brother, and the time passed quickly enough, staring at a pair of amorous pigeons in a tree, and having little chats and chuckles to himself as nothing of any importance went through his happy mind.

When Rachel bustled in he had only just finished dressing. After a little smooch he said, 'Have you seen my phone, gorgeous?'

'No.'

'It must be around here, or did I lose it at the party? It's like a little schoolgirl Nokia.'

'Borrow mine,' Rachel said, handing her heavy, clever one to him. She didn't mind him making calls on her phone, she could see who they were to.

'I can't cos I don't have the numbers I need, in me head.' He had a little laugh at the thought. 'I borrowed a pair of your knickers. Hope you don't mind.'

Rachel thought: clothes. I have to stop him leaving to get fresh clothes. If he goes home – *he must have a bolt hole in London* – I may never see him again. And I can't let him go shopping. She knew from the label in his jacket he shopped in Jermyn Street. A nightmare location, right in the middle of all the big galleries. White Cube was just round the corner, for a start. Their directors were always in the neighbourhood. On no account could she let John Burn fall into their hands.

'Let's go out to lunch. I've found a place that serves your favourite dish,' she said brightly.

'What's that?' asked Brother.

'Fondue, of course,' said Rachel, playing a trump card. 'Herman told me all about how you loved to eat fondue together. With cold cured meats. The best one in London is in Hendon.' Discovering this had delighted Rachel.

Hendon was way outside both the travel and comfort zone of anyone important in the art world.

'I'm not up to cheese and sausage, love, not on a hot day like today. How about we order a takeaway and you give yourself the rest of the day off?'

Her brow knit. The prospect of an unspecified period of time with no interaction with the art world was risky. Who knew what might happen while her back was turned?

'I have meetings,' she said, scrolling her phone.

'What about scheduling a meeting with me. John Burn?'

She looked up. 'Do you want to talk about acquisitions?' she asked.

'Yes,' said Brother. 'Come and sit down next to me, this is important.'

'Is it a, is it a, Zac Manillo you want?'

'No, Rachel, it's not a painting I want, it's you I'm after.' Brother loved being smooth as John Burn, and decided to trowel on some more. 'You're an edition of one. An original. And a really important find.'

Rachel put her hand to her chest. 'Me?' she gulped. 'But what's wrong with Zac's work?'

'Rachel. I said it's you I'm interested in.'

'But why? I don't understand. You could have … anyone.'

'Because you are kind and true, and I'm no expert in the field but it's pretty obvious to me you need some good loving. You've got a good heart, but it's hurting. All that's wrong is it's just a bit rusted up with lack of use.' He was about to say it just needs a squirt of WD40 when he stopped himself.

'Do you think so?' Rachel asked. She was aware of a new feeling in her body: a softness and warmth.

'I do. Come here,' he pulled her even closer and clasped her close. She thought, *this is an unusual sensation.* 'Did you enjoy last night?' Brother said.

She looked at him, and nodded. 'Yes,' she said.

They spent the rest of the day and evening either in each other's arms or each other's knickers.

In the morning Rachel woke early, and with Brother still asleep, gathered up his clothes and stole out of the bedroom. She dressed silently in her bathroom, picked up the bag of clothes and slipped out of the flat.

A couple of hours later, Brother was looking for his trousers when the phone by the bed rang. He picked it up.

'John?' Rachel said. 'Did you sleep well?'

'Like a lord. Do you know where me clothes are? I can't find them.'

'I took them to the dry cleaners.'

'But ... but Rachel, I've got nothing else to wear.'

'It's express service. You'll get them back this afternoon. Make yourself at home. Back later.'

Brother spent a diverting hour in Rachel's walk-in dressing room seeing if anything would fit, but he ended up on the sofa watching TV and drinking a Fernet-Branca, vodka and Drambuie in her underwear.

Rachel turned up with some large bags marked Prada and Etro. 'I got you these,' she said. 'Nothing too fancy, just a little token of my esteem.'

Brother opened the boxes and unfolded the tissue paper from some linen shirts and lightweight suits.

'Go and put them on.'

Without hesitation he selected a blue herring-bone suit and cream shirt.

'Let's see,' said Rachel. When he saw the expression on her face he didn't need to bother with a mirror. He dished out his special twinkling smile, whispered a thank you and kissed her, thinking, isn't life grand? Who would have thought it would turn out like this? She actually likes me.

She said, 'So, exciting news. I've arranged a wonderful tour for you. First, Ryan Young's studio – I know you adore his work and he's dying to meet you. He has so many questions he wants to ask you. Then, we've got drinks and a dinner with a really interesting group of critics. After that, if you're not too tired, there's a live installation in the vault of an old bank …'

Rachel outlined the schedule she had put together, which was designed to show everyone important that she was now in full control of John Burn. On the strength of this, she would be able to sign successful artists and enrage the mega-dealers. A perfect outcome.

Brother threw himself into the evening, and found himself dutifully repeating the performance for the next few days. Well, it wasn't very difficult. Being introduced to one adoring person after another with a pretty girl hanging on his arm? He'd done worse things in his life. All he had to do was laugh a lot and drink whatever was put in his hand, and those were his two special subjects. He had no idea who it was who he was meeting, Rachel handled that side of things. He was like her mascot. But he wanted to help her. He liked her and she was always so generous to him. So why not?

But after a few days Brother was exhausted. As Rachel was explaining who they were going to see that evening, he said, 'How about just you and me go to the pub? Maybe find one with a garden so I can have a tab with me pint. To be honest I could do with a quiet beer.'

'Why?' she said.

'I'm afraid it's a cultural tradition we take seriously in Somerset. It goes back many generations the duty of drinking beer or cider on and in between feast days.'

'But just us two?'

'Yeah. It'll be cushty. We're always at your fancy dinners and parties. How's about just a night off in a pub garden?'

'Which pub?'

'Any pub. It doesn't matter.'

It doesn't matter were not words Rachel understood.

'Who'll we meet?' she said.

Brother said, 'No one. We won't meet anyone. Well, maybe some random strangers at the next table.'

'Ah, you mean another dealer,' she said bitterly. 'That you just happen to bump into …'

'What?' said Brother.

'It's okay. Just not Larry. I beg you.'

'What're you talking about?' said Brother.

'Are you seeing other dealers?' she said, tears pricking her eyes. 'Tell me.'

Brother smiled at the thought. 'You mean other art dealers, I take it?'

She nodded. 'There. I knew it,' she said.

'No,' he said. 'I am not.'

'Thank god,' Rachel said. 'Sorry, sorry, I'm just scared. I'm sorry.'

Brother thought with sinking heart, *why am I incapable of making her happy? What's wrong with me?* He crossed over to the never-used kitchen and opened some cupboards looking for tea bags. 'You need to get acquainted with the subtle art of doing fuck all from time to time young lady,' he said. 'Luckily, you happen to have a master of it here to teach you.'

Rachel was looking in her handbag. 'But I've got far, far too much to do.'

'What would you say about taking a holiday, the two of us, together somewhere really nice?' Brother said.

She stopped burrowing for her phone as she pictured the two of them as they entered the Biennale pavilions at Venice, or the Armoury show in New York, hand in hand. A lovely warm feeling spread through her body as she thought how many people she'd make jealous.

'Where?' she said.

'Have you ever been to Weymouth?' Brother said.

'Weymouth? Has someone got a show on there?'

'No. But there's the beach and sea views, great fish and chips, really top notch, and we can sit on a bench on the quayside looking at the fishing boats. It's one of my favourite things.'

'Looking at the fishing boats?' Rachel said. 'Who will be there?'

Brother handed her a mug. 'No one, just us.'

'Oh – of course.' She put her hand to her mouth. 'You have a yacht in the harbour? Is that it?'

'No, I don't have a yacht,' Brother said.

'But I don't understand. Why go all the way to a dump like Weymouth to see nothing and no one?'

That night, as Brother lay unable to sleep with an uncharacteristically troubled mind, he identified another problem, apart from the fact that Rachel couldn't stop working, poor thing: she just wasn't right for him. She wanted the other chap, not Brother. He also realised that parading himself as John Burn the Collector was going to get *her* into a lot of trouble. The more he helped her by being dragged around to these exhibitions and artists' studios, the more trouble Rachel was going to be in when the truth came out. He had to do something about that. He didn't mind about getting into trouble himself, but he didn't want to hurt her.

His resolve was hardened when, the next morning, looking for a pen or a match or something long and thin to tamp down his spliff, he opened a drawer and found a phone pushed to the back. He picked it up and recognised it as his old Nokia.

'Hey! My phone! How did it get there?' Brother turned it on. 'Great. I can call Kev.'

'Your advisor?' Rachel asked. 'No one else?' she couldn't help saying it. 'John. You can tell me. Are you going to look around other galleries?'

She knew she was going mad. She knew she was acting out on her ADS, but she couldn't stop herself. She had gone through his phone before she hid it. Of course she had. It wasn't locked. She had scrolled feverishly through his contacts. It was all code, of course, but she'd cross-referenced some numbers she knew and was fairly sure he didn't have any major competitors stored.

When Rachel disappeared into the bathroom to get ready for work, Brother responded to Lily, letting her know he was OK, and then called Kev who answered on the first ring.

'Wuppen.'

'Oh man, it's good to hear your voice,' said Brother.

'I thought you'd dropped me, now you're out and about with the big people,' Kev said. 'I heard you had dinner with Jane Tabor.'

'Did I? I don't frigging know. Let's meet. Please.'

'OK. The Wolseley at one?'

'Where's that?'

'You don't know?'

'No I don't.'

'It's the number one art world place.' Kev gave him the address. 'I'll book,' he said. 'I can get a good table. '

Rachel came back into the room, and pretended not to have heard the conversation. She lightly said, but with a catch in her throat, 'Are you going out?'

'Yeah. To see Kev. He's a friend. Just a friend.'

She looked terrified. To Brother, she actually looked hunted.

Brother took her hand, and looked into her eyes. 'Rachel. You know there's a lot more to life than art? Don't forget that, please. Just look around and you'll see it. Now I need to go and see my friend, my lovely.'

26

On the way to the Wolseley Brother decided it was time to get back home just as soon as he had seen Kev. Being outside on his own, on the move, on foot, made him yearn for the yard. He didn't have any money, but the walk from London to Glastonbury was a cinch, an enjoyable five-day wander, mainly on drovers' paths. He had done much longer. It would be good to start in the city, cross the suburbs, then down the Hampshire lanes and onto Salisbury plain, past Stonehenge and into Somerset. A very pleasant trip. Brother liked to observe the subtle alterations of architecture and accents as he made his way across the country. When he got to the yard he would strip off, dive into the lake, go deep under the cold green water and clean all of this London grit off him.

The Wolseley was a huge, clattering, excited space built of marble and mahogany, full of smart people and the smells of fine food. Kev was at the bar, laughing with the uniformed barmaid. He, too, was wearing a natty new set of clothes.

They embraced and kissed.

'It's good to see you, man,' Brother almost wept. 'I can't tell you how much I've missed you.'

'Come on, let's sit down.'

The maître d' led them to a table on a banquette in the middle of the room. As they passed the tables near the bar, Kev said, 'Out of towners,' over his shoulder to Brother.

Kev spread his napkin on his lap. The maître d' said, 'Your usual, sir?'

Kev nodded, 'And one for my friend please.'

'Certainly.'

In a trice, a girl in a starched apron appeared with two glasses of champagne on a salver. Kev ignored the menu.

'I'll have oysters and the steak tartare,' he said. 'Same for you? I recommend the oysters.'

'All right,' said Brother. When she had left he said, 'How are you paying for this? Cos I can't. I'm skint. I bought three drinks in this place Rachel took me and it cleaned me out. Fifty-four spondulicks.'

'I've gone into business with Sophie Hanley-Smart. Art advising.' Kev casually scanned the room for anyone interesting. 'Don't worry, my friend. She gave me a twenty grand advance because she thinks I advise for you, or rather, John Burn. Like my shoes?' He kicked out a foot with an ostrich skin loafer dangling off it. 'I see you're still wearing your boots.'

'Yeah. Cos after this I'm walking home.'

'What? You can't do that.'

'I can and I am. It's exhausting being this bloke. I've had me fun. I'm going to 'fess up and bugger off back home. I want to see the yard and the lakes. It's June, man.'

'Have an oyster. They're from Japan. The best.'

'Might as well just pour salt water into an ashtray and drink that.'

'Just try it,' said Kev.

Brother put the shell to his lips and tipped his head back. 'Hmm, that's not bad.'

'See. Trust me.'

'Still, I'm through with this malarkey. It's different for you. You've got some bread. I'm skint. Plus Rachel. It's like being in prison. She's a ravening beast. She's worn me to a knub. I can't take any more.'

'Shagged you to a standstill has she?'

'Yes, but also all the frigging dinner parties and openings she drags me round.'

After a pause, Kev leant forward and whispered, 'Doesn't sound that bad. She's fit, Rachel. Just break it off with her, but you don't have to say anything about not being John Burn.'

'While she thinks I buy art, she won't let me go. You don't know her. She's probably got a tracker under me skin. I've got to tell her she's got the wrong man to get back me freedom. I've had enough.'

'Don't tell her that.' Kev wiped his neat mouth with the napkin. 'I've got some big news for you,' he said, flashing a smile.

'You're shagging Sophie.'

'No I am not. She only has sex with men who have a billion quid. So, it's you she has in her sights.' He looked around and leant in closer, dropping his voice. 'The good news is, it is safe to sell the collection. The last few days have changed everything. Everybody has seen you on the internet and everybody is talking about you. No one is questioning it. You effectively are John Burn. We've cracked it. Everybody thinks the collection is yours. Sophie, for one, is totally convinced.' He paused, took a drink of champagne, and leant forward again. 'The only thing we need are the original purchase invoices. And if they are in your name, it's all systems go, mate.'

'But I haven't got any.'

'Your lawyer has. Ask him for them. Sophie's already drafted the email.' Kev showed Brother his phone. 'Can we send it in your name?'

Brother read it. 'Okay,' he said. 'Let's see what comes back.'

'Good,' said Kev, pressing some keys. 'That's that.'

Brother said, 'So what about the real John Burn?'

'He's dead. Has to be,' Kev said. 'I keep hearing all these stories about him being in the Amazon and Afghanistan and hot air ballooning. He took risks by the sound of it. If he were alive he would have come out the woodwork now. Your face is all over the internet. You're famous, Brother, and you are John Burn. He's not turning up. For once in our lives, the shit is not going to hit the fan. The fan will blow only cool fresh air upon our upturned faces.'

'Do you think so?' said Brother.

'Now for the really good news. Sophie has found a buyer. I am not at liberty to say who, but he ticks all the right boxes. He can pay in the region of twenty million quid. It's a collector in America. Impeccable credentials. He knows the collection, loves it and has the funds in place. I thought, since we are brothers, and I'm the one who can get it sorted, we should go halves,' said Kev.

'Yeah, that sounds fair. Cool,' said Brother, who always enjoyed sharing what he had, a fact that Kev exploited mercilessly.

'After shipping costs and Sophie's and my commission you'll get nine point two million. Not bad, eh?'

Brother smiled. 'Nine million,' he said.

'Plus two hundred thousand,' said Kev.

'In that case, lend me a fifty will you?'

Kev took out his wallet and pulled out some notes. 'With pleasure,' he said. 'On account.' Then he leant across the table and said, 'It's exciting, eh?' His eyes were ablaze.

Brother twitched involuntarily. There was something wrong. Lily was shouting in his brain.

'What's up?' asked Kev.

Brother said, 'I don't want to go to prison. You know I don't own those pictures.'

Kev's phone vibrated. He glanced at it, then picked it up, swiped the screen and closely studied it.

'You do own them,' he said, still scrolling. 'You do. And we've got the invoices to prove it. And they're in your name.'

He sat back and exhaled with his eyes wide open. 'This is really happening, man.'

Brother said, 'Well I know what I'm going to do with my share. I'm gonna change the world. There are too many people out there hurting, and I'm gonna help them.'

'I know you will, Brother,' Kev put his hand on his arm. 'This couldn't happen to a nicer man.'

'Let's hope it does happen,' said Brother. 'I'm nervous now.'

Kevin drew Brother closer and whispered, 'As far as I can see, the only way it can go south is if people get wind of who you really are. You got to keep it tidy. You gotta keep up the act.'

'How long for?' Brother asked.

'Until the sale goes through. Probably a month or two at the outside. If anyone finds out that you are not a genuine collector in that time and starts asking awkward questions, the whole deal is off.'

Brother spread butter on a bit of bread, nodding.

'You have to keep it going. There's no other way.'

'I can do that,' he said. 'For nine mill, I can do it.'

'Course you can,' said Kev. 'You just have to keep your mind on those homeless kids or whatever. The ones you're gonna help with your share. Personally, I've got my mind on a new Maserati. And can I give you some advice?'

'What?'

'Try and steer clear of talking about art. It's what I would call a danger area.'

'But I'm meant to be this big shot collector and I don't talk about art?'

'Just change the subject.'

'To what?'

'Anything. The weather. Tell them about your collection of Hawkwind albums. Just finesse it, okay? Double espresso?'

27

'Look what I've got,' Rachel said, pulling some papers out of her bag as she came into her apartment. 'Invitations. For us. Well, for you. I picked them up from David Ashton's; he knows we're an item.'

She barely glanced at him, flung off her summer coat and spread the cards and envelopes on the coffee table.

'Some of them are incredible.'

'Rachel, I want to talk to you.'

'Hold on, look at these. Look. Look! A request for you to be on the international jury at Venice. You can choose my artists. Only if you want to, of course. And look at this one. No. Close your eyes. Feel it. Go on. It's from King Khaled Salime Al Deshani. It's for a weekend at his British residence, in Ascot, near Windsor Castle. Him and his wife, Queen Erena. It's actually next weekend. Do you know him?'

'No,' said Brother.

'It's been sitting in Ashton's office, but I got in touch and accepted, explaining the delay. Thank god the invitation still stands.'

'Look Rach, I'm not going to a house party in Ascot with an Arab king. It's not my type of gig.'

'I've already told them we're going. He's got his own museum, financed by billions and billions of oil money. Of course we're going.'

'Rachel, stop a moment, I've got to talk to you, darlin'.'

'What? What?' Only now she noticed his sombre expression. 'John? What's wrong?'

'Rachel, you're a great woman. A man couldn't want for better, seriously, but, but I'm afraid …'

She sat down, then stood up again quickly. 'Don't do this. Please. We're so happy.'

'I've got to call it a day.'

'What? Don't do this to me. I know I've pushed too hard. Haven't I? It's that, isn't it? God. What's wrong with me? I'm an idiot.'

'It's nothing that's wrong with you, it's just that I'm not right for you. And you ain't right for me.'

'You're gay?' said Rachel. 'Look, it doesn't matter. Though it does surprise me. You can have your men on the side, I won't make a fuss.'

'No, I'm not gay. But you're right: I'm not all I appear. I can't say more than that.'

'I know. I love that. You surprise me every day. It's great.'

'I am not the marrying type. I'm a bachelor through and through. I've grown used to me own company, and I miss it. I need to be back at my yard on me own.'

'It's the clothes, right? I got the wrong style? Too formal? I can get the right ones. I'll fire Lauren. That stupid bitch can't do anything right.'

'No. The clothes were amazing. Thank you again for them. '

'Do you want some more?'

'No. And don't fire Lauren. Please. And I don't want anything more from you.'

'Okay then, well buy another painting. Just one. Please.'

'What?'

'Just buy one more painting before you go. I promised Zac you'd buy another of his. I practically told him you had, actually. Or at least say you'll think about it. Let me give him hope, or he'll leave the gallery and go to one of those other bastards. I know he's been talking to other galleries. I'd like to rip his tongue out sometimes.'

'Rachel! Look, I'm not buying any more art, okay?'

Rachel took his hands in hers. 'Pleeeease buy one piece. I beg you.'

'I can't. I'm really sorry. I like you a lot, I really do.'

Rachel's bottom lip went out.

'Do you? Well why are you leaving?'

'Because I'm not built for this world of yours. I need silence and nature and, well, quite a lot of doing nothing, to be honest. And you, well, you know … You're a busy girl, aren't you? All those people … That's how you roll. I understand.'

The invitations drooped in her fingers.

'I see,' she said with a sniff. 'I suppose I knew you were a bit of a pirate. I guess I didn't have quite enough to keep you on dry land.'

Brother smiled at her, took her hand and kissed it.

'Sweet Rachel,' he murmured. 'I'm sorry.'

'All right,' she said. 'At least you're honest. Unlike most others. But grant me one wish before you go. You have to. You owe it to me.'

'Rachel …' said Brother.

'It's not buying a painting.'

'Okay. What is it?'

'Do this weekend with me at the King's. Please. Please. For me.' She put her palms together in supplication. 'God knows who else could be there, but just meeting the King could turn my whole gallery round.'

'Can't you take someone else?'

'Of course not. They want you. Do it. Please. Then I will leave you alone forever. I can't get near the man, otherwise. Just Saturday night at his place.'

'Well, I suppose I could. But we go as friends, nothing more. Separate bedrooms.'

'We have to say we're engaged to be married.'

'What! Why would I say that?'

'We have to.'

'Why? We can just be friends.'

'When I told the King's secretary I was coming with you, he said we couldn't come as partners unless we were married or engaged. They're quite old-fashioned.'

'Yeah. They behead women for driving.'

'The king's very westernized, actually. But I told the secretary we were engaged. Please don't be cross. I'm sorry. Look, I promise I'll call off the engagement after the weekend.'

'I'm not the kind of guy who would be engaged for a weekend. I wouldn't do that,' Brother said. 'It's shit behaviour.'

'We're just pretending.'

'Well, I'm not comfortable with dishonesty, I mean …' Brother started saying, but petered out when he realised how inaccurate the words were.

'I'll say I called it off,' Rachel said. 'I'll take all the blame.'

'What reason?' asked Brother.

'I don't know,' said Rachel.

'Well not something bad.'

'How about you're too much of a handful in bed?' Rachel said.

'Okay.'

He smiled and shook his head. 'Just say that I needed to be alone too much for marriage,' Brother said. 'That's the truth.'

'Okay. After the weekend, I'll write an email to the King and Queen and explain that. I promise. Please. So will you do this for me?'

'All right,' said Brother. 'But then we go our separate ways.

28

On the way to King Khaled Salime Al Deshani's country estate, Brother spotted a pub by a river. Always a sucker for a jetty and a pint, he asked the driver to pull over. Rachel had booked the limo on her business account to be sure he turned up. She had had to nip to a couple of meetings on the way to Khaled's, one in Dubai and the other in Milan, so was arriving on her own later.

'How far to go from here?' he asked the driver.

'Very close. Just up the road on the right. First house,' the neat middle-aged man replied.

Brother got out and assessed the pub. With its clipped roses and phony leaded windows it was too clean and tidy by miles but, from the beer fonts in the bar, was definitely serviceable. His phone buzzed. It never buzzed, so he scrutinised it. A text from Rachel. MY MUM HAS HAD A HEART ATTACK AND IS IN CHELSEA & WESTMINSTER. CARRY ON WITHOUT ME. DON'T FORGET TO TELL EVERYONE ABOUT ME. ESP. KHALED.

Rachel had never mentioned her mum, but Brother was understandably concerned and rang her as he stood by the car. It went straight to voicemail.

He rolled his shoulders and stretched his neck. 'You go on home,' he said to the driver, 'I'll walk it from here.'

'Really sir? It is half a mile away.'

'It'll do me good.'

Brother waved off the man, picked up his bag and made a direct route to the beer. Standing on the flagstones at the bar, waiting for the barmaid to tap off his pint, he began to feel his old self was not lost. He dipped his head to go out into the garden where three or four tables of customers were enjoying the sunshine on a mown lawn that went down to the river. One table had just a single occupant, a middle-aged woman, so he approached.

'Mind if I sit here?' he asked.

She looked at him as though through a day dream. 'No, no, do …' She moved her handbag up the bench closer to her, which Brother took as a sign that she was happy on her own. He took out his pouch of tobacco, rolled a cigarette, sparked it with the Zippo, tugged a lungful, exhaled and closed his eyes in the sunshine. It was good to be Brother again. He turned round, leaned his spine against the table, shot out his legs and crossed his boots, allowing John Burn the art collector to evaporate off him.

The woman sitting at the end of the table was Marie, Herman Gertsch's widow. She hadn't been out much since Herman's death, particularly on her own, and had only left Switzerland and come to Britain because her old friend Erena had begged her in letters, emails and phone calls to come and visit her and Khaled for a weekend house party.

'We hardly see any of our old friends, Marie,' Erena had said. 'We can't go to the Mont Cervin now Khaled is King. And we both miss you. Come and stay in Ascot for a night. It has been far too long and you are such a favourite of the King.'

Marie had agreed to go. Then she wished she hadn't. Her son, Walter, said she should cancel if she didn't feel like doing it, but his sister, Polly, said, 'Mum, you should go. You can't stay here for the rest of your life.'

'Why not?' asked Walter. 'If that's what she wants?'

Marie had flown to London and booked in at Claridge's, the hotel she used to stay in with Herman. She had decided to rent a car to drive out to Ascot. She wanted the independence, and didn't want to share the space with a driver, but had left too much time for the journey, so, seeing a pub with a mown bank curving down to the river, had decided to collect herself, drink a gin and tonic and bide her time until she had to press on to what was increasingly feeling like an ordeal.

She watched the river sliding by in front of her. Floating seeds and bubbles moved gently under a weeping willow, past a jetty, and then accelerated as they curved over a weir downstream.

A ball, kicked by some children playing at the side of the pub, looped in the air, bounced twice and began to roll down the bank. A four-year-old girl appeared and ran after it, a little too fast, until a woman's voice shouted, 'Lola! Stop!' and she stood and watched the ball plop into the water. Her mum, with an infant in her arms, appeared and took Lola by the hand.

A man who was sitting at the end of Marie's table, tall with greying hair and kind eyes, stood up and said, 'Don't worry, my lovely, I'll get that. Simples. We just need a stick. Come on, Lola, help me find one.' He flashed a smile at the little girl and her mother, and hurried towards the willow.

When the man came back with the stick, he took Lola down to the bank and said, 'Now, all we have to do …'

but as he touched the ball it rolled in the water and floated further out. The girl stood on her tiptoes and squeaked. The ball caught the current and started getting further out of reach. Lola shouted, 'It's going! Fucksake.'

'Lola!' her mum shouted.

Brother laughed loudly and sat down on the grass in a way that surprised Marie because he was wearing an expensive suit, and most people would have at least glanced at the grass before they sat on it. He bent forwards supply and untied the laces of his boots. He quickly stripped off red socks and started rolling up his trousers but, glancing at the ball now cruising into the middle of the river, thought he might need to go deeper, and so took his trousers off altogether. As he undid his belt he remembered he had Rachel's knickers on again. They had been a hard habit to break. He hesitated. Then he remembered who he was. I'm Brother, he told himself. Not flipping John Burn.

He stripped off, revealing a pair of black lace French knickers. He looked down at them and laughed, giving Lola a wave before wading into the river, leaning out and bringing the ball back with his fingertips and then hands. He held it up in the air, and waded ashore, while Lola stood on her toes with her hand to her mouth. A few people watching clapped, though not Marie. Brother acknowledged them, returned the ball to its owner, picked up his trousers and, without drying himself, pulled them back on. A minute later he was back at the table lacing up his boots.

'That was very kind of you,' Marie said.

'As soon as I remembered I was wearing women's knickers I thought, I'm gonna find me an excuse to get me strides off in public today.'

For some reason Marie didn't want to smile, but she couldn't help herself. Then she thought, *it's okay to smile again. It's not a sin.*

A waitress came by with a tray of empty glasses. 'Can I get you another?' she asked Brother.

He pulled some change from his pocket and counted it in his palm. 'How much is a John Smith again?'

'Four pounds twenty.'

'Aye yi yi. And how much for a Carlsberg?'

'Three eighty.'

'Make it a half of Carlsberg, please, my darling.' He gave the coins to the girl.

Brother sat down and resumed what he was engaged in before the bouncing ball drama. That is: precisely nothing.

He said to Marie, 'I like water. It's me element. And I like helping out. Single mums have a tough gig, you know.' He noticed Marie was quite attractive, even hot, in a reserved way. She had it, but kept it well under wraps. This met with Brother's approval, though she was definitely a bit out of his price bracket, with her perfect hair, soft, unlined face, expensive bag and shoes. He briefly considered wheeling out John Burn, the art bloke, but rather than launching into the impersonation, felt a pulse of relief that it was all coming to an end.

Marie was staring at the water. Brother noticed sadness in her face. He had a gift for that kind of thing. He could have sworn there was something on her mind hurting her. Maybe a memory, or a fear.

He reached for some cardboard in his back pocket, tore a strip off, curled it, placed it on the Rizla beside a pinch of tobacco, sprinkled in some ganja, and rolled and sealed the spliff at his lip.

Marie couldn't help recognizing the letter Z on the orange business card that Brother used as roach. A rather charming young artist called Zac Manillo had given one just like it to her at a party a long time ago.

Brother exhaled a lungful, a wisp of which must have reached Marie, who said, 'My son smokes the same tobacco.'

Brother smiled. 'Your son will go a long way,' he said. 'But not necessarily too fast.'

'How odd. I've often thought that of him. He likes to take his time before he decides.'

'Good man.'

'And I think I recognise that business card,' said Marie. 'Is it Zac Manillo's, the artist? Do you know him?'

'We have met,' said Brother.

'Are you in the art world?'

'Me? God no. I don't know a thing about art. Why? Are you?'

'No. I'm not,' Marie said. She made an involuntary tutting noise. And then sighed.

'Are you all right, my lovely?' Brother said.

She turned and smiled a moment. 'I'm okay,' she said. 'I've been grieving my husband, though I should be getting over it. He died two years ago. More than two, now.'

'It looks like you loved him very much,' Brother said.

Marie bit her lip and nodded.

'You see,' she said, 'this is the first time I'm out here on my own, since, since being without him,' she burrowed in her bag for a handkerchief. 'I think that's why I'm missing him so much.'

'Sure. Lot of memories no doubt. That must be difficult. Painful.'

'Yes,' Marie said. 'A bit.' She dabbed her face.

'You have a cry. They say it works wonders, but I ain't certain that's true. Some things just can't be fixed.'

Marie nodded again.

Brother said nothing. Nothing more needed to be said. When she gave her eyes a final dab, stowed her hanky back in her bag and clipped it shut she smiled painfully at Brother.

'I'll be all right,' she said.

'Don't you forget, my lovely, never forget, life is out there for all of us. For everyone. And that includes you. You got to go into that dark place, where you been for the last few years, and you got to come out again, bearing trinkets, carrying treasure.'

'Yes,' said Marie, nodding.

'You know what I mean? You go into the darkness, but you must come back out. Because it's a grand and beautiful old world we've got here, and you got to take your part in it. And you know what? The world needs you. People need you. Your friends need you.'

She nodded. 'But I will never marry again.'

Brother said, 'When I lost Susie, my partner, I knew that was it, on that front. Something inside had broken.'

'Did she die?'

'No. She buggered off. Never saw her again. Twenty years ago. Still hurts. I'll never marry. No way.'

Marie looked at Brother as he polished off his lager, jammed his pouch in his pocket and stood up.

'I better get on me way. Good to meet you. Best of luck. Go steady.'

He gave her a kiss on the cheek.

'Goodbye. Thank you for talking to me.'

'No. Thank you,' Brother placed his fist over his heart. 'I needed it. Gold rings to you, young lady.'

Marie watched him go until he disappeared up the road, his gait even and strong. Then she turned round, leant back, closed her eyes as she had seen him do, and listened to the children shouting against the splashing of the weir. She thought *I might have another drink and just sit here for a while* – that man was right, the world is a beautiful place, and I think I might possibly, for the first time in years, be a bit happy.

29

Brother strode over the gravel as he approached the impressive Jacobean frontage of Fryer's Court, the British residence of the King Khaled Salime Al Deshani. Inside, the Queen Erena looked through the mullion window and saw a man in scuffed boots carrying a worn hold-all.

'Do look. Look, darling,' Erena said.

'Who the blazes is that?' Khaled said, who had put some pounds on since becoming king but still possessed the same soft eyes and put-upon expression.

'That's incredible,' she cooed. 'It's John Burn. The guards let him through the front gate. He's walked here. With his bag. All these rich people who talk about conservationism and environmentalism and then travel around by private jet,' Erena said.

'What, like us?' said the King.

'Don't be silly,' smiled Erena. 'We fly private for security reasons'. 'But John Burn really walks. He walks the walk!' she laughed. 'Quite impressive, don't you think?'

'I hope he's not going to be a crashing, politically correct eco-bore,' muttered the King.

Within an hour of joining the house party, Brother had met the King and Queen of a Gulf Arab state, got on first name terms with a member of the British Cabinet, traded banter with a Nobel Prize-winning American economist and was now being led towards a newly acquired oil painting to give a brief talk about it in the company of Sir Benjamin Minto, chairman of the Flint Gallery and acknowledged world expert on contemporary art. It was the kind of situation that, under other circumstances, would have called for a tab of acid.

'No living man's opinion, John, interests me more than yours,' said the king.

Brother stared at the huge painting, terrified.

'Don't start yet,' said a needle-thin woman, taking a pad out of her bag, 'I want to take notes.'

'Herman used to swear by your judgment,' said the King. 'I remember it well. He'd say, if John Burn loves an artist it means buy now. So tell me, what do you make of my latest acquisition?'

Brother blinked and swallowed. Then he remembered the technique he had chanced upon on that night at Rachel's, when he complimented her double glazing and she thought he was talking about the sculpture in her garden. That had gone smoothly enough. His eyes now lit on the cornice running round the edge of the ceiling.

'It's delicate, it's intricate and fragile, and painstakingly painted,' he kicked off with, and noticed the banker nod. The King, thrillingly, smiled. 'Yet, despite its delicacy, it is so repetitive and mechanical it could almost have been manufactured in a factory, by the meter. It is either a brilliant human or a brilliant machine. And how close are those two these days?'

That drew a quiet gasp of admiration from the emaciated lady. Khaled, swelled with kingly delight, actually patted Brother on the back. The King usually found talking about art near Sir Benjamin Minto a nerve-wracking experience, but with John Burn taking the lead, he was well in the clear and could relax. They were in the hands of the master.

Sir Benjamin Minto stood behind John Burn watching and listening. He had come to the conclusion the man was a complete ass. He wasn't even looking at the picture properly. But that didn't worry Minto. He had had to guide many rich donkeys to the trough of art in the past, and no doubt would be doing so well into the future. Making them drink was the challenge. But he would succeed in adopting John Burn into the Flint family. He would find out what art he liked, and encourage him to pay to get it into the national collection.

'But what of the ideas behind the composition?' the needle-thin woman asked.

'Good call,' said Brother. 'You're spot on with that question. Well, the ideas are the joining together of two planes, but not the top not to the bottom. Oh no, that is too simple for this artist. This piece joins the top to the side.'

'Of consciousness?' asked the silver-haired banker in a blazer.

'Quite possibly,' said Brother. 'And quite possibly more. Because its end meets its beginning. So there is no start and no finish.'

'Infinity,' sighed the thin lady writing rapidly.

Erena tipped her head to one side and smiled indulgently at Brother.

Brother finished with a flourish: 'This isn't just fine art, your Highness,' he announced. 'It's damned fine art.'

Minto flinched inwardly, but nodded, apparently absorbing John Burn's wisdom.

'Now. If you'll forgive me, I'm parched,' said Brother. 'Any chance of a bevy, your Highness?'

'Please. Let us go into the drawing room and enjoy an aperitif.'

In a soft and chintzy upstairs bedroom, Marie had unpacked her suitcase and checked her appearance. She was walking down the sweeping staircase when she was astonished to see, framed in the double doors of the sitting-room, talking to the King and Sir Benjamin Minto, the man from the pub. This was an unexpected, but delightful surprise, and Marie entered the room wearing a radiant smile.

Brother spotted her straight away. She flashed an expression of such sweet welcome. It said, *Hello, you are the nice man who didn't come onto me at all, and was kind to a child and gave me some quite obvious but touchingly heartfelt advice, and I feel much better for it.*

Brother's initial thought on seeing Marie was *this is turning out to be my day.* He was later to revise that opinion.

'Hello,' she said.

'Hello gorgeous. What a lovely surprise.' He gave her a squeeze and a kiss on her cheek, his eyes sparkling with the particular brand of innocent affection he specialized in.

'Your Highness,' he called to the Queen. 'It's an all-star cast! I've met this gorgeous woman.'

Erena came up. 'But of course, that's why I invited you,' she laughed gaily.

Marie assumed, particularly as she had seen the Zac Manillo business card, that they had met at some art thing which Erena had organized, and both had forgotten. Brother tried to work out what was going on but momentarily went cross-eyed, so quickly stopped. He supposed that Marie must be one of the many people who knew of John Burn, and talked about him in a familiar way, but had never actually met him.

As guests came forward to greet Marie, Brother took the Queen aside.

'Please forgive me, your Highness, me memory's shot up. What's the name of your wonderful friend over there?'

'Marie. Marie Gertsch,' Erena looked concerned. 'She was married to Herman Gertsch,' she said, looking at John Burn's confused expression, and thinking, *oh no, how sad, early onset Alzheimer's*.

'Of course,' said Brother, theatrically banging his palm on his forehead, thinking *this is insane. John Burn was best mates with Marie's husband. How come Marie doesn't know I'm an impostor?*

'You probably haven't seen her for a few years. No one has. It's a joy to me that she's come to stay. I know you two were particularly close.'

Brother ran through everything he had said to Marie at the pub wondering if any of it was likely to lead to him being manhandled by the King's security detail into the boot of a car, later to be shoved out of a helicopter over a swamp. He had said he knew absolutely nothing about art and couldn't afford a full pint of beer. Neither ideal, considering he was posing as an art collecting billionaire. Unless they could be put down to John Burn's eccentricity, and in that case even enhance his reputation. The mystery was why Marie didn't know he wasn't John Burn, the art collector. He slugged back his third martini and went on a hunt for a fourth when, through the sash window, he saw a black car draw up and Rachel, in a hat and high heels, get out of the back.

'Oh shit.' Now this might present a challenge. He necked the fourth Martini and headed to the front door where Rachel was pushing past a butler.

'Have I missed anything?' she said to Brother.

'Hello Rachel. How's your mum?'

'What? Oh, fine. Well dying, actually. But taking her time, so I left her to it.' She shoved her bags at the butler and said to Brother, 'Come on. Where is everyone? Introduce me.'

Rachel jabbed Brother towards the drawing room.

'And remember to say I'm your fiancée,' she said.

'I don't think we need to bother with that any more,' said Brother. 'They're good peoples, actually.'

'Yes we do,' Rachel hissed.

Brother guided Rachel towards the Queen, but when he saw Marie moving in her direction too, steered away.

'Let's say hello to Minto,' he said, and swerved towards the diminutive puppet master of the art world. 'Sir Benjamin!' he called. 'May I introduce you to my friend, Rachel Baker?'

'We know each other,' said Rachel. They murmured hello and gave each other a kiss so icy it sent a shiver down Brother's back.

'I look forward to having a talk with you about your collection, John, and the direction you are taking it in,' said Sir Benjamin. 'I am hoping you have some new ideas for us at the Flint Gallery.'

'Me?' he said.

Brother felt a tug on his arm; it was Rachel dragging him towards the King. She was weaponising, or at least monetizing, him.

'He wants to get his teeth into you,' she said under her breath. 'Could be useful. Usually I'd want to talk to Minto for longer but fuck him when fucking King Khaled Salime Al Deshani is in the room. Your Highness!' She curtseyed.

'May I present Rachel Baker,' Brother said.

Rachel flashed him a look of white-hot anger.

'My fiancée,' Brother quickly added.

'Your fiancée! My wife had told me. Miss Baker. Congratulations are due,' said the King. 'I compliment you on your choice of intended. I know John is a brilliant businessman, connoisseur of art, philanthropist and adventurer of the highest order. Has he told you about his time in the Amazon fighting with the Wakapa in their struggle for freedom?'

'No. And why not?' Rachel play-punched Brother on the arm. 'Mister mysterious.'

'It's a wonderful story,' said the King. 'Herman told me all about it. You were there a few summers ago when I invited you onto my yacht. I remember. Was that the time you choppered in a pallet of Swiss food to break the siege at Niquitos?'

'Why on earth Swiss food?' asked Rachel.

'Because he had discovered that nutritionally it was the best diet for life in a tropical jungle. Is that not correct?' asked the King.

Brother said, 'I had every diet scientifically tested and the Swiss came out on top.' After he had said this he thought, *that was a blast. I'm pretty good at this. What else can I do?*

'Dodging those RPGs,' the King smiled, 'to get the emmental through! Now that, my friend, was a very brave thing you did!'

'We airdropped 500 fondue sets.'

'You what?' said Rachel.

'You must tell us all about it one day,' said the King. 'But you mustn't tell us in Wakapa.' Turning to Rachel he said, 'you know your intended speaks it fluently?'

Brother thought *I'm certainly safe with this*, and said, 'Siy mi deh canscraggi. That means, enough talk, let's get another drink.'

Marie, on the other side of the room, took Erena aside under a ludicrously large vase of flowers and said, 'Who is that man, that man there, the one laughing with Khaled? I bumped into him earlier today in the pub. He's quite sweet.'

'But you know who he is,' Erena smiled, and squeezed Marie's cashmere forearm. 'Of course you do.'

'No I don't. Who is he?'

'John Burn,' said Erena. 'It's John Burn. You haven't forgotten?'

Suddenly Marie felt like she was leaning over a precipice with a yawning chasm beneath her. Colour drained from her face and her mouth flapped open. 'What?' she said, struggling to breathe. 'Him?' She swallowed. 'That man? He's John Burn?'

'But you must know,' the Queen said. 'Wasn't he Herman's best friend? That's what Khaled told me.'

But he told me he knew nothing about art. And pretended to be poor, Marie thought to herself. *What sick and manipulative games he plays.*

'And who's that who he's with?' she croaked.

'That's Rachel Baker, his fiancée.'

His fiancée, thought Marie. *That fits the pattern of malicious duplicity he specialises in.*

'Come on,' said Erena, 'let's go and say hello.'

'No,' said Marie. 'Do you mind if I don't? I'm not feeling well. I think I'm a bit overwhelmed being back in a crowd of people. Will you forgive me if I go upstairs for a rest?'

Brother had seen the two talking and was heading in their direction when he saw Marie sweep out of the room.

Finding himself on his own, he turned to see the Minister and the economist looking at a painting right beside the door. The door. This was an open goal.

'You want to know what I make of that?' Brother said.

'I don't see anything in it at all,' said the Minister of State under his breath. 'It's like scribbles, how is it so brilliant?'

'The thing about this piece,' Brother said, taking a sip on his martini, 'it's a piece about movement, about departures and arrivals, about going in and out. And all you have to do to make it work is have the key…'

'… sounds like a door,' said the economist.

Brother almost spat out his martini.

'You see, every time I open my mouth on art I make a fool of myself,' sighed the American.

30

Back in the bedroom, Brother was going through his pockets a third time, looking for his blim of dope, when he heard a knock on the door. He opened it to see Marie looking up at him.

'Well well well, look who it is!' he said. 'I wondered where you'd disappeared to. Hey, what's wrong?'

'I wish to talk to you in private,' Marie said.

'We can talk. Rachel's in the bathroom.'

'Oh yes. Your fiancée. You, who this afternoon, correct me if I am wrong, swore you were never going to be able to face marriage.'

Brother held up his hand and gave a little laugh.

'Rachel. Me fiancée? No way. No way. Man. No way. We're just friends. I just said that to the Queen because…' Brother could see his words were not penetrating the sheet metal of Marie's stare. He petered to a halt and swallowed.

'That's not why I'm here,' she said. 'I'm here to tell you I'm leaving this house'.

'Don't go,' said Brother. 'You've only just got here. You godda give it a chance.'

'I have told Erena and Khaled I have an ill child at home,' Marie said. 'But the truth is I am departing solely because you are here, and I cannot bear to be under the same roof as you.'

'Me? Me? But darlin', what have I done? Apart from the Rachel thing which I swear I can explain at another time when she's not likely to hear.'

'You dare to ask that? After the way you treated my husband and my family?'

'It can't have been that bad. We were mates, weren't we?'

'You treated Herman despicably. Come here, go there, with a flick of your fingers. It didn't matter that it was in the school holidays or on a weekend, or even, three years ago, you will remember, on Christmas Day. Herman had to get up, leave us and go and do your bidding. And in twenty years of working with Herman you never took any interest in me or his family. You wouldn't even come for a drink.'

'I was gonna offer you one at lunch today, darling.'

'I asked you to come to our home. I asked you to dinners, to house parties, even just for a drink as you were always so fucking busy. I made an effort with you. But you? You ignored, refused, or cancelled every invitation I sent you.'

'That sounds pants. I'm sorry.'

'Yes. You nearly ruined my marriage with your demands on poor old Herman. Well, you did. You killed him.'

'What do you mean?' said Brother. 'It was an accident.'

'Not really. You rang and summoned him at short notice to a meeting in Zuog, and he was hurrying to your side, as per usual.'

'Marie, hold on. Hold on. You got a totally wrong idea about me.'

'I haven't.' Her eyes blazed fury. 'I'm the only one here who has a totally correct idea about you. You never even came to the funeral,' she said. 'Why didn't you come to Herman's funeral?'

Brother looked pained. He really had no idea what to say. Every direction was signposted calamity. He tried to make it better: 'I should of, it was wrong, I know. I'm really sorry.'

'Eugh,' she said, 'and I had been hoping it was because you were on one of your expeditions and hadn't heard about it. Why didn't you write me a letter of condolence?' Brother put his hand over his mouth. 'I'm sorry Marie. I should of done that too.'

'You never came to see me and the children. You are a pathetic excuse for a man. You self-centred, malicious, greedy, lying coward. And what for? For your fucking art collection. I hope you rot in hell with it.'

'I want you to know that I would never hurt you. Believe me, Marie. You've been through enough. I only want to help.'

'Please. Listen to yourself. You virtually ruined my life,' Marie sniffed. 'And then come up with some sanctimonious bullshit, like you spouted in the pub this afternoon.' She looked down at the carpet and tutted. 'It's a total mess,' she said.

Brother put his hand on her shoulder and immediately knew it was a wrong move.

'Don't,' she said, and pulled away. 'Herman told me how you beat your wife, you pig.'

'What?'

'No wonder she walked out.'

Marie turned to go, and stopped. 'I knew I shouldn't have come. I knew it. You're all shits, and you, you, you

227

are the worst. You nasty, sleazy, lying creep. It makes me sick to think of the power you wield. You ruined my life.'

He had, in his life, quite often been bollocked by women, sometimes fairly scarily, but they shouted words at him like *slow, thick, lazy, late, stoned,* and most commonly *useless,* but never *nasty* or *creep.* He had never been accused of being a lying shit. Or, worse, hitting a woman. It didn't sit well.

'I'm going back home and I'm staying there,' Marie said.

'No no no, don't do that, darlin'. Please don't say that. You're just getting back into the swing of life! I could see it at the pub.'

Then he registered the deep sadness sunk in Marie's brown eyes. She had picked up all the broken bits of her heart and painstakingly stuck them back together as best she could only to have it shattered again. And somehow Brother was in the frame for both disasters. He decided, right then and there, without reference to Kev, who he thought would counsel against it, to explain the truth to her, and he had to just hope it wouldn't jeopardize the 17 million quid.

'Marie. I have to tell you something. You've got me very wrong. Please give me a chance to tell you the truth. But I have to ask that you keep it a secret.' He glanced behind him to check Rachel was still in the bathroom. The bathroom door was shut.

'All right. Come on. Tell me.' Marie said, her arms crossed.

'It's a bit of a weird one, I'll be honest,' Brother said, scratching his head. 'It's that, well, as far as I can tell, there are two people called John Burn, the one you know, and me. And your one who did all that stuff to you has disappeared, and I'm getting the blame for all his shit. So I actually had nothing to do with not going to the funeral or being shit to you or an asshole to Herman. And I definitely have never raised a hand to a woman. That wasn't me. I didn't do any of that. That was the other one. He did all the bad stuff. The real me is the one you met in the pub.'

She narrowed her eyes. 'Have you got some kind of personality disorder?' she said stepping back.

'This is mental, aaaaargh,' said Brother. 'I promise you, Marie. I've never met Herman.'

'Oh for god's sake. Get yourself some help. Goodbye, John Burn. I hope I never see you again.'

She pulled herself up to her full height, raised her head, turned on her heels and walked away. Only when she had gone around the corner did she stop, and take out a handkerchief and wipe away her tears.

Brother rolled his shoulders and went back into the room.

He was surprised to see Rachel on the bed doing her nails with a towel on her head.

'Bravo!' she said, applauding. 'Bravo maestro! I like your style,' she laughed. 'I had nothing to do with all the stuff that pissed you off. It wasn't me! It was another John Burn. How did you think you'd get away with that?'

'Oh,' laughed Brother nervously, 'you heard?'

Rachel put her arm around him and let her towel slip.

'It doesn't matter. I don't mind that stuff. Honestly? I quite like it. So you behaved badly? Big deal. So you lied to get out of it. Who doesn't? Although your story was like never going to work,' she laughed and ruffled his hair. 'And what do funerals really mean?' she went on, 'Herman was hardly going to know you weren't there. Right? And why should you go and see that selfish bitch? It's not like you were her friend, right?'

'This is doing my head in,' Brother said.

'Hun, you are over thinking it.'

He said, 'I'm going to get a drink,' pulled on his jacket, walked downstairs and into the garden to smoke a spliff. With the joint glowing nicely and a couple of good lungfuls inhaled, he took his phone out of his pocket and dialled Kev.

'Whuppen?' said Kev.

'It's dicey,' said Brother, 'how's it going with this deal? Because I can't do this much longer.'

'What's the problem?'

'I've just had a strip torn off me by Herman's widow. For not going to the funeral.'

'How did you meet her?'

'She's at this house party thing Rachel made me come to in return for letting me split up with her, with the King of some Arabian country, called Al Deshani.'

'The actual King?'

'Yeah. And Sir Benjamin Minto's here.'

Kev said nothing.

'Yeah,' said Brother.

Kev said, 'You're not talking about art are you?'

'Not really.'

'Good'.

'Kev, just get me out of this.'

'Sophie and I are on the case. You keep it together. Don't fuck up. Just don't fuck up.'

Brother repocketed his phone and headed to a man in a white jacket standing beside a trolley of bottles whom he had earlier identified as being the kind of chap he'd probably get on with. Their conversation about mezcal was cut short by the arrival of Minto who appeared as though borne on a cushion of air, wearing a curious grin, and when asked what he wanted to drink stared at the bottles with lips pursed and finally said, 'Still water please, with a dash of sparkling.'

The barman proceeded to fill a glass with water, then unscrew a bottle of sparkling and pour it. 'Woah,' Minto said putting out a tiny hand. 'Just a touch.'

The barman derived pleasure from Brother's expression as he looked at Minto sipping the drink.

'Now, John,' said Sir Benjamin. 'I insist we have a discreet talk with each other.' He wanted to seed Brother's mind with ideas about art. 'Which artists are catching your famed eye at the moment? Any you can recommend?'

It was to Brother the absolute nightmare question, posed by the worst possible person. There was no describing a door knob to get him out of this corner. Minto was unbluffable. Brother swallowed and looked desperate. His mind was a desert stretching scores of miles in every direction, totally empty but for the odd irrelevant thought drifting across the middle distance. He now had to think of a name of a living artist. Despite being one of the world's greatest collectors he couldn't come up with a single one. *Zac. Zacman? Zamillo? Manzillo? Hammy Manzillo? Was that one?* Brother wasn't certain, and he couldn't take the chance of being wrong. He hummed as if in deep thought.

'So many in my head,' he said.

'Which was the last artist you bought?' asked Minto.

Oh god. That's a bastard too, thought Brother.

'I ask,' said Minto bending his head to one side and trying to look up into Brother's eyes, 'because at the Flint we are always looking for new, or overlooked talent, to bring through.'

'Okay, but why ask me? It's a job for an expert. A trained man. Like yourself.'

'But you are such an eminent collector.'

'But not trained. I buy for meself, and it's me own taste. I shouldn't be advising on what goes in the national collection. Not me.'

'We do find,' said Sir Benjamin, 'that often the patrons who endow our institution also have such wonderful ideas for artists to include in the national collection. I thought you might be able to make some suggestions.'

'Why's that?' said Brother.

Minto stared at Brother, thinking *it looks like I am going to have spell it out to this dunderhead.*

He then said, 'If you give me the name of an artist and were so generous as to make a donation to the gallery, I could make sure that your recommendation would be included in our list of acquisitions.'

Brother looked blank.

Minto asked himself how someone so thick could have made so much money. 'This would of course further that artist's career.'

Brother nodded benignly and Minto thought, *God, he still hasn't got it.*

Minto forged on: 'Because as you know, having a piece in the national collection does, shall we say, no harm to the value of an artist's work.'

Brother's mind was off on a little wander. It had found a door in the desert scene and was now walking through the long grasses of the yard, dawdling amongst the dragonflies and butterflies. He saw the path to his caravan, and a blissful smile filled his face. He had completely stopped listening to Minto, who as far as he could tell had been drivelling on about some art scam which to Brother had zero interest, until the door of his caravan opened and there he saw, in the bright morning sunlight, dangling from a nail on a cupboard, *Tor Kebab (2009)*.

'I do know a painter,' Brother said.

Minto stopped and inclined his head.

'And his picture was the last one I acquired.' Brother didn't want to say *bought* because he hadn't given Paul the forty quid for it yet. 'It hangs in pride of place in me living quarters. Where it is very much admired by all and sundry, especially sundry.'

'And who is this artist?' said Minto hungrily.

'Chap called Paul the Painter.'

This intelligence was devoured and processed. The artist was in the collection of John Burn but Minto had not heard of him. That made him very interesting.

'You won't know him,' said Brother. 'His full name is Paul Connell.'

'I don't think I've come across him, but I will make it my business to look at his work.'

Minto hurried off to an empty room, and set the wheels in motion. He had two assistants, whom he contacted and briefed. He asked for everything they could find on Paul 'the Painter' Connell to be emailed to him. Sir Benjamin's assistants were, by the terms of their employment contract, available to work 24 hours a day 7 days week. They were a pair of young men who could have passed for twins. Pale skinned, with black hair greased to their scalp, they wore black clothes and always carried Flint tote bags across their shoulders. They were part secretaries, part bodyguards, part sons, part god knows what else. It was a condition of their employment that they slept at Minto's South Kensington apartment, in fact on Z beds at the end of Sir Benjamin's super-king, in case he needed to dictate in the night. The job also included dressing and undressing him at morning and night, although there was no suggestion any sex took place. The assistants looked bloodless, and Minto's passions could only be aroused by art. He did the nearest thing to having sex with a painting: he purchased it for the national collection at the Flint Galleries whose size, variety, sophistication and value was the envy of every curator on the globe.

Dinner was a glamorous affair at which the guests glowed and the gold embroidery on the King's traditional cloak sparkled in the candlelight. Liveried butlers served course after course of the finest Middle Eastern food. Brother was enjoying some spiced lamb when the table fell gently into silence as the King tapped a gold knife on a crystal water glass.

'Now, if I may,' his eyes gleamed with kingly pleasure, 'I want to invite our esteemed guest, John Burn, to tell us about his time in the Amazon with the Wakapa tribe. I remember Herman telling me you were there to bring back a ton of a rare herbal medicine called, what was it? DMT?'

A ton of DMT? A TON! Brother's head almost exploded at the thought. DMT was actually Brother's Class A drug of choice, though it was almost impossible to get hold of. A teaspoonful cost about fifty quid, and then it was probably some chemical copy cooked up in a lab. But a ton of genuine organic DMT from the Amazon, where the finest quality originated, was an astonishing thought. A gram would effectively launch Brother into multiple alien universes for thirty-six hours. No wonder no one had heard anything from John Burn for years. The man was clearly off his tits burrowing through his DMT, lucky bastard.

The King was burbling on about how Herman had told him of John Burn's many Amazonian adventures. 'Regale us now with an anecdote, John. And that is a royal command!' Khaled laughed.

Luckily, Brother had earlier located his blim, and half way through dinner had had a chance to nip out and get a good deep pull on a well-lit fat one, so was ready to let rip as the other Burn.

'Yes, I was with the Wakapa, trading DMT, your Highness. They use it in their ceremonies. It's a wonder drug that can basically cure anything. We'd just packed a crop when we heard news that a neighbouring tribe, the Strongbow, were preparing an attack, possibly to steal the harvest. A shy and peaceable people, the Wakapa leader implored me to stay and help defend the village. By custom, the Wakapa women wear not a stitch of clothing. I used this knowledge to my advantage, and while I kept the men in the village, I sent the women secretly through the jungle to take up a position on a cliff above the settlement. The attack duly came, an hour before sundown. I drew the enemy towards our lines and then, at the given signal, the women on the cliff came out of hiding and jumped up and down bellowing their flippin' heads off. I was gambling on the Strongbow not being used to seeing 140 gorgeous naked women shakin' their booty and I was right, because as the Strongbow warriors turned and stared, so the Wakapa men, led by me and their chief, pounced and did our deadly work. I knew my plan had worked when they brought me two of the dead and both had erect penises. Those women were what you call crack troops.'

The King applauded and the queen smiled coyly. The thin American woman was scribbling in her notebook.

'How do you spell Wakapa?' the lady asked.

'There is no correct way, as Wakapa is not a written language,' Brother said. 'And you won't find anything about them on the internet or in books because, apart from me, no white person has ever penetrated their territory and society. Or at least none has returned to tell the tale.'

Rachel beamed at him adoringly.

Minto nodded, privately annoyed that the party of eminent people were talking about some nobodies in a distant country. Minto was, unfortunately, a bit of a racist on the quiet. He had absolutely no interest in humans with darker coloured skins except to use them to appear politically correct, a tiresome necessity in the securing of funding.

'After the battle we, of course, celebrated in the manner traditional to the Wakapa, which modesty forbids me from describing.'

'I think we can guess,' laughed the King.

'Well a lot of the men sloped off to sleep after the battle. So I was left virtually alone with 140 naked women. I begged them to break with custom and wear some clothing but they resolutely refused saying they could not dishonour me thus. Put it like this: it is not a night I shall soon forget.

'The next day I walked forty miles through the jungle to my chopper, which I had left in the protection of two gorillas I befriended,' he stopped and glanced at the woman with the notebook. 'That's gorilla the animal, with whom I could conduct basic conversation,' and then I flew out to Santa Jose and on to Lima where I boarded a commercial flight and, nine hours later, was in The Wolseley eating oysters, ready to purchase a few plum pieces of contemporary art in the morning.' He winked at Sir Benjamin, who flinched.

Things went a little hazy from then on, but Brother did remember enjoying himself fulsomely. He recalled telling the King all about Hawkwind, even the early albums, and slipping off an ottoman while singing Silver Machine using a poker as a bass guitar. It was possible that that was how the huge vase of flowers fell off the sideboard.

The following day, Brother opened his eyes and thought *get me out of here*. Rachel emerged from the bathroom with soaps, flannels and little bottles in her arms which she tipped onto the bed.

'Can you fit these in your bag?'

'Why?'

'Mine's full. They've all got the royal coat of arms.'

She spun round and soon reappeared carrying towels, bath mat and toothbrush mugs.

'I'm not taking anything,' Brother said.

'Just as a memento'.

'I don't want a memento. I want to forget this weekend.'

She was examining the door handle. 'You haven't got a screwdriver have you?' When he didn't answer, she went over to where he lay in bed and climbed on him, pinning him down with her sharp knees on his elbows. 'And we are soooo much in love'.

'Ow, stop it. We are not in love. Ow.'

'We are. You just won't admit it.'

'I'm not, and you aren't with me'.

'You're not with me because I'm not rich enough. That's it, isn't it? Ooh. That's nice,' she said snatching the coaster off the table. 'Looks like gold.'

As she reached to get it, Brother wriggled out of the bed and started dressing. He grabbed his hold-all and opened the door.

'Bye bye, Rachel. I got to be on me way. See you on the avenue.'

'Which avenue?'

'It's just a saying. Like, see you around.'

'Okay. Where? When? Let me get my diary. Hold on.'

'Bye Rachel,' he said to her bottom as she burrowed in her handbag. It was the bottom he had admired so much, now swathed in the fluffy whiteness of the King's bath robe which was soon to be folded up and stuffed into her suitcase.

Outside the house, the cars were being loaded by the staff, and guests were bidding goodbye to their hosts. Brother hitched his holdall on his shoulder.

'Goodbye, your Highnesses,' he said, 'you wonderful pair of generous and kind monarchs! I'm gonna love you and leave you. It's been a very special spread. Thanks very much.'

'You're not walking again are you?' asked Erena.

'I am.'

'Where are you going?' asked Minto.

'Somerset. A hundred mile, near enough.'

'How long will that take you?' asked the king.

'Five days should do it.'

'Walking?' the King winced.

'A little wander.'

'Which way do you go?' asked Minto, his tongue protruding slightly between his lips.

'Well, I'll be in Abingdon tonight, then down into Hampshire on Tuesday and by Wednesday I'll be at the Burn Inn, a hostelry named after a relative of mine, in Wiltshire, by the River Test. Very pretty spot. I'll overnight there, then make Stonehenge on Thursday, and take a drovers' track over the Plain and into Somerset. All being well I will be back in me little bed on Friday evening.'

31

'Paul the Painter,' said Sophie.

Kev looked at her. He wanted to kiss that kittenish face and stroke his hands all over her catlike body, but she only purred for the super-rich, and then only if they looked like buying art.

'How do you know about Paul the Painter?' he asked.

'Two people mentioned his name yesterday. One from the Flint and another at an opening. Apparently he has work in the John Burn Collection. But I don't remember it.'

'You'll like this,' said Kev, pointing at his screen. Sophie came up behind him, and for her own amusement stood at a distance accurately calculated to madden Kev as he tried to work out if she was flirting with him. She wasn't.

'Exam results,' Kev said. 'I've got the university and college degrees from the last fifteen years. I'm pulling out the names of any men who got a third class degree or failed their degree, and am cross-referencing it with your rich list.'

'Students from high-net-worth families with poor degrees,' said Sophie.

'I'm trying to find you some clients,' said Kev.

Sophie's phone started ringing.

'Hold on, it's Julia,' Sophie said.

Julia was the person handling the other end of the John Burn Collection sale. Kev focused on the delicious pout of Sophie's bottom lip to keep the anxiety at bay.

Sophie put down the phone. 'She says he's not at this stage ready to commit the funds because of the instability of the markets. Fucking liar. They're markets. They're always unstable. She's got him to buy that goddam Joachim Muller triptych that's coming up. I fucking know she has, and I bet she's on twenty per cent.'

'Can't we offer her more?'

'No. The deal's off. Julia's screwed it. She wants to build the collection herself.'

'Is there anyone else?'

'Of course there is, and we'll find them, but each time it comes back on the market it's a little more shop-soiled. We might have to be more flexible on the price. And be patient.'

'How long do you think it could take?'

'No more than a year.'

That could present a problem, Kevin thought. *I might have to get Brother out the country.*

'Paul the Painter? Is that his full name?' she asked, looking through the John Burn Collection file.

'That's what everyone calls him.'

'How come he's not in here? Does John actually own any?'

'Sure. He has one in his main residence. I've seen it.'

'Is he British?'

'Paul? He works in Glastonbury. He paints pubs and cafes and shops in the High Street.'

'I was thinking maybe we should put on a show of this guy, since he's so hot. It might get a bit of a buzz going about the collection, and if we can pick a few pieces up, make some sales. You said he's painting the High Street?' Sophie strained her face.

Kevin softened her expression with some buzzwords. 'I'd say it's more a scientific documentation. There are architectural and anthropological subtexts.'

'Remember that for the press release. I'm beginning to like the sound of this guy. Would John give us a quote?'

'Sure, of course he would. Leave that to me.'

'But John Burn doesn't do interviews, right?'

'He will for me.'

Sophie's eyes sparkled. 'That'll be worth thousands.'

'Paul the Painter's work is honestly the art he talks about the most.'

'Out of all of them?'

'Yes. Hold on, I've got a photo of it.'

Kev played with his phone and handed it to Sophie. She stared at *Tor Kebab (2009 oil on canvas)*. Her mind whirred into action, assembling a matrix which included the following axes: who was showing her the work, who made the work, in whose collection the artist had work, and, finally, what the thing looked like.

'How much do they go for?' she asked.

'I can get them cheap,' said Kev, thinking eighty quid, but not saying it.

'What?' said Sophie. 'Like ten grand?'

'Possibly. If I'm tough.'

Sophie smiled. 'Do you own any?' she said.

'I've got *The Backpackers* at home,' he said.

'Good investment,' said Sophie.

'And he doesn't have a gallery in the UK?'

'Definitely not.'

'Great. Get this Paul the Painter to send us some images. I want to see if we can make this work.'

'Hey, look who I've turned up for you.'

Sophie looked at the screen, on which was a photo of a fat, red-haired youth with tiny eyes holding a fish by the tail.

'Cuthbert Stonehouse. Heir to a three billion pound mining fortune. Failed a degree in Geography and Farming Studies at Cirencester Agricultural College. Twice. I don't think you get any thicker than that.' He looked up. She had the smitten kitten look.

'That man is badly in need of an art advisor,' she purred.

32

Paul was sleeping off a drinking bout on his caravan couch, fully dressed in coat and boots, his red face and thick lips in fitful repose under a cloud of dirty grey hair. The phone was rattling on the Formica counter. With a heave and a cough he reached and answered it.

'Hi bud, it's Kev.'

'What's wrong?' Paul said.

'Nothing. I'm in London. Working in the art world.'

'What?' croaked Paul. He swung his boots onto the laminate floor. One was split. 'I'm sorry, I can't hear you very well. Hold on.' He held the phone out and embarked on a sequence of coughs starting with ones that seemed from their rumble to come from beneath the caravan, rising to some painful barks and ending in a kind of squeal of slow agony. 'Sorry. What did you say?'

'I work for an art advisor called Sophie Hanley-Smart. She's quite well known in the art world. We are interested in putting on a show of your paintings.'

'It won't work,' Paul said. 'You put them up, nobody even fucking looks. You just lose money paying the framers. Where were you thinking?'

'London.'

A short silence was broken by a wheezy laugh. 'Kevin, no, no, no,' Paul took a breath, 'It won't work. No one's interested. I'm not a name any more, if I ever was.'

'Well that's where you could be wrong,' said Kev. 'You're in the collection of John Burn. It's a stamp of approval from a blue chip collector. And I have a plan, or rather Sophie does. And she's clever. But first she has to see your work. Have you got pictures of it?'

'As a matter of fact I do. A woman came round last year and photographed them for a gallery in Bath. Never heard from her again. I think the place went bust shortly after.'

'Send them to me'.

Paul finished the call, felt for his spectacles on the couch and then stared intently at his phone. 'What do we do here?' he said to himself, touching the screen. 'Gallery. Yes.'

Paul scrolled through his private gallery, spinning past photographs of the yard in the changing seasons. Ice on the lake, a twisting cloud of starlings, a dewy dawn, spiders' webs, the Tor under thunderclouds, rushes thrashed by the wind. Then, his paintings. About two dozen of them. He pinged them to Kev.

He looked through the dirty window at Geoff's mildewed caravan and said, 'No no no, we don't get our hopes up Paul. No. We do not. But, but, surely a positive attitude might help? Oh. It might.' He heaved himself onto his feet and stood for a moment, blinking while his vision returned. 'Circling crows,' he said, lifting the kettle to feel its weight and placing it on the hob. He lit the flame and said, 'Please be a kind god. Let something good happen.'

Something good had not happened to Paul the Painter for quite some time. The last time something good happened often was in the 1970s when he lived in Chelsea, or rather Fulham, and had made a respectable living from painting. He had a one-man show in a street next to Cork Street, admittedly in a basement, but it had garnered a favourable review in *Prospect* magazine. But rising rents and a contraction of the economy had made things increasingly difficult, though they were nothing compared to the hammer blow which was to follow: conceptual art. It blew away old-school figurative painters, sending their easels and berets twisting into the hurricane. Some tried to bend with the wind and adapt their style to the brash simplicity of Britart, but they were still not admitted. It was total annihilation. Nobody was interested in a well composed oil painting in the old style. Paul had moved into a damp cottage in Wiltshire and tried to hold it together for a decade, sliding into drunkenness and despair. Brother had offered him a caravan on his site for free.

'You're brilliantly talented, man! They don't know nothing. You can be the yard's resident artist. Who better? This is such good news for us all, to have a man of your pure talent amongst us. Utterly inspirational.'

For two days after Kev's call Paul glanced at the phone when he passed it to see if there was a message or missed call. 'That's why we don't do silly things like get our hopes up, isn't it?' he said out loud. 'That is exactly why. Precisely, in fact. Because nothing is going to happen. Except bad things. Oh yes. The gas will run out. And I'll get a puncture. Nothing nice. Good, happy-making. That's what we mean isn't it?'

The phone went. Paul dabbed at it and brought it to his ear.

'She likes them,' Kev said.

'She does? She does? What did she say?'

'She said she liked what she saw and apparently there's a bit of a buzz around you at the moment'.

'What?'

'I know, I thought that must be the flies.'

'Kev, that is not kind'.

'I'm joking, Paul. She said that someone from the Flint Gallery in London had been asking about you, saying you were one to watch.'

There was a gap.

'Did she? Really?'

'I promise she said that. And we want to do a show. And we want to buy three pieces, and put another couple on reserve.'

'Kevin, it's very kind of you, but does this woman really know what you are up against? It's very difficult, work like mine. My salesroom prices were once fairly respectable. But I think would struggle now. In 1983 I sold a painting for 2,500 pounds. Which was a considerable sum in those days.'

'She wants to buy *36 High Street*, *Heritage Fine Foods*, and *Crystals*. She's offering 18 thousand for all three.'

Paul sat slowly down.

'Thank you Kevin, thank you.'

'Give me your bank account and I'll transfer ten grand, the balance to follow. And I want you to come to London as soon as it suits you, and meet Sophie and talk about how we are going to do this.'

He clicked off the phone and stared through his open door out across the lake. For the first time in years, decades, his body felt light, and his mind bright. There was a delightful tingling in his tummy, usually the source of only unpleasant sensations, and, he realised, tears of gratitude and joy springing from his eyes. 'Eighteen grand,' he whispered out loud, 'Well well well. But it could go wrong. We have been here before and been disappointed. Oh yes. Of course it could. You have not seen the cash yet. Do not get your hopes up. It will only hurt more later.'

Geoff looked over from where he was tinkering on the fuel project. 'You all right, old boy?' he said.

'I'm not sure,' said Paul the Painter, 'I think so. That could be the call I've been waiting thirty years for.' He fixed his eyes on Geoff. 'I always thought, if I just kept at it and didn't give up, if I just somehow keep working, someone, somewhere, would notice my work. That was my dream.'

Geoff nodded hard. 'We all believed in you, Paul. Even when things were, you know, when you struggled. We all believed. On the yard. Brother always said you were an undiscovered genius.'

'Thank you, Geoff. If I may say, we all, to a man, believe in you,' said Paul, trying not to think of the time Kev had commented, after seeing Geoff struggling with a monkey wrench, *that's a spanner with a nut at both ends.*

'What I think,' said Geoff, 'is that in a hundred years' time, Brother's Yard will be written in legend. People will say it was like the Italian Renaissance. They will pilgrimage to this hallowed place, the way they do to Florence. This community where writers, painters and engineers all helped each other to produce ground-breaking work. All of us gathered here under the patronage of our own Lorenzo de' Medici: Brother.'

33

The Lorenzo de' Medici *de nos jours,* aka Brother, was literally and figuratively humming with happiness as he marched with a bounce in his step down the grassy footpath. After three days of walking, every anxious thought had been set free to fly away, leaving just the happy prospect of 17 million sponduliks alighting on his bank account any time soon. That would clear the £7.92 overdraft that had frozen all banking activities for three years. He felt calm, content and pleasantly exhausted as the thatched pub in Chipley came into view. He shifted his hold-all one last time on his shoulder and thought about soaking in the bath with a spliff before going down to the bar for a pint of cloudy cider and steak pie.

His eye was caught by two men with service haircuts, sitting in a black estate car in the car park. As he made for the pub, or more accurately the beer fonts, the pair got out and wandered casually over.

'Excuse me, Sir. Sorry to bother you,' said the older of the two, a tall fit man with greying hair and cold eyes that Brother didn't like. 'Are you John Burn?' he asked.

'Stone me that's a coincidence!' Brother said. 'These lay lines man! They are strong. A lot of energy. I have just seen and spoken to John Burn about four miles up that path. Just passed the fellow. He said he was making for Southampton. If you run, you may catch him, though he walks at a fair clip.'

'You're a slippery customer, aren't you?' said the man.

The other one, shorter, with a broken nose, had walked behind Brother and now grabbed Brother's arm. 'You're under arrest.'

'I do not consent!' Brother stepped back and flung his arms in the air. 'Resist! I assert my rights under the Magna Carta. I am a free man of this land,' he flashed a triumphant smile. 'You shall not arrest or otherwise interfere with my quiet enjoyment of life, nor impede me on a highway without a king's warrant.'

'Well I'm a Detective Inspector at the Met, and you, mate, are nicked,' said the big one, as he rushed Brother. In a matter of seconds, Brother was standing with his wrists cable-tied behind his back.

'Shall we read him his rights?' the wiry one said.

'No. Let's not,' said the other. To Brother he snarled, 'Get in the car.'

'It's okay. I'm good right here.'

He was bundled onto the back seat. The smaller man jumped in, started the car and drove out of Chipley on the curving lane Brother knew so well and, at the junction with the A303, turned right to London.

'Hold on, cabby,' said Brother, 'I haven't told you where I'm going.'

'Shut it,' said the grey-haired man.

'What am I being arrested for?' Brother said.

'Don't you worry about that. We'll get to that. First, allow me to do this.'

He took a well-used roll of gaffer tape out of the glove box, tore off a strip and stuck it across Brother's mouth.

'We are taking you for a talk with a very prestigious man,' he said, giving Brother's cheek a little slap. 'He wants to ask you a few questions.'

He then shoved a warrant card in Brother's face. *Detective Inspector Doug Boyle. Metropolitan Police.*

The Met, thought Brother. But if it was about impersonating the other John Burn, they couldn't lay a hand on him. He was John Sparkler Burn, he had never said anything different. He had not lied to anyone. He was in the clear. Up until the moment he took money for the collection it could all be explained away as a misunderstanding. And even then, he had the receipts. The CPS couldn't make a case of that.

A few miles later, on the treeless landscape of Salisbury Plane it occurred to Brother that his arrest might be about the Battle of the Beanfield. Right here, near Stonehenge, back in 1985 he had assaulted two police officers with a tin of Tenants Special in a Budgens bag. He'd given a better account of himself on that day. The pigs had been smashing the windows of women and children's vehicles. That had got Brother's blood up. He thought about the many times he had boasted about lamping those coppers over the years. Maybe his proud words and possibly rather inadvisable exaggeration had caught up with him. Coppers didn't let grudges go.

Or was this about some planning injunction at the yard? He never did what he was told by the council or the courts. But even that bastard Councillor Pratt at Mendip couldn't get the Met involved. Then Brother worked something out. With the forensic mind of the aggrieved hippy – rained under extreme conditions, like the SAS with a hundred and twenty pound rucksacks on the Brecon

Beacons, solving life's mysteries through the fug of two ounces of dope a week, plus acid and sometimes speed, not to mention cider. He had a mind that saw every facet. Eventually. Who knew he was going to be at the Burn Inn that afternoon? He hadn't told anyone at the yard he was on his way. Ahh. The King and Queen. He had told them his route. Arab money, power and corruption, at work. The very prestigious man could surely only be King Khaled.

Was it the remark about his crack troops? His manner had lacked formality and protocol, Brother would admit. The Arab eyes were blind to his charm. For this he was headed to the helicopter and a short hooded flight over the marshes.

They drove into London and glided down the quiet Embankment beside the glistening river. A few turns found them descending a wide ramp into the deep basement of a huge floodlit building. Was this the embassy? God knows what went on in there.

The car drew up inside a brightly lit, high-ceilinged loading bay which looked like a shipping warehouse. Was he to be crated up and sent back to the desert for a YouTube beheading? Brother was pulled out of the car and walked between packing cases and forklift trucks to a portacabin office with a sign on the door saying PRIVATE MEETING. NO ADMISSION. Inside the windowless room was a white table, three chairs, four large paintings and one of Joachim Muller's signature gold radiators on the far wall. Brother was made to sit down while his wrists were cable-tied to the back of the chair.

The short man left the room. D.I. Boyle stared hard at Brother, and ripped the tape off his mouth.

'Get me a cold beer, would you?' Brother said.

'Mister hilarious, eh?'

The door opened and in walked the tiny figure of Sir Benjamin Minto, flanked by his two personal assistants, a preening praetorian guard.

'Eh?' said Brother. 'What's going on here?'

'That is precisely what you are going to tell me,' smiled Sir Benjamin, taking off a little pair of leather gloves. 'Let's start with something simple: who are you?'

Brother sensed real trouble close at hand, even if it wasn't having his digits whizzed off with a grinder. He decided that to remain the Other Burn would give him his best chance of getting the money.

'You know perfectly well who I am, Sir Benjamin. And I have no idea what this unwarranted intrusion into me privacy is about, but I am prepared to overlook it if you let me go this instant, and I will not press charges.'

'You are a fraud,' said Sir Benjamin. D.I. Boyle nodded and smiled. For some reason Brother particularly disliked that.

A couple of years ago, the D.I. had done some freelance work for a Kazak warlord called Akan Pumclap. Mr. Pumclap had gassed a medium-sized village because its inhabitants had demonstrated against his oil refinery. He hired D.I. Boyle as his close protection officer. It turned out that as well as collecting enemies, Mr Pumclap collected art. In the long hours in hotel rooms, cars and on the airplane, Mr Pumclap talked about his passion and showed a nonplussed D.I. Boyle pictures of his collection. While staring at some de Koonings in a Christie's sale catalogue, Mr Pumclap said something very wise to D.I. Boyle, that he had never forgotten: 'Art is the new oil.'

The D.I. requested a secondment to the Art Crime Unit at Scotland Yard, where he had worked his way up and come to the attention of Sir Benjamin, when handling a couple of minor cases for the National Gallery. Sir Benjamin had asked D.I. Boyle to do him the favour of picking up John Burn and bringing him in for interrogation, all under the radar.

'You didn't purchase that collection of art you purport to own,' Sir Benjamin said. 'Did you?'

'I did. I've got all the receipts at my lawyer's.'

'You may have the receipts, but you did not buy those works.'

'I'm a high-net-worth individual. I'm an art lover. I invested funds in art. Call my lawyer – David Ashton.'

'Art lover, are you?

Sir Benjamin took a piece of paper out of his slim leather briefcase and placed it on the table. 'Who did that?'

It was a photograph of a bit of art.

'I don't know,' said Brother. 'I've forgotten.'

'He's lying, Sir Benjamin,' the D.I. said. 'I can sense it. D'you want me to beat the truth out of him?'

'Detective Inspector Boyle,' Minto said impatiently, 'please.'

'Shall I give him a couple of softeners?'

'No. In fact you can leave us now. Thank you. I'll call if I need you.'

The D.I. grudgingly left the room.

'Now,' said Sir Benjamin. 'Where were we? Ah yes. This picture,' he pointed at the image. 'Who is the artist?'

'I am afraid it's slipped me mind.'

'Have you seen it before?'

'I can't remember.'

'You have a bad memory, Mr. Burn. You own it.'

'What about this one?' Sir Benjamin laid another on the table.

Minto was enjoying himself. It was always refreshing exposing a forgery. Sir Benjamin had thought for some time that something about John Burn was not quite right. Even in the years of his seclusion. The stories that circulated never matched the works he was buying. His life was lived in comic book technicolour, but he bought pictures of muted sophistication. When Sir Benjamin had finally met John Burn, at Rachel Baker's opening, he had seen him pretend not to know Callum's name. At the time it seemed odd, but now he realised that the man had not been playing a game: he hadn't actually known who Callum was. In fact he didn't know anything. He hadn't recognised the Ryan Young at the King's house. The penultimate straw was when Minto heard John Burn was marrying Rachel Baker. Only a complete idiot would do that. And on that straw was then thrown the outrage that was Paul the Painter. Minto had physically recoiled from images of the man's work. If this was the kind of thing that John Burn was going to try and spread around the place it would undo all Minto's work. He had to be stopped.

'Come on,' said one of the assistants. 'You've been asked a question.'

Brother looked at the image. It was a bit familiar. He felt ashamed not to know it.

'We were surprised, when we asked our friends at the Inland Revenue, to discover you don't pay tax,' said Sir Benjamin.

'Taxes are for little people,' declared Brother. 'I've got everything offshore. I got my own frigging island for gems and gold bullion.'

'You see, we have had a firm of forensic accountants check you out,' said Sir Benjamin. 'You are not a tax exile. You are officially classed by the Department of Work and Pensions as economically inactive. You once claimed housing benefit.'

'That was a tax avoidance scheme I entered into and now regret. I was led into it unwittingly on the advice of financial advisors since fired. I admit it, I was exploiting a loophole.'

'So how did you pay for your pictures?' asked Sir Benjamin. 'Pray tell.'

'None of your business,' said Brother. 'I am a legit art collector and I don't talk to narks. Let me go.'

'Look at this,' Minto pointed back to the portrait, which was of a woman. 'Who is it?' he asked. His two assistants sniggered.

'I don't know.'

'She's known as *The Girl with a Pearl Earring.*'

'Oh yeah. That's it. I knew that.'

'Who painted it?' Sir Benjamin asked quietly.

In as menacing a voice as he could muster, which was not very menacing since that was never a natural register for Brother, he growled, 'You mess with me, you'll regret it. In a couple more minutes everyone present in this room will go on a kill list, whatever happens to me.'

'But who is possibly going to kill us?' asked Minto as though talking to a child.

'The Wakapa. My blood tribe. You'll end up with a poison dart in your neck. They like pygmy,' Brother said, staring at Minto. 'Particularly in a winter stew.'

'You seem to think this is a game,' said Minto. 'You are guilty of – at the very least – tax evasion, money laundering and fraud. Stop playing. The music has stopped. You are trapped and there is no escape.'

Minto gave a signal to one of his assistants, who placed a stapled document on the table.

'This a confession?' Brother asked.

'No,' said Sir Benjamin. 'This is a transfer document to place the John Burn art collection in my possession. For my safe-keeping. And this is a letter to your lawyer authorizing its removal from your storage facility to mine. Please sign here and here.'

It was when being shaved by an assistant that morning, while his other assistant clipped his toenails, that the idea to steal the John Burn Collection had come to Sir Benjamin. He was no longer prepared only to be the architect of the country's art collection. He wanted one of his own. But on his salary, Minto could only afford a handful of minor pieces and a few novelty items given by major artists, which actually looked like insults. In retirement he was going to have to stare at them, while at the same time pining for the peerless collection he had provided the nation with. This was his last chance to get his hands on some of the good stuff so as to stand shoulder to shoulder, artistically, never literally, with the rich folk.

Brother looked at the two documents. The trouble was, Sir Benjamin was right, he was cornered. Of course he couldn't explain how he paid for the works of art. It could only end in jail. The game was up.

But, at the same time, an elegant new plan was materialising in Brother's mind. If successful, it would result in vengeance against Minto, freedom from prosecution, and a year's supply of top quality hallucinogenic. He would sign over the pictures and then track down the other John Burn and tell him his art was being stolen by Minto. And leave that madman to deal with Minto. A smile played on Brother's face as he thought about that. In return for which information he would ask the other John Burn for a reward of some of his DMT, if there was any left.

Brother put out his hand and took the pen.

'Can I ask one question?'

'What?'

'How many grams in a ton?'

Minto looked irritated.

One of his assistants said, 'A million.'

Brother whispered 'Kiss me neck...' leant forward over the table and signed the documents.

Sir Benjamin inspected the signatures, folded the documents and slipped them into the inside pocket of his tailor-made coat.

'I will now bid you goodbye,' Minto said. 'I hope we never meet again.'

Minto left the room. Brother stood up. 'Much as I love it here,' he said to the two assistants, who were standing sentry by the door, 'I'm gonna love you and leave you.'

When Brother went to the door they tried to bar his way. But Brother had done the math, and no one, particularly not two pipsqueaks from the art world, were going to get between him and 750,000 grams of DMT. He pushed them aside, opened the door, and saw a large fist coming straight at his face with D.I. Boyle not far behind it. Brother staggered back into the room clutching his eye.

'You're going nowhere,' D.I. Boyle growled.

'I've frigging signed, man. I'm free to go.'

'You will be free to go when Sir Benjamin has the pictures in his possession with all the i's dotted and t's crossed. And not before.'

'This is bollocks. You can't hold me. It's false imprisonment.'

'I can't hold you? I can't hold you? Stroll on! I can do what I fucking like. I can have you on a private jet to Iraq by six o'clock. Special rendition. Courtesy of one of Sir Benjamin's benefactors. We are talking top fucking collectors. Normal rules don't apply. So shut it.'

The D.I. took a set of cable ties out of his back pocket and dragged Brother's chair to the radiator. The D.I. approved of its finish: gold. Only the best for Sir B and his top fucking flight collectors. Boyle secured Brother to the half-million-pound artwork, grabbed a handful of his cheek, then patted it and said, 'I don't want to hear a peep out of you. I'm very near by.'

34

Paul the Painter, bathed, shaved and attired in a smart olive-green corduroy suit and wide-brimmed fedora, stood outside the Fulham Road Artistic Club, allowing memories to stir in his elated mind. It was good to be here again. Though he was nervous. He crossed the road and headed for the gothic door in the long two storey Victorian building. For over a hundred years this had been a lively hub for artists, but had recently fallen into disrepair, and was now a sort of day centre for aged painters who were no longer needed in the bright and brilliant era of Sir Benjamin Minto.

The woman on the intercom appeared to be expecting him.

'Hello! Do come in!' she piped, and Paul heard her say, before she put the receiver down, 'he's here!'

Paul had an unpaid bar bill from the seventies which he hoped they weren't going to remember. It was one of the reasons he had avoided the place, and then his membership had lapsed in about 1983. He entered the echoey bar and saw the scrofulous snooker table under which he had occasionally slept in the glory days, now bathed in the gloom of a splattered skylight.

Gerald de Gruchy, chairman of the club, a tall man in a painter's smock with a beard like a spade, held out his arms. Gerald was the portraitist who had immortalised Lord Mountbatten in oils and now drew people's cats for a hundred pounds a pop.

'Paul! Welcome!' he boomed in his theatrical bass, 'After so many years! What a joy to see you, old, old friend. And congratulations. We have heard the great news, and rejoiced.'

Paul smiled bashfully.

'An exhibition in the West End, six pieces already sold. Is it true?'

'Ten pieces now, I can hardly believe it,' said Paul.

'I read your prices range from forty-five to a hundred thousand pounds,' a woman with an eye patch called Monica said from the bar.

They had read Kevin's press release, which Paul had forwarded to the club magazine. He hoped they wouldn't think him boastful. He just wanted to share his good news.

Gerald embraced Paul, thumping huge hands on his back. Over Gerald's shoulder, Paul watched the decrepit club members teeter off their bar stools and clutch the arms of their chairs with a groan to stand up and greet him.

These were the artists whose work had been popular before the 90s. In those far off happy days, life for Gerald de Gruchy consisted of a few hours' painting in the morning, preferably of a naked lady whom he could have a stab at seducing, a long and cheap lunch at the Artistic Club, a siesta on the day-bed in his studio and then, was it six o'clock already? That called for a large G&T before he wandered back through the quiet, slightly run-down streets of Chelsea back to the Club.

Without warning, it became all about youth and, aged forty-eight in 1993, Gerald discovered he was considered washed up. Without a gallery to show in, Gerald had had to tout his art around himself, and cut costs. He downsized his studio, and bravely moved into a bedsit, hanging onto his old Tite Steet address from which the diminishing number of invitations to private views were forwarded.

On the rare occasion Gerald had set foot in a studio of one of these new artists, he had found the atmosphere to be disagreeably industrious and efficient. Some studios were even said to be alchohol free, a condition that every member of the Fulham Road Artistic Club considered hostile to artistic activity. Assistants worked in teams, computers hummed on long white desks, the spaces were spotlessly clean and the artist himself rarely present. Gerald De Gruchy's studio had been somewhat different. It was his personal lair and sanctuary. Nobody set foot there in his absence. It had a day-bed, chaise longue, a red curtain on a brass rail for women to disrobe behind, a large easel, a trolley of paints, a good lock on the door and a disconnectable doorbell to ensure uninterrupted hours of either work, rest or preferably play. It was not a factory; it was a place of reflection, creation and small acts of seduction.

Now his days were spent like many others of his ilk, with other fruity-voiced, broken-veined old artists at the club, moaning about what had happened to the art world. Many had fallen behind. Paul was one of those taken by bankruptcy and the bottle. These men and women, now in their seventies and eighties, had sat out the years of the new art as though in a siege – getting poorer, making do, cutting back, praying, and hoping, above all, for relief – and here, on this glorious July morning, like the cavalry at Mafeking, it had at last arrived, in the unlikely form of Paul the Painter.

'So you've really made it,' said Dorothy, a vodka-sodden miniaturist who hadn't seen Paul for twenty-seven years.

'Barman!' called Paul with tears of happiness in his eyes, 'a drink for everyone, please.'

They hadn't heard those words in a few years and responded accordingly, rushing the bar to get their order in before anything went wrong. Paul looked around at the wonderful grimy interior of the club.

'I've missed this room so much,' he said. 'I have thought of all of you often.'

'We've lost a lot of good members in the Flint Art terror,' said Dorothy.

Gerald sipped deeply on a large cloudy glass of red and said to Paul, 'Do you think this Sophie might be interested in my work? I don't actually have a gallery at the moment.'

'None of us do,' said Dorothy.

'I'd love to show Sophie your work, it would be an honour to introduce you. She's a wonderful woman. So positive. You will meet her at my opening.'

'Could I tag along too?' asked Magiver, the famous maritime painter, now reduced to painting pub signs for a Chingford micro-brewery.

'You must all come,' said Paul. 'I will be happy to introduce you all…'

'Is it true you know John Burn?' Monica asked. 'I read about him in the article. He sounds very interesting. A lover of art.'

'He's an old friend, and a fine man,' said Paul, feeling safe with this recommendation.

'Do you think …' two members said at the same time. 'Sorry,' said one. 'I was just going to say, do you think he might be there at your opening?'

'Yes,' said Magiver. 'If he likes your work he might be interested in some of ours.'

'He will be at my opening, I'm sure. And I will introduce him to you. I think he would love it in here.' It was an observation Paul could make with total confidence.

'We must offer him free life membership,' said Gerald, to murmurs of assent.

Taking another couple of bottles with them they all moved out through the French doors into the magnificent club garden. This serene setting for long summer afternoon naps, late night drunken fumblings, and retches into the bushes, was currently under threat. Joachim Muller had recently bought half the street behind the club and, finding it convenient, wanted to buy the club's garden to erect a fabrication studio. He had offered a brutal amount of money for their shady sanctuary, so large it would surgically remove the club overdraft, a financial tumour that had been growing for more than fifty years.

'It must not be allowed to happen,' Dorothy said. 'This is our home.'

'There might be no way around it, I am afraid,' said Gerald. 'Our debts are unmanageable. We simply don't have the income anymore.'

'We must start a fighting fund,' said Dorothy, into dead air, until Paul said, 'Good idea. I will donate a thousand pounds.'

There was a pause while this sank in.

Gerald, standing in sunlight dappled by branches of a sycamore said, 'My dear friend, that really is such a magnanimous, noble and generous gesture.'

Dorothy started crying, looking down and shaking her head from side to side.

The chairman drew breath. 'This club has gone through some dark years recently. Years in which a certain kind of art – our kind of art – has been held in derision. Years in which men and women of good intention and fair talent have been denied any public support from the tyrants who run art in this country.' He drew another lungful of air, and his voice quavered. 'We have suffered years of exclusion from the Flint, from the major art prizes, from TV programmes, from shows in national galleries … But I believe,' continued Gerard, 'that we are turning a corner. Paul here, our old friend, our dear colleague, our brother in arms, our fellow painter, is proof of the fact.'

The septuagenarians, in their cords and velvets and with slightly stroked faces, glasses of house red in their trembling hands, wine-stained lips carefully held tight to conceal missing teeth, all nodded hopefully.

'We must be ready to mount exhibitions again,' Gerard said. 'And not ones with names like *Urban: Navigating Transality*, with their infuriating incorrect use of the colon,' he smiled, 'but shows with our, the artist's, name alone, a set of dates, and if absolutely necessary, the caption *New Work*. To your easels! Pick up your brushes, palate knives and pencils!'

A man in a beret with a florid face and curving fag ash smiled to himself at the thought of again selling work to a stranger. 'May I ask a question?' he said.

'Of course,' said Paul the Painter.

'What advice would you give to the senior artist?'

The emotion tightened Paul's throat. The sheer excitement of the last few days when laid against the many preceding years of toil and disappointment all made this present triumph almost unbearably joyful, especially as he was sharing it with such kind old friends, all of whom had faced the struggle.

'Ne…' he swallowed, and tried again, a little hoarsely: 'Never give up. Never give up. Always believe.'

He nodded and beamed at all his old colleagues. 'Always believe. In yourself, and very importantly, in each other. That's what I've learnt.'

'Well said, beautifully said,' said Monica.

'Shall we have another two bottles?' Paul said.

35

The same sunlight that dappled the Artistic Club's garden shone too on Sir Benjamin Minto. After a morning at home, he had decided, for a change, to walk to work. South Kensington, with its creamy mansions, tree-lined streets and absence of anyone poor, looked spectacular in the sun. He had sent his personal assistants ahead on errands: one to buy a pair of shoelaces of the precise calibre that Minto decreed, and the other to purchase a new spectacle cleaning cloth, as the duster they had presented to him after they had bathed and dressed him was an unacceptably pale shade of grey.

That setback aside, Sir Benjamin had enjoyed a fine morning. A low vibration of satisfaction, originating from the signed Transfer Document of the John Burn Collection tucked in Sir Benjamin's coat pocket, spread through his body. From time to time, for an extra burst of pleasure, he tapped his breast to feel the envelope. He had looked at the inventory, and even drawn a rough plan for the hang in his apartment. A thought crossed his mind about whether one of the Callum Smiths would fit over the chimney piece in his bedroom. He stopped to scroll through his phone on which he had both the dimensions of the work and the precise height of the space. It was an emergency, so he halted on the pavement by a pub, where drinkers had left some empty glasses on a table. A wasp that had had a skinful of best bitter flew off the glass intending to go down Chilbrook Street but swerved out of control and crashed into the back of Sir Benjamin's neck. Angry to have made such a fool of himself, he gave Minto's pale soft skin a hefty sting, and buggered off down the Fulham Road looking for a fruit stall.

Minto yelped and put his little hand on his soapy neck where it touched the sting. He staggered down leafy Chilbrook Street, but found his vision blurring, his mouth drying and his heart fluttering alarmingly in his chest. Then panic started.

The Wakapa. Had he heard the whisper of a blowpipe? He may have. He stopped and got on his phone. He had to call D.I. Boyle to beat the antidote out of John Burn. Fortunately for our hero, that call never got through, because Sir Benjamin's legs started to tremble, so he steadied himself on a long dirty white wall, limping to a small wooden door beside which was an intercom that he leant against until the door clicked open. He did not notice the tarnished brass plaque on the other side of the door that declared: The Fulham Road Artistic Club, and a bit of paper underneath upon which was written *New Members Welcome*.

The light applause at the end of Gerard's stirring speech in the garden of the Arts Club was broken by a rotund, jolly woman in a floral dress at the French windows calling, 'There's a man in the lobby having a turn!'

Gerald led the group back into the club.

The fat lady, a woman called Joyce Billingham who painted gay seaside scenes from her studio in Ealing, was rushing back into the bar from the lobby.

'Quick!' she said to the barmaid. 'Get me a glass of water!' This sentence was one of the rarest ever spoken in the club, and the members rushed out to see what had occasioned such an emergency.

Sir Benjamin sat slumped in a worn velvet armchair by the front door. He opened his eyes and flinched when he saw the array of old people crowding him. Though in his seventies, Sir Benjamin was allergic to old folk. He tolerated them only on the condition they made annual donations to the Flint five hundred times their age, were modishly dressed, and had the decency to get some plastic surgery. But these people, with their shrivelled mouths, kind, rheumy eyes and baggy clothing, were transparently poor as well as old.

'Are you all right?' Gerald inquired.

'No,' gasped Sir Benjamin fumbling for his phone, 'I need to call for my assistants. An indigenous Indian has ambushed me.'

'He's sweating, take off his coat.'

Like undressing a large doll, Monica peeled off Minto's coat and hung it in the club cloakroom, along with a score of abandoned garments, some of which had been on the hooks for years.

With shaking hands, Minto took the glass offered by the corduroy-clad man in front of him, who looked, like some of the others, vaguely familiar. He sipped at the water, but even in his state could see how dirty the glass was. He tried to stand up, but his legs went from under him, not from muscular failure, but because someone had deliberately kicked away his ankles.

'Dorothy!' shouted Gerald. 'What on earth are you doing?'

Minto lay sprawled on the threadbare rug. 'Help … Please …' he begged.

'Someone help me pick him up,' said Gerald.

'No!' said Dorothy.

'Why?'

'Don't you see who it is?' cried Dorothy.

'It's Benjamin Minto,' a woman with an eye patch said. 'Did he help us when we needed it?'

Gerald stood back thinking about this. The man in the beret pushed his way to the front of the group and kicked the glass out of Minto's hand, sending it spinning across the grimy parquet.

'What was that for?' Gerald said.

'That was for cancelling my retrospective in 1991,' he growled.

Someone else kicked Minto in the side. 'That's for Jane Tabor,' she said. 'And the retrospective you gave her at thirty-two years of age.'

The man in the beret jabbed Minto in the groin with his cane, saying, 'That's for your so-called education programmes that brainwash people against us.'

Minto doubled up with a groan. By this point he had worked out which nest of devils he was in. He knew he had to fight back, and began by dropping a name, the way an army dropped a bomb, to scatter the enemy. He tried to remember who was on the board of governors at the Artistic Club.

'I am sure Lady Humbledon will be shocked when I tell her about this common assault,' he said struggling to get on all fours.

But another kick flattened him, and an aged voice hoarsely shouted, 'That's for video art.'

Minto tried again: 'What about lunch? All of us ...' he croaked. 'At the Flint. I can get the Princess Kirsten Grindlewald-Wengen. She's a renowned billionaire philanthropist and has a soft spot for figurative oils. The best wines. Four courses. I promise she will come. I promise.'

'You crooked little dictator,' Dorothy said. 'Do you think we care about your corrupt financiers here? You have turned them all against us.'

Minto changed tack and hissed, 'I denounce thee!' in the faces of his tormentors. 'I denounce thee! You washed-up losers. You pathetic has-beens. You won't even make a footnote in art history,' he sneered with curled lip from the floor. 'Post-war figurative painters? What an utterly ridiculous idea. Your art is locked out, and will never be readmitted.'

That was too much for Paul who shook his fist and shouted, 'You trod on so many good people.'

Minto, who was having a seizure, went into a spasm. 'Antidote!' he croaked.

'I think we had better call an ambulance,' Dorothy said flatly.

Fifteen minutes later Minto was being stretchered out of the club whispering, 'I've been attacked by an Amazon blowpipe.'

The paramedic, a friendly man called Talib, leaned over him.

'What was that?' he asked.

Minto looked up and into Talib's face and froze. Was this another silent assassin from John Burn's private army? As Minto spat the words, 'Don't touch me you evil Wakapa!' he suffered a second, more debilitating attack that rendered him speechless and, to make things even better, unable to move his limbs.

'Don't worry, gramps, we'll soon have you safe and sound,' Talib said, binding Minto down with straps for his own safety.

Gerald briefed the paramedic. 'He came in seeking a glass of water and had some kind of fit. He was also babbling in a rather alarming paranoid manner. I think his mind has gone.'

To Gerald, the paramedic said, 'Dementia probably, poor man. And a stroke. I'll put it on his notes.'

36

Sir Benjamin had not missed a day's work in forty-three years. Even when he had bowel cancer, it was rumoured that he had elected to go under the knife lying face down on his desk with local anaesthetic between meetings. So when the news broke that he was struck dumb, irreversibly paralysed and never to work again, the Flint went into shock.

As the old regime teetered, long-held scores were settled. The eyes on the portrait of Minto that hung in the staff room were stabbed out and the word TWAT written across his forehead. D.I. Boyle left his post on guard at the portacabin and went up to the executive suite to shred and delete all correspondence between him and Sir Benjamin.

The first Sir Benjamin's secretaries knew of the crisis was when the door to Minto's river view office banged open and a braying mob of embittered curators and disaffected staff stormed through. Both assistants were pinned down and assaulted anally with a Brancusi. It was generally agreed that it could have been worse had a Giacometti been to hand.

Three ladies searching long-prohibited regions of the basement opened a door and discovered Brother standing in the middle of the portacabin with a gold radiator attached to his wrists behind his back.

'Are you from special rendition?' Brother asked, his black eye now shining.

'No, we're from conservation. What's going on here?'

'I'm being held against my will. Minto and Boyle have been torturing me.'

They drew back in horror when they saw his raw wrists.

'Oh my God,' said one of them, 'go and get Dorothy, tell her we've got an emergency. Please keep still.' A lady ran out and returned with another stout, no-nonsense woman gripping a cantilevered box.

'Thank you,' said Brother.

She slipped on some white gloves, then took up a pair of scissors and some balls of cotton wool. She approached Brother and, with meticulous care, clipped the ties.

'That's a relief. Thank you love,' said Brother.

'That cost three quarter of a million pounds,' the lady said.

'Kiss me neck, plumbers, eh?' said Brother. 'Now can someone please tell me how to get out of here?'

The three of them were crouched round the sculpture, tending closely to it. One said, without turning, 'Go up the stairs and along the corridor.'

'They're on the top floor ransacking his office,' said Dorothy, 'if you hurry you might be able to join in.'

Brother had no time for that. But striding down a corridor strewn with paper and empty drawers he glanced through a doorway and saw the unmistakable sweat patches on the back of the blue service shirt worn by

D.I. Boyle as he feverishly fed documents into a whirring shredder.

Standing silently in the threshold, Brother selected his weapon. He wanted something decisive so slid a copy of Callum Smith's largely ignored 648-page 2008 Catalogue Raisoneé, complete with stainless steel slip case, off a shelf. Brother lifted it above his head, aimed carefully, and brought it down spine-first into brutal contact with Boyle's cranium. The Met officer sank with a groan to his knees and fell forwards onto the polished concrete. The book had finally made an undeniable impact.

Brother went through the officer's pockets and took his phone back. He turned it on. It had 70 per cent battery and twenty-eight missed calls from Rachel. He pocketed it and strode out of the Flint gallery as police were running up the steps.

Minto's second-in-command, a woman who had never made a decision more important than which hand dryer to install in the toilets, ran onto the roof and called the Ministry of Arts and Culture in a flat panic.

The Minister was Ludo Daventry (Con. Surbiton). He was briefed about the crisis by his permanent secretary.

'The Flint is a most important institution,' declared the Minister. 'Nothing must be allowed to threaten it. We need a safe pair of hands to keep the ship steady.'

Ludo was pleased Minto had gone; he had always thought there was something a bit creepy about him, and had heard a disagreeable rumour that Minto's assistants sometimes chewed his food for him. And he was always trying to get honours dished out for dubious types who had donated money to the Flint.

'Who can I get to clear this mess up?' The Minister said.

'I have been so bold as to make out a short list you might be interested in looking at.'

Ludo looked at the list; a name from the past leapt out at him. Adrian Krietman. The nice quiet fellow who was Herman's partner until Marie bought him out. He was a nice chap. Not too pushy, and free of Minto's tedious stratagems.

In the thirty years since Adrian had left Herman to run the gallery, he had quietly done rather well. Riding gently on Herman's coat-tails, because the gallery was still named after him, and not always correcting people's assumptions that he was still involved with it, he had not only climbed from one influential public sector arts job to another, but had learnt to understand, appreciate and even delight in cutting-edge? contemporary art, as long as it didn't involve video and he wasn't obliged to sell it. He was even heard, after a sherry too many, boasting that he had given Martino Zachman his first Swiss show back in 1989.

'Let's send in Adrian Krietman,' Ludo said.

'Very good.'

'Will you do the necessary? I have an important lunch appointment to attend to.' Roman and Gianni were in town and they were meeting up in a rather intriguing cellar bar in Pimlico that Gianni was thinking of buying.

In a leafy Esher suburb, on the ground floor of Grey Gables old people's home, Sir Benjamin Minto sat motionless in a wheelchair, staring out of the window at a larch lap fence and row of leylandii.

'Who sat Sir B there?' a friendly carer called across the day room. 'He doesn't like it there. Sir B likes art, don't you, love? It's in his notes.'

She released the brake and turned Minto into the warm room.

Inside Sir Benjamin's head a voice shouted: *No No No. You ugly philistine.*

The sweet, flat-footed lady wheeled Minto to face a lilac wall on which hung a Jack Vettriano print called *Cocktails For Two*.

Minto started praying either for some residual movement in his neck or merciful death, so exquisite was this torture.

Five hours later the carer plodded back. 'Enjoying yourself, love? You'll be pleased to hear you've got visitors.'

Sir Benjamin's two assistants limped into the day room on matching Philippe Starck crutches.

'Would you two boys like to sit down?' the nurse asked.

'No thank you,' they said in unison.

'Has he spoken?' one asked.

'I don't think there's much going on in there, sadly. But he's very happy, aren't you Sir B?'

No I'm not, you ignorant cow.

Minto willed the young men to look in his eyes, hoping he could communicate to them: *My boys, my boys, look in my eyes. It's me, it's me. I'm perfectly all right in here. Just look in my eyes. Like that diving bell and butterfly book. One blink for A, 26 blinks for Z. I am not finished. I am still perfectly capable of running the Flint. All I need is one of those things you blow into. Get me back at my desk and we can finish what we started. There's so much to do. You can start by retrieving the John Burn document and getting the collection up at home.*

Come closer! he shouted at them, silently.

'Look at him,' said the one who looked like the other one. 'He's a complete cabbage. Search his room. I'll keep a look out.'

No! They're not in my room! They're in my coat at that terrible club. Gerald de Gruchy took it off me, the idiot.

'Did you find the papers?' One of his assistants said to the other.

'No, I can't find it anywhere.

'Typical. We let him out of our sight for a minute and he loses the most important document he owns.'

'Pathetic dwarf. It's not here. That's that.'

Right, that's it. You're fired. Yes, both of you. Go. Leave. Now. You're nothing without me. You will never work in the art world again.

The transfer document was indeed tucked into the breast pocket of Minto's coat which hung unnoticed in the under-lit and under-cleaned cloakroom of the Fulham Road Artistic Club, and which, over the months, was hidden by other unclaimed garments until, like its owner, it was pretty well forgotten.

37

With a spliff in his hand, Brother reviewed the victuals laid out on the tartan couch in his caravan. He told himself they were for him on his travels alone but he also had Marie in mind. It would be nice to break bread with her. Satisfied he had all he needed, he packed them in his knapsack: a block of East Pennard cheddar, a jar of Geoff's chutney, a jug of Mudgley cider and a loaf of sourdough bread, tucking his Opinel pen knife in a side pocket before tying the top tight. At Bristol airport, the security man confiscated all of the above items. Brother was going to make a song and dance about it, he was sure there was something in the Magna Carta about a Freeman having the right to cider and cheddar, but feared getting thrown out of the airport, and he knew he had to get on that Zürich flight.

The only way of tracking down John Burn was by talking to Marie. He had tried speaking to her on the phone, but no dice. She wouldn't answer his calls. So he got her address from David Ashton and was going to knock on her door and find out where the other Burn lived. There was nothing else for it.

He had little money, but it was only a twenty-two kilometre walk from Zürich airport along the lake to Marie's house, so he set off down the dual carriageway. Inevitably, he was stopped by a squad car. An impassive Swiss policeman told him that the place for walking was in the hills. Using a judicious combination of Spanish, English and semaphore, and with the help of a map, Brother explained where he was trying to get to, and was given a lift off the dual carriageway and onto an older, small road that ran in places right along the pebbly shore of the lake where tiny waves lapped. It was a hot, overcast, still summer afternoon. A few light breaths of wind made amorphous shapes of silver and grey ripples appear and disappear on the dark lake. On the far bank, dark hills rose from the water, and beyond them Brother could see what looked like real mountains. It was unusual for Brother to see a body of water and not want to plunge into it, but today his mind was on other things.

It didn't matter that he had had his picnic taken. He didn't need to have a meal with Marie. He just wanted to meet her again, clear his name and locate John Burn. He could grab a bite to eat on the next leg of his journey, in whatever direction that was. In fact, it made his knapsack lighter, which was good, because he was in a hurry as it was a top priority to get to Marie and set the record straight about his character. That was the thing that mattered most.

It was dusk when he finally arrived at the ornate gates, set in a high wall with a small brass plaque saying *Delincourt*. Beyond them, a gravel drive disappeared behind cypress trees.

As he was about to press the doorbell, he saw headlights behind him from a car approaching the gates. Brother sighed and turned, assuming someone had seen him and called the cops.

He put his hands up, knowing the Swiss police carried guns. Two men got out of the car, laughing. Then he noticed that the car was an orange jeep. Undercover cops. Typical Swiss thoroughness. They didn't fool Brother. One was a tall young man with long hair in a top knot, wearing a T-shirt, paisley bell bottoms and bare feet, and the other a young bearded man with a heavy build who seemed to be smoking a fat one. Brother was just about to flee when he heard one say, 'Hey. Hold on. Is that you ... Brother?'

'Who's that?' said Brother, peering into the gloom.

'It's me, Walter.'

They then said in unison: 'What are you doing here?'

'Hi Brother,' said Ali.

'We're so sorry,' said Walter. 'We should have come and found you.'

'We're really sorry, what happened was shit,' said Ali.

'Don't worry about that, lads. That's not why I'm here. But hold on, what are you doing here?'

'It's my home, Brother. I live here.' Walter took out a fob and activated the gates.

Brother put down his knapsack and leant against the van. He was buffering.

'So ... is Marie your mum?'

'Yeah.'

Brother blew some air out. 'Look, I'm on a mission Walter. It's a code red. I've got to talk to your mum, sort something out, and then find a certain guy. And your mum knows where to find him. But she won't talk to me.'

'Why not?'

'Cos she thinks I'm like a bastard billionaire who collects art and beats up women. But it's not true, man. Will you tell her I'm not?'

'I would have thought that would be fairly obvious,' said Walter.

'You'd be surprised. Everyone's got the wrong end of the stick when it comes to me.'

They drove in the van and pulled up in front of the portico.

Walter said, 'Let's go inside.' After trying three keys, he let them into the house. The place was panelled like a cigar box, with pale carpets, expensive antique furniture and cosy lighting. There was a soft feminine hush.

Brother started to take off his boots.

'You don't need to do that,' Walter said. Brother was quite relieved because he wasn't quite sure what he was going to find in them after his early start and the walk from the airport.

Walter opened a door. Brother heard movement and suddenly Marie was in front of him, once again furious. It was becoming a bit of a habit.

'Show him out, Walter.'

'Hold on, Mum. Do you think this man is a billionaire art collector?'

'Yes,' Marie said. 'It's John Burn, Walter. Dad's client.'

'What?' said Walter. 'There has been a major misunderstanding. This man here lives on a travellers' site by school, in Somerset.'

'Tell her what I do.'

Walter looked at Brother.

'Go on.'

'What do you do?' Walter asked Brother.

Brother sighed. 'I pick magic mushrooms in the woods in autumn.'

'Yeah – he does that,' Walter said. 'And he lives in a caravan by a lake.'

'Am I a billionaire?' asked Brother.

'I would say you are a comfortable distance from billionaire status,' Walter said.

'I'm skint,' said Brother. 'I've been trying to tell you, Marie. You've got the wrong man. I am a low-net-worth individual. I never met your husband in me entire life.'

'He's not rich, Mum, I know that.'

Marie sat slowly on the arm of a sofa. Then she stood up.

'I'm not sure I understand what happened here or why.'

'Nor do I,' said Brother. 'I'm flummoxed.'

'Come through to the sitting room, I think we need to talk.'

'Ali and I owe Brother a very big debt,' said Walter.

'Not for drugs, I hasten to say,' said Ali.

'No, Brother here took the rap for us when we had the van busted getting into Latitude Festival just after we left school. I told dad about it.'

'What happened?' asked Marie, as they settled into the sofas and armchairs around the fire.

'On the way into the festival we had loads of magic mushrooms in the van. We saw the security coming down the line searching all the cars really thoroughly, and Brother told us to get out and walk away. So we ended up standing under a tree watching him get busted. He got a suspended sentence. And we've never apologised or thanked him.'

'Or paid his fine,' said Ali, 'which I shall do now. How much was it?'

'Oh that would be handy,' said Brother. 'All told, it was four hundred and fifty quid.'

'But why did you do that?' Marie asked.

'I did it on instinct. I thought I stood a better chance of bluffing the security guys for a start, and if I was caught, better me than them. I could see what a drugs charge would do to their lives. I never wanted to go America. I don't like going west of Yeovil. Too many second-homers. I don't care. But them. Well they had their whole lives ahead of them. And I was fond of the lads.'

'Thank you,' said Marie, softening for the first time. 'That was kind of you. What is your actual name?'

'People call me Brother, but my birth name is John Sparkler Burn.'

'Thank you, Brother,' Marie said.

'I'm glad we got that cleared up. Now, what I want to know is where the other John Burn is. Where the right Burn is. Because I'd like to talk to him.'

'I would, too,' said Marie. 'Oh, please, make yourself a drink,' she waved at an impressive array of bottles on a huge silver salver.

'I think I'm going to lie down, I didn't get much sleep,' said Walter.

'Me too,' said Ali, and they trooped out in an after-party daze.

With a smile on his face, Brother selected a tumbler and poured himself three fingers of thirty-year-old Laphroaig. 'Do you want one?' he asked Marie.

'I think I better,' she laughed. 'Gin and tonic please.'

'Coming right up.'

When they were settled on facing sofas, Marie said, 'So you were just pretending to be the art collector?'

'Correct. And I apologise for that. Profusely. That's what all that stuff with my so-called fiancée, Rachel, was all about – just me pretending to be the other John Burn. It did me head in to be honest. I thought I might be able to make some money out of it. Quite a lot. But that's gone now. It's one of the reasons I have to find the right Burn. To tell him someone is trying to nick all his pictures. And one or two other reasons.'

'So you never dealt with Herman?'

'I've never met him, though he did try to move my caravan once.'

'In Somerset?'

'Yeah. I live on the Levels.'

'Oh, I think I remember that. That was most unfortunate.'

'Apart from that, zero contact. Until, after he died, I got told that I owned all these valuable paintings. But they have the wrong Burn. Where is the right Burn?'

Marie smiled. 'That's what we need to find out,' she said. 'You'd better stay here tonight. Let's meet early tomorrow and try and get to the bottom of this. I'll show you to the spare room.'

'I'm fine on the sofa, love. With an open fire I actually sleep better. You don't want to go wasting a bed on me.'

Marie had already recognised Brother's suit from the pub garden. And it had clearly not been to a cleaner since then.

'You will sleep in the spare room, please. If you don't mind.'

Brother woke in a white room on a soft bed with sunshine pushing round interlined curtains. He went downstairs and found Marie in a summer dress, making coffee. There was no sign of Walter or Ali.

'Top of the morning to you,' he said. 'And what a fine day we have here…' Brother stood at the window staring at the lake and the distant mountains.

'Yes,' she said. 'Shall we go out into the garden?'

They took the gravel path between the parterres to the jetty.

Brother said, 'Nice pitch, Marie. You've got a very tidy spot here. Do you rent or own?'

'It's not rented,' she said.

'Good move,' he said. 'Always best to buy if you can.'

Marie smiled.

'Can I walk on the jetty?' he asked.

She was watching him carefully because she didn't trust his story. She could see Walter and for that matter Ali both liked him, but there were still too many unanswered questions for Marie.

'Do you do the gardening yourself?' Brother asked.

'No, of course not. I love a bit of gardening, mainly veg.'

She decided he was being himself, which though naïve and simple, was not as annoying as the people who pretended not to be impressed when they were.

Typically, Brother overdid it. As they stood by the shore and looked out at the sparkling lake he gushed, 'I don't think I have ever clapped eyes on anything as beautiful as this place you got here, Marie. It's a paradise! And what an amazing boathouse. That must have cost a mint. Can I have a look inside?'

'Of course,' she said. It was heartening to see someone enthusiastic about things she had grown so used to, and maybe even a bit bored of.

'There's a great boat in here,' he called.

'That's Herman's *Riva*,' Marie said. She had never much liked its white upholstery and pink piping. 'He bought it in La Spezia. We went to the factory to choose the engine.'

'Not that one, the rower. Very sweet lines on it. Got my own little boat on me lake. Water's always a good place to do thinking. It's where I get a lot of my big ideas.'

He closed the boathouse door. 'The big one's a bit bling for me,' he said. 'Now, Marie, how am I going to find this bloke John Burn? What's my best bet?'

'It seems so silly,' Marie said, 'but I never actually had a number for him, and I never knew where he lived. Communication always went through the gallery, and

Herman never said to me where they met, just which city or country, and they were all over the place. When I asked him, he said John was obsessed by secrecy and privacy.'

'Do you still have Herman's phone?'

Marie looked serious. 'Yes,' she said, 'it was returned with his watch and wallet after the accident.'

'Is it here?'

'Yes,' she said. 'In a drawer. I haven't touched it since.'

'I think we'd better look at it. Burn's number will be in it.'

'Yes,' she said, 'of course, I hadn't thought of that.'

Brother said, 'Come on, let's get to the bottom of this.'

Marie came into the sitting room holding an iPhone. She handed it to Brother. With some difficulty he failed to turn it on, so handed it back. Marie turned it on. 'It's locked,' she said, 'and I don't know the code. Hold on, maybe it's this ...'

She tried a few numbers, but none worked and she soon blocked it.

'Damn thing,' she said.

'Yes,' said Brother. 'Have you got his computer?'

'It's in his study,' said Marie.

'Can we look at his phone bill?'

On Herman's laptop they found his accounts folder and navigated to his phone bills. The screen threw up an itemised list of numbers Herman had dialled, ending on the day of his death.

Marie looked over Brother's shoulder. She pointed to the column of numbers. 'That one's me, that's Walter, that's Polly, that's the London gallery, that's Los Angeles. That's Highworth. What's this one?'

'Do you know the area code?'

'Switzerland.'

Brother scrolled down the screen. 'It comes up a lot. A lot.'

'And he called this one a lot, ending in 642.'

'No. That's the architects.'

'So what about this one?'

'I don't recognise it. Maybe we can Google the area code.'

She leant forward and tapped the keyboard.

'Zuog,' she said. 'He was on his way to Zuog to meet John Burn the day he died,' said Marie. 'It was on the flight plan of his plane.'

Brother scrolled down the column of numbers. 'There it is again. And again. And again.'

'Let me see if my phone recognises it.' She looked closely at her phone while dialling a number. 'No,' she said.

'Have we found him?' Brother asked.

Marie nodded. 'Maybe.'

'Let's call it. Can I use this phone?'

'Yes,' said Marie.

Brother picked up the landline and dialled the number on speakerphone.

'Der Whimper Stubbe! Guten Tag!' piped a Swiss lady.

'Hello. Do you speak English?'

'A liddle, ya.'

'Can I speak to John Burn?'

'Is he dining with us today?'

'No. This is serious. I need to speak to him.'

'Does he have a reservation?'

'I know he's there,' said Brother firmly. 'Put him on the phone. I'm not messing around.'

'I am very sorry, I do not understand. We have nobody called John Burn here. We are a restaurant open for lunch at 1 p.m. if you would like to make a reservation.'

Marie nodded.

'Table for two, please. Name of Brother. One o'clock.'

He put down the phone.

'It's an hour and a half away,' Marie said, having found the address on her phone.

'We'll go and confront him. There probably isn't even a restaurant,' said Brother.

As they got in the car, Walter hurried out of the house holding a mug of coffee.

'Where are you going?'

'To find John Burn,' Brother said.

'We think he's in Zuog,' Marie said.

'You're coming back, aren't you?'

'Of course.'

'Okay, we'll be here,' said Walter. 'Good luck.'

Marie drove them towards the Alps, Brother enjoying being pressed into the pristine leather upholstery of Marie's Mercedes as she accelerated around the corners. They flashed through little villages, the pitch of the roofs getting steeper and the eaves wider as they gained altitude. When they arrived in Zuog, the high street was empty, although the main square was bustling with two people, who walked past each other without any acknowledgment.

Brother and Marie stood outside the Whimper Stubbe, which at least looked as though it was a real restaurant after all. The air was cooler in the mountains. Brother looked up at the two storeys above the restaurant, thinking: *That's where he's holed up. Him and his stash of near-on a ton of DMT. So trashed he's lost track of 17 mill-worth of art. Slipped his psychedelic mind.*

They went down the steps and through the door where Julianne welcomed them warmly.

'Hello,' said Marie. 'We've come to see Herr John Burn.'

'We know he's here,' said Brother.

'Do you know him?' Marie asked.

'I'm afraid not. Are you the Brother party? You booked a table for two? Your table is ready.'

'You don't know him?' Marie said. 'We're looking for him and believe he came here often.'

'I'm sorry, no,' said Julianne.

'Did you know a Herman Gertsch?' Marie asked.

'Herman Gertsch?' she shook her head. 'I'm sorry, no.' She led them to a table.

Dejected, but hungry, Marie shrugged her shoulders at Brother. 'Shall we eat?'

'I'm starving,' said Brother. 'Hold on, I've got an idea.' He got out his phone, Googled Herman and hit images. When he had a photo of Herman he showed it to Julianne. She looked at it, felt for her spectacles, put them on and jumped.

'Otto! Otto! Do you know where he is?'

'That's Herman Gertsch,' said Brother.

'No, that is Otto. Our Otto! Our Otto!' she cried out. 'It's been so long and no word.'

'Was he a regular customer?' Marie asked.

'Did he used to meet someone here?' asked Brother.

'No. He worked here. He was our second relief chef.'

Brother and Marie exchanged glances. Brother scratched his head. He was trying to remember if he had any LSD on him. It occurred to him he may have accidentally swallowed some.

Julianne babbled on: 'But he was so reliable. He loved his work here.'

Brother showed her the photo again.

'Are you sure it was this man?'

'His teller was famous with our customers. He put so much love into them.'

'That's Herman,' Marie said, bringing a hand to her chest.

'Here,' said Julianne, and led them to a framed photo on the wall of Hugo, Julianne and Herman standing in front of the restaurant. Herman was attired in unapologetic *trachten*: leather shorts, braces, knee socks, hat and feather. There was bliss writ across his face.

'Then one day he left and never came back.'

Brother had thought the woman would lie, to cover John Burn's tracks, but she wasn't fibbing.

'Was that around June 2016?' said Marie.

'Yes,' she said. 'We never found anyone like him again.'

Marie's eyes began to fill with tears.

'Did you know him well?' Julianne asked. 'He was such a kind man.'

'Christmas Day, 2015. Was he here?' Marie asked.

'Oh, he saved us. Max was in the hospital with breathing problems. We had the restaurant booked out by the Mayor for his family. And Herman came in to cover. We offered to pay him double, but he wouldn't take it. Thank God Max pulled through. Do you know Otto well?'

'I was his wife.'

'His wife! Oh but I am so glad to meet you. How is he?'

'I am afraid he is dead. He died in a car accident nearly three years ago.'

Julianne put her hand to her mouth. 'No.'

Marie said, 'I think I need some air. You have been very kind.' She shook hands. 'I'll be just outside.'

Marie went and sat down very slowly on a park bench in the deserted square.

38

Brother stood at the bar and watched Julianne open a schnapps bottle with a squeak and pour him a glass to the brim, which he necked, and said, 'Mint. Danke schon.' She filled the glass again. Brother kept an eye on Marie through the pavement-level window. When he judged she was ready, after two more schnapps, he said his thanks, left the stubbe and that heart-warming hollow sound of the cork leaving the bottle, and joined her.

He took a seat beside Marie on the park bench and said nothing. He stared down the street lined with shops, all firmly closed, and looked up again at the apartments above the restaurant. The pristine net curtains and tidy balconies were not the signs of a heavy hallucinogen user.

'I know what this is …' Marie said. 'It's my fault. I blame myself. I never let him have his own restaurant. I should have listened. I laughed at him. So he went off to do it in secret.'

'Humans have quirks and kinks, Marie,' said Brother. 'There are worse ones than cooking Swiss food. What I can't work out is why he kept it secret.'

'I know why. He did used to mention it. I always said it was a stupid idea. That's why he went into the art world. In fact that's why he became a superdealer,' she said, 'because I wouldn't let him open a mid-range Swiss restaurant.'

Brother smiled. 'Well he didn't do badly.'

Marie shook her head slowly from side to side. 'Now I want more than ever to find John Burn. He must know so much more about Herman's last few years than I do. There are so many unanswered questions.' She turned to Brother. 'I was very unkind to you, I am sorry. I thought I had my reasons, but I realise I was wrong. Do you still want to find Burn?'

'I sure do, Marie. I would really like to meet him.'

'We should start with David Ashton. He knows everything.'

'He doesn't know him,' Brother said. 'He thinks I'm him. He's met me and everything. I tried to explain I wasn't but he wouldn't believe me.'

'That's strange,' said Marie.

'Tell me about it,' said Brother.

'The only other person I can think of who might have been in the loop is Herman's PA. If Ashton doesn't know, we should talk to her. I bet she knew what he was up to.'

'We tried to get in touch with her at the beginning,' Brother explained. 'Lily, that's me daughter, spent weeks on it. The woman seems to have disappeared. Even Ashton tried to contact her. She even had no social media. What was her name?'

'Celia Somerton,' said Marie.

'Yeah, that's her,' said Brother.

Marie paused and then said, 'That's why you didn't find her. Because that's not her real name. Her name is Sharon Pratt. Herman made her change it. He said it wasn't art world-friendly.'

Marie stood up. 'Come on, I bet she won't be hard to find. Let's go back.'

They drove back the way they came, a grey ceiling of cloud hanging motionless in the valleys. Marie was quiet, and Brother filled the silence with a long, rambling monologue about his planning woes with the council. 'I mean it's me own land, I paid for it, but will they let me and a few of me mates live quietly on it bothering no one? It ain't right, Marie.'

When he realised she wasn't answering him, or even nodding, he quietened down, and watched the road.

They drew up at Delincourt to find Walter, still in his pyjamas but eager, at the door.

'How did it go?' he called to Burn.

'It was a bit mental, Walter. We didn't find him.'

Marie said, 'But we did find out that dad had a secret life working as a chef in a traditional Swiss restaurant in Zuog.'

'You what?' Walter scratched his head as he followed them into the house.

'That's where he was going when he said he was seeing John Burn, it seems,' Marie said.

'He was what?'

'It's a bit shocking,' Marie said. 'A secret Swiss chef. I promise you. We've just been to the restaurant. Dad did shifts there for years. I thought he was doing art stuff, but he was working as a chef. It's not even a big restaurant. It's tiny, and really—'

'—mid-level?' said Walter. 'Do you remember he used to bang on about me starting a mid-level Swiss restaurant?'

'How am I going to tell anyone this?'

Walter laughed. 'I think it's brilliant. It certainly could be worse, Mum.'

Brother raised his eyebrows and nodded in quiet assent to that.

'It doesn't surprise me,' said Walter. 'Swiss food was his first love. He never stopped going on about it. He was a bit weird. You have to laugh.'

Marie smiled and nodded. Walter put his arm around her shoulder. 'He loved you, Mum, he just loved emmental as well.'

In the laptop in Marie's study, she went on Facebook. This time Brother stood behind, looking over her shoulder. She typed in 'Sharon Pratt Glastonbury' and then clicked on a photograph. A page came up.

'That's Celia, or rather Sharon,' said Marie.

'Hold on,' said Brother. There were only about four thumbprints accessible for them to see as they weren't her Facebook friends. All featured Celia/Sharon. Brother pointed on a newspaper cutting. 'Click on that.'

The image enlarged to reveal Sharon Pratt posing at a formal dinner with an older man. The caption read: *Councillor Eric Pratt with his charming daughter Sharon at Mendip Farmers annual dinner-dance in Shepton Mallet, Somerset. The evening was sponsored by Avalon Waste Management and Tor Plastics.*

Brother pointed at the man. 'I know that man. I know him. Eric Pratt. He's the councillor who's got it in for me. He's made my life hell for ten years trying to get me off my land. And he's Sharon's dad?'

'I think we should go and pay a visit to the councillor and his daughter,' Marie said.

'I know where he lives. Not far from me, in Glastonbury,' said Brother.

'We'll go tomorrow morning, first thing,' Marie said. 'Leave the arrangements to me.'

39

The following morning, Brother came down to the sunlit kitchen and found Marie placing a few things in a wicker hamper.

'We leave in half an hour,' Marie said. 'I'm just taking a decent bottle of wine and a few snacks.'

'Oh, you can't take that on the plane,' Brother said.

'I can.'

'No, seriously, the airline'll take it off you.'

'Actually, it's my plane.' The Bombardier twelve-seat private jet was one of the few things Herman had bought that Marie had not sold. It was fun to use.

'Oh.'

Any faint lingering doubts that Marie had about Brother's veracity were removed when she watched him board her jet. From his wide-eyed wonder she could tell he had never been on one before.

As they sipped the fine white burgundy and ate triangles of pate, Brother said, 'You know what this reminds me of? This plane has got almost identical dimensions as my vardo. Great little gyspy wagon. Very similar.'

'But slightly faster,' said Marie.

At Bristol airport a car met them at the bottom of the airplane steps, and drove them south.

Councillor Eric Pratt lived on the flank of the hill at Glastonbury in a solid but soulless modern house. As they drew up in his drive, a portly man with strands of hair combed back over his balding head appeared on the front porch.

Brother was the first out of the car. 'Morning Councillor Pratt!' he called.

'John Burn,' sneered the councillor. 'What are you doing here? I thought your type slept all day.'

It was actually quite fun being treated as Brother from Brother's Yard again.

'I've come to ask some questions.'

'This is irregular. Highly irregular,' said the councillor. To Marie, who had got out of the car, he said, 'Are you his lawyer, then? Because it's no good trying to open negotiations. That train has left the station. That's over. No compromise is acceptable. He and his gyppo friends and all those skivers and scroungers and all their rusting, moulding rubbish have to be off that land or I will be applying, on behalf of the people of South Mendip, for a court order to bulldoze them from it. Do I make myself clear?'

'I'm Marie Gertsch,' said Marie chirpily. 'We haven't come to see you, actually, we've come to talk to Sharon. She used to work for me.'

'Is she here?' Brother said.

The councillor called into the house and an apparition appeared in the porch, so wan and thin was the woman. 'Do you know these people?' her father asked.

'We have not yet had the pleasure,' said Brother, putting out his hand. 'My name is John Burn.'

The sunken eyes in Sharon's skull-like face stared first at Brother, then at Marie and then at her father. Her mouth opened. Her mouth closed.

'John Burn?' she croaked, and ran back into the house, her voluminous skirt swishing around her. Marie started after her.

Sharon had had what might be described as difficulties coming to terms with Herman's death. Her coping strategy had been to simply carry on as if the gallerist were alive. The stress of working for Herman for fifteen years had pushed her close enough to the edge of sanity, and his death had shoved her over the drop. Six weeks after arranging Herman's funeral, Sharon had had to be led by two nurses out of the London gallery where she had been sleeping, fully clothed at her desk, for a week. When she saw the ambulance and realised what was going on she said, 'I'm sorry, I can't possibly leave the gallery, no one knows how to make Herman's coffee. And no, you don't pour his champagne any old how, he likes it in an iced coupe, not a flute, at twelve-thirty on the dot.'

In hospital, the psychiatric nurse came to talk gently to her about her old boss. 'Herman is dead. He has been dead for two months. He is not coming back.'

'He is not dead,' tutted Sharon, adjusting the headset she wore even with her pyjamas, 'he's just running a little late. I'll call him on his mobile. Was it Frieze preview tickets you were after?'

In time, she had recovered sufficiently to go home, where she lived a subdued life in the muted light behind heavy net curtains. She had been gently forgetting the stresses and strains of working in the art world, but the name John Burn had catapulted her back to her days with

Herman. She had dashed into the pantry and hidden under the slate shelf behind the door. But the door opened and the man who had said he was John Burn stood looking down at her.

'Out, you two,' the councillor called from the kitchen. 'I don't know what you want, but you need to learn some manners.'

'Yes – get out, you filthy gyppo,' Sharon said.

'Leave now. Can't you see how you've upset the poor girl? She's not well,' the councillor said.

'I'm not ill, dad,' Sharon said. 'I've told you, there's nothing wrong with me. I'm on a diet. I've got to get down to five stone for next week's opening.'

Marie said, 'Sharon, listen to me, this is very important. You witnessed a document between my husband and John Burn to buy art.'

Sharon withdrew into the corner, blinking.

'What's going on, Sharon love?' The councillor asked his daughter.

'We're not leaving till we hear the truth,' Brother said. 'I want answers.'

'I can't say anything,' Sharon said. 'Herman banned me from talking about it.'

'Herman's dead,' Marie said.

Sharon looked around like a startled bird.

'Come on, love,' said Councillor Pratt, 'come and sit at the table. I think some explanations are needed.'

When they had drawn out chairs and were sitting at the kitchen table, Marie said, 'What we really want to know, Sharon, is where can we find John Burn?'

She looked at Brother and said, 'He's sitting there.'

'No, she means the one who bought the paintings,' said Brother.

'It's you,' Sharon said. 'There isn't another one.'

'I'm the only Burn?' said Brother.

'Yes.'

'So what about the guy who dug minerals in Africa and went up the Amazon for stuff? Where's he?'

'He never existed. Herman made him up. We invented him.'

Brother said, 'All of it?'

'Yes.'

'Even the stuff he was bringing a ton of back from the Amazon?'

'All of it,' said Sharon. 'He doesn't exist.'

Brother bit back some pain.

'So who paid for the pictures?' asked Marie.

'Herman. But he told everyone John Burn had.'

'Why would he do that?' asked Marie.

'He wanted to create a private collection. That wasn't owned by the gallery.'

'But why?' asked Marie.

Sharon looked at Marie. 'To impress you. To get respect. He wanted to show that he was good at what he did. On his own.'

Marie thought: *what an idiot. How stupid Herman could be sometimes. How could he possibly have thought he didn't have her respect?*

'Why did he put them in my name?' said Brother.

'It's true isn't it, he's dead?' Sharon said.

'Just tell me, why were they in my name?' said Brother. He was furious about the DMT, and now he was remembering everything he'd been through in the last few weeks.

Sharon put her hands over her ears.

'Why my name?' Brother said.

'Answer his question, love,' said Eric. 'He's a right to know.'

303

'They weren't in your name at the start,' she said. 'At first it was just an anonymous collector, but anti-money-laundering laws meant we had to come up with a real person.'

'So why me?'

'We had to find someone who would never meet anyone in the art world, and was impossible to track down. Dad, you said Brother was the slipperiest man in South Somerset and therefore the Western Hemisphere, and when you had his file at home one day I copied his signature and NI number out of it.'

'You what, love?'

'I photographed it and showed it to Herman.'

'Sharon,' said Councillor Pratt.

'That's a criminal conspiracy right there,' Brother said, raising his voice now.

'Did you really, Sharon?' asked the county councillor.

'Yeah. I did. That's what happened,' Sharon said. 'We knew it weren't right. We tried to stop it straight away. But it just kind of snowballed.'

'This sounds like a proper cock-up,' said Eric.

'John Burn got so well-known so quickly, because he was always buying art, or rather Herman was. All the artists started talking about him, boasting that John Burn had bought the best work from their show. Loads of people claimed they'd met him. It was a sign they had made it.'

'But didn't people think it weird that this guy never showed up?' asked Brother.

'Herman told everyone that John Burn hated parties, or that he was abroad,' Sharon said. 'All kinds of rumours did the rounds: I heard people say that John Burn had been scalded as a child and didn't like to show his face, that he suffered from agoraphobia, that he was in an iron lung, even that he came to every party and every opening dressed as a waiter.' She took a sip on her tea. She was actually enjoying getting this off her chest.

'I think Herman often wanted to kill the whole project, but we both began to see how useful John Burn was. If I wanted to get Herman out of a meeting I would announce that John Burn was on the phone and no one felt put out when Herman left the room to talk to him. If Herman wanted to avoid something boring he just explained that John Burn had demanded to see him and, as he was so important, he could not be denied. Everyone understood, because of John Burn's reputation. And I think Herman enjoyed it. Everyone always wanted to hear gossip about John Burn, so he just made it up. It made Herman seem in the loop. He was always bringing John Burn's name into conversation. And you know how he had this thing about Swiss food? Well guess what? John Burn loved it too.'

'So when Herman said he was in Paris with John Burn, or one of the other places he went to, what was he doing?' Marie asked.

Brother looked down and grimaced inwardly.

'I'll tell you,' said Sharon. 'The first trip he took was on a sausage-making course in Vienna. Then he started visiting sausage factories wherever he could find one, if he thought they were any good. And if he wasn't doing that, he was investigating gherkin manufacturers.'

'Or serving tellers in a restaurant,' muttered Marie.

'But what about me?' Brother said. 'While all this was going on?'

'You were never going to know about it. The idea was that Herman would sell all the work and you'd be forgotten. We never thought you'd get involved.'

'But when he died, they found his name in the files,' Marie said.

'You allowed my private data to be passed on to a third party,' Brother said to Eric Pratt. 'That is a criminal offence, under the Data Protection Act, and trust me I am going to pursue it.'

'Come, come,' said Pratt.

Brother stood up and pointed at the councillor, his anger turning to delight. 'After all these years of you harassing me, it turned out you were the criminal.'

'Your caravan site detrimoniously affects the value of my property,' Pratt said, also raising his voice. 'And many others.'

Brother swept back the curtain. 'You can't even see it from here,' he said.

'You can. There,' Eric Pratt pointed to a white dot, miles away across the plain.

'There?' exclaimed Brother. 'That? That's what all this has been about?'

'And the principle. You have no right to develop a settlement without legal prior planning consent…'

'Dad,' said Sharon.

'She's right. You want to be careful what you say to me. I want redress.'

The county councillor sat down.

'Identity theft, that's what you did, the two of you,' Brother said. 'And it's a serious crime.'

Pratt had a think.

Brother remembered another phrase from *On Your Feet – The Magistrates' Court*. 'And I will be demanding exemplary damages. Plus costs.'

'Look,' said the councillor. 'Let's be reasonable here.'

'No,' shouted Brother. 'You did me a wrong.'

'Well is there some way we can make up for the … the oversight?' the councillor asked.

'Apart from you going to jail? No!' shouted Brother. 'There isn't! You don't know what I've been through. Sir Benjamin Minto had me tortured because of you.'

At that, Sharon burst into floods of tears. Councillor Pratt attempted to comfort her while staring at Brother with impotent fury.

Brother felt a hand on his arm. It was Marie's. 'Can I have a quiet word with you?' she asked.

As Marie led Brother across the hall into a deadly parlour with thick net curtains, he shouted over his shoulder, 'I've got you banged to rights, mush.'

When they returned a couple of minutes later, Brother said, standing at the end of the table with his arms crossed, 'On reflection, and after taking advice from my friend and confidant, Marie, I have decided to cut you some slack, which is more than you deserve.'

'Tell us what you want for it?' Pratt asked.

'I think you can guess,' Brother said, glancing towards the window while he drummed his fingers on the table.

'I'll spell it out,' Brother said. 'As you know, I have owned the land at my yard for twenty-three years now and for nearly all of that time you have tried one way or another to get me off it. That stops today. And in perpetuity.' He glanced at Marie in a way that made Pratt think she had told him to say that. 'Ipso facto,' Brother continued, 'et cetera, forever more. And we call it quits. Also, I don't want any of your mates coming after me.'

'I'm very sorry, I'm not sure that this is within the scope of my powers,' said Eric. 'Wouldn't you be happier somewhere else? Have you thought about relocating to Ireland?'

'No, but I am thinking right now of ringing the police and reporting a crime.'

'Plus, pursuing a civil damages case,' said Marie. 'That sort of thing could end up costing you hundreds of thousands. How much is this house worth? You could lose it if Brother won.'

'And how am I going to lose?' shouted Brother. 'You forged my signature off a council document. You've admitted it! And I've got a witness.'

'All right, all right,' said the councillor. 'Let's talk this through. Sit down, please.'

Half an hour later, after matters were concluded satisfactorily, Brother and Marie left the house and stepped into the sunshine, for the morning mist had evanesced, and the day was evolving into a soft summer afternoon. From the councillor's drive, Brother could look down onto miles of flat land spreading like a picnic rug around Glastonbury. The Tor was behind them, out of sight, but they could see Dragon Hill, a spur of land that looked like a sleeping saurian. Brother and Marie got in the car and drove down the hill to the yard.

40

'I don't give this to anyone,' Brother said, stepping out of his caravan and passing Marie a mug of his special cider. 'But I think you'll appreciate it. This is the stuff I was telling you about. It's mint.'

Marie glanced in her cup and caught a whiff not so much of the bouquet but of fumes, and thought, *I'm going to have to pour this away when he's not looking.* But she got trapped into tasting it when he held up his metal cup to her mug and said, 'Gold rings to you, Marie. Solid gold. 189 carats. Cheers.'

It tore a strip off her throat but settled in a fiery ball in her belly that was not totally unpleasant.

'Nothing but apples in that, love,' he said.

He sat down on a picnic chair opposite Marie that he had tatted from the festival. Brother knew and observed the tatting rule: before Sunday anything you took was thieving. On Monday and Tuesday it was tatting, and thereafter picking litter, for which he charged.

'So,' said Marie, 'what are you going to do with your pictures, Mister Collector? Now we know they're yours.'

'What do you mean?'

'There's only one John Burn and you are he, so you own them,' she said, finishing her mug and holding it out to Brother. 'Just a bit, thank you.'

In the caravan, he measured a quarter mug for Marie, and refilled his to the brim.

'They're not mine, Marie. They're yours. You know that,' he said, handing her the mug.

'Thank you,' she noticed and appreciated the measure. 'I don't think so. By the letter of the law you are most definitely the owner.'

'I don't really follow the letter of the law,' Brother said. 'I go more by my heart, and it says … hold on, I signed them away to Minto!'

'That was when you thought there was another John Burn, and besides, he's hardly in a position to collect. Plus, now you are the only John Burn you can challenge it. And you signed it under duress, didn't you? Anyway, he's completely ga-ga. Under the law, I think you'll find they are yours.'

'Hold that thought,' he said, and went to get a refill, which he drank off in one and then topped up to the brim again. Later, he thought that that could have been an error.

He sat back down again and looked at Marie who was smiling at him with the sunlight in her hair. This was suddenly such an intensely beautiful moment for Brother. To have Marie, a woman of true substance, and a great beauty, on his pitch, sharing his cider while having a good heart-to-heart was enough to make him quietly weep with joy.

He thought, *oh I know what to say now. This is easy.*

'It ain't me,' he called out to her, feeling magnificent, flamboyant, a fully resolved man. Like Bob friggin Dylan.

So he added 'Babe,' to amp up the vibe. 'I don't need them. That's what the law of my heart says. You have them, Marie. You take 'em.'

As he said these last seven words he was aware of another thread of thought in his head. This one said, *you are not Bob Dylan, Brother, you are a complete idiot, about to do something unusually stupid, even by your standards.*

'I absolutely don't want them,' Marie said waving her hand no.

Okay, the voice in Brother's head said. *You have made the gesture. Now accept the pictures gratefully. Because if you don't you are going to regret it for the rest of your life.*

But I have to declare who I truly am to this magnificent woman, Brother said to himself.

He drained off his cup.

'Neither do I want 'em. They've caused me nothing but trouble.'

'They're worth a lot of money,' Marie said. 'Are you absolutely certain?'

'Never been more sure of anything,' he said, stopping just short of adding, *except maybe the attractiveness of your delightful bum.*

Ignoring a crescendo of screaming voices in his head, he coolly said, 'Maybe I should give them to Walter.'

'That's such a kind thought, but I honestly think Walter has got enough on his plate now. It might cause an overload.'

Brother nodded seriously, sagely. The co-parent, concerned for the wellbeing of the stepchild. This was going so well.

'Mmm,' he said sounding thoughtful, his mind a complete blank. Then he wondered, *how further to impress Marie now I have given away 8 million quid and agreed with her about her son?*

'If you really are serious about giving them away, you could donate them to the country,' she said. 'To the nation, to be exhibited in a museum. Then people could enjoy the whole collection, and it would stay together.'

'Now that's a mint idea,' he said pointing at her, he wasn't quite sure why. 'How would I go about that?' he asked, hearing, *you are one hundred per cent going to regret this.*

She will see who I truly am! He shouted silently at the thought.

The thought replied: *no friggin' kidding.*

'Sir Benjamin Minto's replacement at the Flint is an old friend of mine. Adrian Krietman. If you are sure, and I mean really sure, I could approach him for you.'

'Approach him!' Brother said.

'Well I can write to him and maybe next month you could go and meet him. How about that?'

'Next month?' said Brother.

'Yes, I don't think you should hurry this, Brother. It's a very big decision.'

'It's only money!' Brother cried, waving his arm around. 'I love my life just as it is. I don't need anything more, me. Particularly as you got Councillor Pratt off me back. That's worth more than millions to me. Let's call your mate now.'

Marie looked at Brother fondly, and thought, *he is so sweet but so idiotic.*

Brother revelled in her gaze, which for some bizarre reason made him sure he had done the right thing. Getting it past Kevin was going to be more of a challenge.

'You've had a drink,' Marie said, 'I think you should wait till you decide. Sleep on it, why don't you?'

'No way, Marie,' said Brother. 'If I do that I might go back on it! And I know this to be my truth. Remember,

Marie, they ain't me friggin paintings. I don't want the greed to start again. I don't want to change me mind. I want to talk to him right now, and get it done. Have you got his number?'

Adrian Krietman was presiding over his first opening at the Flint since he had been put in charge. He was enjoying being at the centre of cultivated attention. Young Kev was presently schmoozing him, while the thin lady was busy writing in her notebook about the event.

'Excellent show, congratulations,' said Kev. 'I particularly liked the title: *Interrogating the Space*. Very provocative.'

'Do you think so? Thank you,' Adrian said.

Sophie approached the polite crush of art folk pressing to talk to the new chief of the Flint.

She plucked Kev's elbow and said quietly in his ear, 'Very, very good news.'

Kev hadn't seen Sophie for a few days because she been spending all her time with Cuthbert, the obese man with the small eyes holding the fish.

'What's he, dynamite in bed?'

'Don't be jealous, Kev, it's not attractive,' Sophie said, without smiling. 'And it makes it less likely I will sleep with you, not more. I thought you would be clever enough to understand that. Listen. The Nigerian has come through for the John Burn Collection. 16 mill. In bullion, in Geneva airport free port.'

Adrian felt his phone ring in his divinely cut lounge suit. He glanced at it, and would never usually have answered it, but saw it was Marie, who Adrian kept a watchful eye over since Herman's death.

'Hello Adrian,' she said, as he turned away from the group around him.

'Very nice to hear you, Marie. Are you well?'

She paused, 'Yes I am, thank you. Yes I am.'

'Good. I am at an opening right now, so don't have too much time, but what can I do for you?'

'It's about business I'm calling. Because I have John Burn here with me, and he wants to ask you something rather important. I will hand him over.'

'Hello.'

'John Burn here. I want to know if you wish to receive, as a gift, my collection of 147 pieces, known as the John Burn Collection. Basically I want the people to see them.'

'But that is a wonderful, public-spirited act, Mr Burn. The nation will be deeply grateful.

I must ask you if Sir Benjamin made any quid pro quos about this gift. Because I am afraid I can offer nothing in return but my deepest thanks and a promise to display the work so the public get the access you ask for.'

'I know how Sir Benjamin worked, and that's not my speed,' said Brother. 'They're yours, man. Enjoy them.'

'On behalf of the nation, thank you very much. Please ring me up at your earliest convenience and come and talk to me about the details. But thank you; thank you very much.'

Adrian put the phone away. Kev was beaming at him hoping to build on the solid foundation of the positive reaction to his first remark, when Adrian said in a weak voice, 'Excuse me, everyone, may I have your attention? I have some very good news to share with you.'

The crowd fell silent. Kev tilted his head winsomely, ready to smile, and even applaud, whatever the news.

'I am pleased to announce,' said Adrian, 'that I have just had the eminent collector John Burn on the telephone. We share a very dear mutual friend who he is currently with.'

The thin woman scribbled hard in her notebook. *John Burn is not with the Wakapa. I fear the Strongbow will be seeking revenge.*

'Mr Burn,' continued Adrian, 'has officially offered his entire collection of art as a donation to the Flint Gallery. And I am happy to say, on behalf of the nation, I have accepted.'

Kevin blinked.

'For any journalists here,' Adrian continued, 'I would like to put on record that no money nor honours nor any inducements were asked for or offered. That part of the Minto era is finished, but our continued programme of finding the best cutting-edge contemporary art will proceed unchanged, and the acquisition of the John Burn Collection is, I think, proof of that.'

Back at the yard, Brother passed the phone to Marie.

'It's official,' he said. 'I am now a low-net-worth individual.'

'But you are a man, if I may say, of exceedingly high worth,' said Marie lifting her cup in a toast.

'Thank you, gorgeous.'

He went in for a kiss. Not on the mouth, but on the cheek, ostensibly as a thank you for the compliment, but really just to get a touch of her. As he got in range of her refined scent he panicked and feared he was making a mistake, but by that time was committed. It was tragically clumsy. There was a faint knocking of heads in which Marie had seemed to try to be avoiding contact of any nature with him. He wheeled back and attempted to regroup by turning to the lake and saying, 'Lovely sunset, I see the ducks are coming in.'

'You have a beautiful spot here,' Marie said.

'It would all be in jeopardy if it wasn't for you. You gave me a masterclass in negotiation back there. The sight of

Councillor Pratt's face is not something I shall ever forget as long as I live. Thank you, Marie.'

'And you have taught me a lot too.'

'I don't believe that?' Brother said. 'I'm a thicko compared to you.'

'You have taught me about my husband, about myself and about life.' She put down her cup and she said, and picked up her handbag. 'For which I thank you.'

'Please, don't mention it. But thank you, thank you. Really?'

'Really.'

'Bless you Marie. Bless you.'

'I think I must go now,' she said standing up and picking up her handbag.

'Well, if you must. Goodbye Marie,' Brother said.

He gave her a hug, which she warmly returned.

'And gold rings to you,' Brother said. 'Solid. Two hundred-carat.'

'It's been very nice,' Marie said. 'Thank you for the company.'

As she walked to her car, her driver jumped out and opened her door.

41

A year later, Brother was standing by his caravan wondering what it was he was in the middle of doing, when he noticed a van coming up the drive kicking up some dust.

He ambled in its direction as it parked.

A big, brown-haired man climbed down from the cab. 'Mr Burn!' he called. 'I was hoping you'd be here. Good to see you again. It's Mike – Mike Chambers.'

'Welcome. Welcome! I remember you!' It was the lad who Brother had told never to give up on his dream.

They shook hands.

'Of course, and call me Brother, that's what me friends call me.'

'You've given my picture to the Flint!' Mike said. 'That's so amazing.'

'Yeah, well, art's for the people, man,' Burn said, in a now fairly polished routine. 'Not just for billionaires to lock away.'

Mike glanced at the bit of paper in his hand. 'I've come to pick up the last three pieces, I believe. The rest I moved from storage to the Flint yesterday.'

'This way,' Brother said, and led Mike back down the path. 'You been in the studio painting?' he asked.

'Painful subject,' said Mike. 'But this has been a boost, getting into the Flint. We all just wish there were more collectors around like you.'

Brother showed him Kev's picture, and the one in Lily's piper, which Mike packaged and stowed. Then he came to Brother's pitch. Brother opened the caravan door. On the left hung the Ryan Young *Dandelion Head*, value £200,000. Dangling from a nail over the basin was Paul the Painter's *Tor Kebab*.

'One more?'

'Yes.'

Brother hesitated and then reached for *Tor Kebab*.

'I think it's the Ryan Young we were expecting,' Mike said.

'Pass me that bit of paper.'

Brother found his specs and a biro and wrote across it: Number 147, THE FINAL PICTURE OF MY COLLECTION TOR KEBAB PAUL CONNELL. And signed it.

'If anyone asks about this, tell 'em to call me.' He handed the painting to Mike.

'I'll get this properly wrapped and stowed,' he said, heading back to the truck.

'You, my friend,' Brother said to the Ryan Young painting, 'are gonna look after me in my old age.'

42

On the day of the opening at the Flint, Brother was in a state. His name had turned up in Forbes Magazine's Top 100 Global Philanthropists, and a journalist had rung him to arrange an interview. He had tried to say no, but the lady was so charming and sounded on the phone like she'd be hot, so he ended up agreeing to have lunch with her and a tape recorder. Luckily, Lily rang him shortly before the lunch, and when he told her what had happened, she took the journalist's number, called and cancelled the interview.

'You're right,' said Brother. 'Thank you. It could have got complicated. Will you come with me to the Flint this evening?'

'Of course. Meet at my flat and we'll go together.'

'How do I look?' he asked her as soon as he was inside her door.

He had made a real effort. Lily recognised a new shirt. That usually happened about once a decade, and his boots were polished brightly.

'You look great. Very handsome.'

'Do I? Really?' He glanced at the mirror.

'Yes.'

But Brother was still a pack of nerves as he climbed the wide steps outside the Flint and entered under a sixty-foot banner that said:

Spatial Interrogations: forty years of postmodern painting. The John Burn Collection.

Adrian stood at the huge doors, waiting for Brother, and pumped his hand while three photographers caught the moment. A journalist stepped forward to ask questions, and Lily dragged Brother inside.

There were lots of people there, but it was the paintings that Brother first noticed. He had only ever seen them in photographs and was taken aback by their power in the flesh. He went around the room looking at each one, thinking, *So this is what it's all been about. You lot.* A couple of people tried to get his attention, but Brother was lost in a bubble going from picture to picture, feeling emotions swimming around his body.

'The power of art,' he said to Lily. 'It's awesome. Awesome. These are beauts.'

In a second room he came upon Paul the Painter with the folk from the Fulham Road Artistic Club. Gerald had put himself in charge. When they had arrived earlier, he had announced to the woman with the clipboard, 'We are with an exhibiting artist. This is Paul Connell. Thank you.'

Their group now stood in front of *Tor Kebab* (2009). Paul the Painter glowed. The lady with the eye patch whispered congratulations.

'You are in the Flint, dear boy,' said Gerald. 'At the pinnacle of artistic success.'

'Hello 'ello 'ello,' Brother said.

Paul said, 'This is Brother,' then added, 'John Burn.'

There was a pause while everyone took a small step back, their eyes brightly taking in Brother.

'What a marvellous show,' said Monica.

'Thanks,' said Brother.

Lily thought it was safe to leave her stepdad for a moment and was looking at a Jane Tabor when she noticed, in the corner of her eye, Zac Manillo. Her instinct was immediate evasion, but then she remembered she didn't have to avoid him any longer. She wasn't a big heiress anymore, so he wouldn't be interested.

On the other side of the room, Adrian tapped two glasses together and, after a short speech of thanks, introduced Brother and gave him the microphone.

'It's fantastic to be here, my friends.' He looked into the crowd. There was Geoff and little Terry and a good crew from the yard.

'You are lovely, lovely peoples, you know?' Brother smiled. 'And as for the collection … It's honestly like I am seeing some of these pictures for the first time,' he said, 'they're so fresh. And they're cushty, aren't they? They're gorgeous. I love 'em, and I'm glad the people can see them all together. I don't know how I managed to amass such a brilliant collection of works. I know I couldn't do it again. Anyway, I never believed that that they were truly mine, and they are now where they belong, on public show, for posterity, thanks to Adrian Krietman, here, the boss. Give him a round of applause.'

Adrian dipped his dome in acknowledgement.

'And the gorgeous Marie Gertsch,' Brother went on, 'whose idea this was, actually. Marie, where are you?'

No hand went up, no voice was heard.

'Well, wherever you are, thanks, thanks very much.'

Lily heard a slight catch in her father's throat and could sense his disappointment. She felt sorry for him. She had thought the shirt, suit and shoes were for someone, now she knew who. Marie Gertsch. Of all people. Poor Brother. That kind of thing never worked out for him.

While everyone applauded, Zac smiled hello at Lily and crossed the gallery to her. 'What a great dude your dad is,' he said. 'And what a totally cool thing to do. Respect to the max.'

'Yes, he is great, isn't he? '

'How have you been, you elusive woman?' Zac said.

Lily always regretted not taking Zac up on his offer when he was texting her almost hourly, but as he thought she was the daughter of a billionaire art collector, and she couldn't tell him the truth, it was a non-starter. She had the strong suspicion that had he known the truth his laser-like interest would probably have dwindled to the power of a torch with a year-old battery.

'Has he kept any works back?' Zac asked.

'I don't think so. And he has no other money. I think I need to inform you I am officially no longer an heiress,' she said. 'I guess I'm not such a catch.'

'You're still a catch to me,' Zac said.

'Oh yes?' said Lily sceptically.

'Yes. You not only like my work … I mean, lots of people like it … but you actually know it.'

'I do, and I don't like it, I love it. I admire it hugely. I honestly think you're a truly great artist.'

'Now you're teasing me,' Zac blushed.

'I'm not. I mean it.'

'Oh, I've been wanting to tell you, I've been offered a restrospective in Germany, next year.'

'Not at the Pinakothek Der Moderne?'

'No. At the Hamburger Bahnhof.'

'Berlin! That's even better! I am so pleased for you, Zac. That's brilliant.'

'Would you help me pick out the work for it?'

'What? For the show?'

'Yes, you've got such a good take on my development as an artist. I've always thought that.'

'I'd love to, and I think I pretty well know where I'd start.'

'We'll start by having lunch and talking about it all. I'll be in touch. And this time ...'

'Yes?'

'Please answer my text.'

'Of course I will,' said Lily.

Brother watched Lily with Zac from across the room and felt a pang of self-pity. Not only had Marie not been in touch for a year, she hadn't turned up tonight, as he had hoped she would.

After an hour or so, the throng started thinning and Brother reluctantly headed for the door. A number of people asked him to join them for dinner, but he hung back alone, searching the crowd.

'Brother!' said a familiar voice.

'Walter. All good?'

'Well good, my general,' Walter said. He was wearing camo, flip-flops and a straw hat.

'What're you up to?'

'Big step forward this week, Brother, career-wise,' Walter said.

'Great,' said Brother.

'After a lot of umming and ahing, I have finally decided to commit to another year off.'

'Good man,' said Brother.

'Well, one of the factors was that I wanted to spend time at home keeping an eye on mum.'

'Has she not been well?' Brother said.

'She's okay. What? You haven't seen her?'

'No, no,' said Brother, 'Why? Is she here?'

'She was here. I think she was finding it a bit heavy,' he said. 'I know she wanted to see you. Didn't she say hello?'

'No. I never saw her.'

'Well go and say hello to her now. She's outside, over the road by the river, having a breather. I've just left her there.'

The cool air settled Brother as he stepped outside. The light was fading, the traffic on the embankment was a procession of headlights and back lights, and brake lights. He spotted Marie as he crossed the road and stepped onto the generous pavement. She waved from where she stood by the wall along the river.

'Hello, gorgeous,' Brother called. 'Walter said I might find you out here.'

'It was all a bit much for me, I'm afraid,' she said.

'I can imagine it. It was a bit trippy for me, everyone thanking me for something I ain't done.'

'That's not true. You gave them away. You could have sold them.'

'Yeah, well, not in my book.' He took a breath and continued brightly. 'Great to see Walter. He's coming along very nicely, isn't he?'

'He likes you.'

'I like him. He's got a good heart. '

The black river glistened silver and yellow with the lights of the bridge.

'Marie, did I say something wrong last time we parted?' Brother asked. 'Only …'

'No, not wrong,' she said.

Brother said, 'Would I have had more of a chance if I hadn't given those pictures away?'

She laughed. 'It wouldn't have made any difference at all. With or without, you're the same to me.'

He absolutely knew her to be telling the truth. That's what he liked about her.

'Oh, good, cos I thought I might have made a strategic error there, of fairly large proportions. Losing you as a friend and seventeen mill in one afternoon. Though, of the two, you were the biggest loss.'

Marie made a small surprised noise.

'Tell me, would you ever think of spending a week with me in Switzerland?' she said. 'No friends, no parties, no talk about art or money.'

'Good, cos I can't do any of them. As you well know.'

'I was thinking we could go for some alpine walks. Do you like walking?'

'A bit,' said Brother.

'I mean can you hike?' Marie asked.

'I can hike,' said Brother.

'Only I am quite serious about my walking,' Marie said. 'I do long distances.'

'I think I'll keep up,' Brother said.

'We'll see about that,' she said with a little competitive smile.

At last, Brother thought, *a break*.

About the author

Guy Kennaway lives for pleasure, producing books to add to the gaiety of nations. In all of Kennaway's work he likes to champion the underdog. He searches out communities under pressure and celebrates their struggles by having a good laugh with them. He is best known for *One People* about a Jamaican village threatened my mass US tourism, *Bird Brain* about a community of optimistic pheasants, *Time to Go*, the funniest book about assisted suicide ever, and most recently (with Hussein Sharif) his take on black and white thinking in the 21st century, *Foot Notes*.